T0157553

SACMAN

"A Tale of Two Fates"

UNKNOWN SOLDIER

authorHOUSE®

AuthorHouse™
1663 Liberty Drive
Bloomington, IN 47403
www.authorhouse.com
Phone: 1 (800) 839-8640

Published by AuthorHouse   05/22/2015

ISBN: 978-1-5049-1462-8 (sc)
ISBN: 978-1-5049-1463-5 (e)

Library of Congress Control Number: 2015908366

Print information available on the last page.

Any people depicted in stock imagery provided by Thinkstock are models, and such images are being used for illustrative purposes only. Certain stock imagery © Thinkstock.

This book is printed on acid-free paper.

Special Dedications

To my Lord and Savior; I thank you for all the words you have given me to express my true feelings and recollections of this mysterious Myth, while headed for home the hard way. To my two Sons, Jayme and Marsalius; I thank you guys for not giving up on your Daddy, but it goes to show you that Life is a rollercoaster ride where you have your highs and lows; but when your low do you have the strength and courage to fight back and win? To my oldest son, yes I know in my heart that you possess this strong spirit, so keep on swinging at it. To my "Wrong Way" Sister, Escape was the caper; and now that I'm free, I truly see what you see! A world of hope with many choices and decisions to make while being aware of hidden evils, for they will consistently clip at your wings; but now I sing forever, where I was held back from receiving the Lords blessings.(LOL) I also give a special, special dedication to my man Mar Mar; you know who you are. It was all those Daddy, tell me a story nights that got me motivated to know that I could accomplish something special; with all your wonderful and humorous ideas that were noted and taken, and yes I know in your heart that I am true. Thanks to Ni Shim Summers for his beautiful artwork; you truly captured what I envisioned for this dream. I just thank you all for everything, and may God bless this Tale of Adventure with understanding and love. Hearts are forever….

Introduction

The night was inviting, and long as a quiet storm waiting for its story to be exposed. It was the end of May 1978, close to the Dog Days, and summer heat of this West Virginia isolated coal mining town; where sight-seeing, adventure, and curiosity combined to transform this desolate community, known as Deepwater West Virginia into deep mysteries, and deep imaginations running astray trying to determine the realms of reality, and the depths of make believe. This nightmarish night was set at a sleepover at Uncle Bobby's, and Aunt Brenda's house where mischief, and solving enigmas were a must for us young danger seeking Daredevil's with a passion for the unknown. Now what started out as fun, ended in a horrifying story that would soon send icy chills up the shivering quivers of our spines, making our judgments', and testimonies wonder; would we survive the wavering night? The Legend of Sacman would soon consume the minds of the young, curious, and naïve; but as the Roger's family settled in for an understanding, and an explanation of the journey; the story soon began!

We were all gathered in the bedroom getting ready to turn in for the evening, when Kevin Rogers the sleuth of fabrication started his rant about something he really knew little about; but he unfolded what was handed down to him from his Dad, and Roger Walker, a Train Conductor that often passed through Deepwater on a constant basis, and had witnessed Sacman unleash his curiosities, and perils on the young, and the innocent at **heart** (Ha, Ha, Ha, Ha)! Family man turned psychopath; Thomas Wolfe well-known as half man, and half wolf had transformed into a serial killer it seemed almost overnight. As suspicions grew; intrigue of quest opened the expedition of a deserted soul trying to navigate his way to a peaceful place in his mind, away from the pains of death that plagued his thoughts with unstable issue. With the community being unsettled by the current events, and mayhem; we all wondered would Sacman survive his passage draped with uncertainties, and rare conclusions. So, let us open the Gates of Hell and visualize the agony, and the distress that has summoned such a vicious onslaught of lifeless victims, as we search for that once in a lifetime story of horror, and betrayal. The late night antics of this War Room of wits was consuming our weary, and heartfelt lost souls; because hearts was really what Sacman was searching for, while trying to obtain a reckoning of peace, and agreement over the tragic death of his youngest son, Sqirt Wolfe, who died at an alarming, and disappointing early age. As the Tale frightfully developed, Kevin continued his mental manipulations to control his inquisitive spectators; all ready to hear the animations of this fabled: "SACMAN"!

Author: James E. Rogers Jr.
Pen name: Unknown Soldier

CHAPTER I

The Legend Begins

"Be particular", said Kevin as he whispered a song he supposedly had heard bellowing through the remains of trains not far from the Rogers' residence. Now, this railroad graveyard was triumphal in its final destination; which was a secluded stronghold with its fortified rage piercing the coarse infrastructures; wailing with eerie evaporating echoes rolling sharply off the barren wreckage of discarded, and written off as useless throwaways. As Kevin began his rendition of the song he swore he had heard while out exploring the abandoned wreckage; all eyes and ears were fully focused on his words, and the gruesome expression etched on his face as he began to sing:

> ➢ *They call me Sacman, They call me Sacman I can make time stand still,*
> ➢ *Why do I feel that I have to kill?*
> ➢ *I ride these trains in search of fear,*
> ➢ *With my sack full of hearts that I hold so dear.*
> ➢ *So come out and play if you children dare,*
> ➢ *Or I can get you while you sleep like you had a nightmare.*
> ➢ *They call me Sacman, They call me Sacman if you see a train you better run,*
> ➢ *Cause I'll take your hearts and then you're done.*
> ➢ *So, when you hear that whistle slow-ly blow late at night,*
> ➢ *You better lock your doors, and turn on your lights!*
> ➢ *Cause I'm Sacman, Sacman……..!*

Now, these winds of change, deranged and delusional as they were, howled Lone Wolf intimidations of sweet victory as Kevin the sleuth continued his vigorous barrage of the vast ages where the darkest hours were evidence of what's to become, and what has already been for told, as he was rudely interrupted. "Wow Kev, you're a great storyteller", said Nece with her devilish crocodile smile; who already knew that Kevin was trying to scare his opening audience, so she wasn't too scared but her nerves were still dangling a little bit on the edge. Kevin's momentum of confidence was building in the sway of his swagger and what started out as ridiculous, and witty ended in toughness of truth: You know that heightening of anticipation where your heart sometimes repels and beats that unknown feeling of exhilaration when it's shook, and rattled by fear and mayhem. Kevin continued to ordain into the wee hours of the morning, trying to force intimidation into the depths of our unknowing elements, as his ending words crept up the hairs on our necks stirring the souls, and burning the blood of four innocent and timely graces that were trying to sleep; but be very far from the concepts of peace, calmness in thoughts; or for-see a "Good night!" The search would soon begin after we woke up the next morning while everyone was clamoring about and focused on what they had heard the night before about this drifter known as Sacman. Now, this predetermined hunt would be awakening to the sleepy eyes that were jumbled from this mystery, and intrigue that was forging a grand performance through our minds like a blank canvass ready to be painted with the true horrors that patiently lie in wait. We all sat at the dining room table the next morning eating our bowls of cereal, as Kevin began his quick witted dares by challenging the family to uncertainties and rare conclusions that would soon be unveiled. He said, "Come on guys, we got to get the bikes ready for our Sacman trek; and I know exactly where the monster dwells!" I could tell that everyone was scared but courage isn't the absence of fear; and actually I could barely hear the thumping heart beats rapidly thrusting inside the timid chests of my kin. I said, "Hey Kev, do you think it's really a good idea to intrude on Sacman's lair bro?" He quickly replied, "Relax guys, it's not far down the road and if we run into any trouble my trusty slingshot will topple this so-called Marvel." He continued by saying, "This has to be an aggressive takeover, and when we invade this Hornets nest we'll always be known as the Deepwater

Daredevils!" Now, Lia the youngest of the group didn't talk much but she had a great response to Kevin's boasts. "Big bro" she said, "You're full of Donkey poop and I Neigh not say how you smell right now." Everyone started laughing including Kevin, but his persistence to ignite fear would alter the waves of hostility that lingered thickly in the air of his safe haven of home. Finally Rene, my big sister spoke up after hours of listening to her little cousin submit his perilous images, as if she was about to shred them into little pieces and discard them into a river of cowardice that knows no limits to intimidation. She said, "Boy please, I remember just last year you peed in the bed because you were too scared to get up and use the bathroom in the middle of the night, and now you're some kind of Superhero with a rock shooting slingshot going up against a killer who kidnaps children and keeps their hearts for trophies; You've really gone out of your mind you crazy naïve kid." Everyone wanted to laugh but we could all see that Kevin was motionless and didn't say a word, he just sat there absorbing what Rene had said with a scowl on his face; but his new found bravery would not be denied its first performance on a live stage where it would definitely be "do or die", he just couldn't let it be refused of that Daredevil mentality. It seemed like the sacrificial canyons were ready to rumble while an awakening of dangers would soon be discovered by our inquisitive and thrill-seeking group; and this so-called Time for learning would be a major step toward maturity, ripe for the picking with Sacman unleashing his sweetness for revenge against unlike souls who had no idea of the terror and rage that was about to succumb; and then be reborn as quicksand to the innocent, sort of like a snake pit that had been hidden for years of starvation now killing with a hunger that couldn't be satisfied. I felt something strange was happening to us all because I could sense the thorns of agony were amongst us watching diligently from the shadows of the Dining room walls while gently scraping our fearless minds and leaving marks of pain that we would soon suffer if caution wasn't taken in our new adventure. I really thought we were making a big mistake by searching for this man of myth while fiercely escaping the inner compounds of torment; and I really didn't know what we would be looking for, but it might kill us if we found it. We were facing major problems that had been seen so many times before, at every stage of life guaranteeing if we take the chance, we'll locate somebody and be a part of something where shortcomings, failures, and leisure's of hope are the champions of their choosing. I desperately tried talking Kevin around it by heading straight, where my words would align to counter the fast balls that were being thrown by him meant to excite the pressures of pure concentration, leaving the heart to accelerate to spectacular levels of concern. When Kevin's words had finally found him again he spoke urgently to communicate his thoughts as he said, "Sacman will be hiding in wait like Kane; you know how he smothers his victims is pure hatred but refusing to embrace that hate would be failure for all the things left inside of him, and all the things to come." The windows of opportunity were looking slim for us like soft disappointments where we would be put in inferior positions to be casualties in this urban warfare that we called hide-and-seek. Rene aggressively replied, "I heard Sacman was not predictable but his denial was direct, just, and honorable slowly eating away at the animosity swirling through his inner thoughts of killing." She quickly continued before being interrupted by saying, "I heard the best legend of all is where you can't predict what his aspirations are even if they're a little bit more ambitious than everyone of his dreams, but I foresee one more dream that will finish off the plate of tid-bit morsels that think they can do anything while not recognizing his limitations of talent." Rene had a great way of putting things into perspective, and was really being kind to the temper tantrums that were being thrown to get their way. Kevin was now huffing and puffing fighting for his words to be heard as he angrily said, "I'm going to give this Sacman a dose of his own medicine and this unfamiliar commencement we are about to face will probably be insurmountable, but last night I witnessed a star proving that light evolves the inner parts of a celestial body emitting animations like a guide to hope and a guide to understanding the love that's left behind, so guys I want you to think about the children that have disappeared and the many lives we could save from this rare monster of mystique by just standing up to our fears and uniting as one to put an end to this timeless terror." We all knew that Kevin was an excellent motivator to get what he wanted, but his stubbornness was like a slight touch of insanity. "Wow Daredevils", I said, "This is getting us nowhere by arguing back-and-forth, I just wonder if Sacman is trying to communicate his innocence or just simply trying to lure more faultless sacrifices into his web of injustices that is inescapable by a rooty-poot prey; and by rooty-poot I mean dumb as a dog trying to scratch a flea off a cat's balls; dumb as a turtle trying to race a rabbit to the finish line, and family I think you know what the finish line is: Life or Death!" "So, I don't know about the rest of you but if Kevin's willing to scratch some cat balls, I say ruff, ruff let's get to scratching." Lia started laughing so hard I could've swore I seen wet patches on her Wonder Woman pajamas sagging the inner parts of her crotch like a baby's soaked diaper, and with a child like sense of wonderment where the boundaries are not set quite right, she desperately had to get her opinion heard at a table full of authentic feelings that were trying to draw strong results. Lia said, "I feel like I'm spiraling out of the air!" She was expressing an outrage of alarm that I had never seen in my little cousin's eyes before as she continued saying, "Guys, please don't mock me but only I know what I'm capable of accomplishing, and I really want to go with everybody to search this monster man out but I don't want to lose anybody, and ya'll know I'll bite and fight until my last breath; but I'm really scared." Kevin said, "Sis, I'm so proud of your courage and I don't mean to scare you but just remember huge hurdles still remain, and while our emotional wounds remain fresh we are also prey just like the lost souls that have mysteriously disappeared." Nece was rocking so vigorously in her rocking chair near the Dining room table that you could feel the vibrations shimmering through the place mats on the table. Finally, she spoke up after patiently waiting for her turn to be heard as she said, "Let's go get the bikes and leave now before I have second thoughts about this run-in." "I'm beyond terrified but we have to go now or my nerves will get the best of me. because this type of pressure will really let you know if you're a man, woman, or mouse." Kevin didn't hesitate or blink an eye as he said, "Off to the bikes then my fearless Daredevils, off to victory and the glory of adventure." As we all scrambled toward the front door thumping our chests and chanting "Deepwater Daredevils, Deepwater Daredevils" we all made a quick change of clothes, gathered our specialty weapons that suited our personalities, and then darted outside and mounted our trusty stallions. After a few minutes of cautious preparation, we galloped gallantly toward the sun as if we were John Wayne or Clint Eastwood starring in one of their finest Western films. Our well tuned bikes seemed like thoroughbreds racing steadily at a contender's tempo knowing not to waste all of the stored energy that was yearning to be released. As we headed down the narrow country road for about twenty to thirty minutes, I could see that everyone's faces were so serious and concentrated on the task at hand that we didn't even notice the pavement was about to change dramatically. We could now hear the swoosh of the leaves, and the crumble of the gravel as we rode like we were climbing up the walls of what seemed like an infinite mystery while having a rigid mindset as we made a bee- line toward Sacman's supposed lair. I was in awe of all the beautiful scenery that surrounded this secluded area that was rarely occupied by explorers such as us, but every once in awhile a tourist or sightseer might frequent these back-wood regions to take an unforgettable picture that would last a lifetime on their minds as far as capturing that unique moment of wonderful wildness. Now, the road was steadily growing very dusty from the full charge of our bicycles zooming over this unfamiliar route, as I observantly glanced over at Kevin and noticed that he was slowing his pace in pedaling, as our bikes quickly hugged the center of a hidden path heading left and then down a mild slope of muddy mass hysteria. The end of our journey at this moment was hidden by a grisly clump of trees that looked like an unmaintained graveyard waiting for a cemetery grounds man to replenish the last bit of life that lingered from its unwanted welcoming. Perching high in an impressive safeguarding tree, I recognized a jet black crow with a penetrating stare cawing, and bobbing its slender neck back and forth; as if he was guarding the entrance to a sanctuary of evil spirits that didn't want to be found. It was worse than bad it was unforgettable, like vipers ready to strike, ready to unite, and serve that single blow that paralyzes its victim's soul into an abyss that staggers deep into the darkness, like nine ways to Sunday with confetti falling gently to the surface of this instant proof we had found with special instructions to waver under the silent sun. We faithfully knew that God was on our side but we didn't perceive the words that would be spoken at a later time because all we could think about was that wars were won in the trenches even though they're sometimes filled with motionless bodies not expecting such a methodical execution. Now these wise words have cursed my bravery, and my relentless hope of being indestructible, which was ringing sharply through my eardrums like hummingbirds singing that everlasting melody with exhausted possibilities, that I'm never going to respect you, or the secretive choices you've made against countless innocent souls. I said aloud, "God is good, God is great!"

"So, how will we all survive on this Hell's filled plate?" No response was given at this particular time but I knew Father was there observing, and protecting us from afar with the Sun's heat being so overwhelming that caution would have been the best option of approach; but Kevin was on a mission to conquer and destroy, as if he was trying to rid his veins of pure resentment, or just trying to surpass the fear that had been laid on his simple mind at such an early age, definitely being overwhelmed about these graphic stories of "Steal your Hearts" <u>Sacman.</u> Even though we were all witnessing Kevin acting hyperactive, we still executed our Daredevil approach of caution while scanning the surroundings, until our attentions were immediately drawn and mesmerized by these commanding train cars that were set in a rotund pattern like a wagon train protecting itself from an onslaught of vindictive Indians trying to regain a time adjustment of lost respect from lost revenge. As we dismounted our bucking, and belligerent Broncos it seemed that our wild hearts couldn't be broken as we began our Tribal walk down memory lane drawing nearer to the abandoned wreckage that was embroidery framed and artistically canvassed like a Van Gough, or a Da Vinci painting; inviting the imagination to create a perfect picture of unwanted destruction. Rene observantly said, "There's been activity here recently, just look at the remnants of wood still burning in the interior of this dull made campfire." As we looked the area over, we could hear the mournful cry of the summer wind parading briskly through the open doors of this vacant wreckage: whistling as if to say, "Welcome to the Party of Fear!" "Death lingers near!" Now while we were learning to accept the curiosity inside, tragic plans of surprise were about to unleash a completely out of its mind fiasco. It seemed that we were in pursuit of a fight while crossing the threshold of hope as we crept closer and closer to the nearest train car, quietly peeking inside the enclosed chamber, where the walls crooned like the National Anthem roaring with battle drums beating an elusive cadence. I could see out the corner of my eye that Kevin was growing very agitated as if he were sitting on pins and needles, but we could all admit that we were feeling a little edgy by this invitational picture of a psychopath trying to control a serious standoff, while his words floated aimlessly through our deaf ears. "John Moe, Will Moe, No freaking more," said Kevin as he lunged from his kneeling position into the center of this haunted snake pit of a train car, while keeping a close reconnaissance on the entrapping surroundings. It was like an octopus of octagons filled with mental confusions to cloud our brains, but we were still willing to get dirty and take the risk of being snatched by Sacman, until we noticed a large structure that looked like a pillory; which was a frame with holes for the head and hands used to punish offenders such as ourselves blocking the second exit to the train car. The Lord knew we all had a point to prove because Sacman was said to have taken one of our closest friends Lamont Hickman, who lived on the hill across the road from my cousins; but vengeance is often served short after seeing and touching this torture device that brought an eerie, put you to sleep type of feeling to finally get the message across; that Love sometimes kills. We were in shock from the amount of bright red blood stains that plastered the walls of this wreckage, but there were also light splatters of blood dripping a recognized trail across the encirclement of cars to a larger and more menacing, erratic stronghold. It's been said that if you find an enemy, you'll find a foe, so approach with precision timing when letting them know that every story has an ending, and these electrifying images that manifest will be remembered eternally in the heartfelt thumps of your chest. Therefore, honor with no pity because the layers have already been peeled away with no return, and no guarantees; thus if we really want this by putting an end to the madness; we'll have to extinguish the flames with cleverness while being easy with the quick tempered outbursts, and the unwillingness to unite. At the moment, this eye catching dwelling that laid before us was as black as the massive coal piles that encircled it, which looked like perfectly crafted totem poles sending out a warning to mischievous intruders to "Keep Out or Pay the Price to Wrath!" Witnessing this unsettling work of art made the bloody tears of Hell seem like it was taking its time patiently pulling us closer, and closer to the grasps of the likes of Lucifer. Even the crows that perched above sat honorably like beautiful butterflies; few and far between to the naked eye leaving our hearts in neutral eagerly anticipating its next beat; but what you have to understand is that we had tons of crazy dreams that every hour turned into magical hours for us Deepwater Daredevils. Suddenly, Kevin jumped out of the first train car as we started edging nearer to our goal while leering and peering like we were incredibly moved as we reached the grand entrance to this Fortress of Fate train car where the trail of blood stains were laying out an introduction to the so-called "Unkempt One." Nece, who had been soberly silent throughout our journey, was quick to quote her elders saying, "Back in the old days trust was still a fragile thing, and family I trust you'll get us home safely without regrets or repercussions." Before anyone could respond and without delay, the insanity began to thicken as a flimsy ball of tumbleweed flurried across the barren courtyard with a slight sigh of hope to make it through the roughness of the terrain by letting off a little steam to give it that extra push, so that it could feast upon the moment of achievement. Time was firmly sitting like a grave digger arguing with the thoughts deep in my mind, but for some reason all I could think about was the story of Alice in Wonderland and how she wouldn't understand the demand of having the upper hand, as I command a well executed plan to withstand sinking from this bland quicksand. (Which was a rhyme held true to this specific situation of loose ends and the cold challenges of man?) We were well organized and discipline as we slowly entered the massive courtyard in a column two formation with Kevin as the unanimous squad leader, who was overly comforted by his trusty slingshot; and with the rapid wave of his hand balled up in a fist we all took cover behind tree stumps, and other various objects that would camouflage our offensive maneuvers. Up to this point Rene was the true protector of this makeshift of a squadron, but she decided to bite her tongue and let Kevin learn from the traumatic experiences of real- life we would soon face. Lia suddenly spoke in a low concealing voice as she said, "Your only as good as your last idea guys;" while deceivingly lagging behind as if she knew what lay ahead. She let out another soft whisper to get everyone's attention again saying, "Hey Daredevils, what if Sacman is here; what should we do?" I said, "not you too Lia, Nece is already scared, so we have to stick together; I mean our victory depends on it." Unexpectedly, the wind started to pick up its pace causing the isolated hovering trees above to shimmer like the lines on a seismograph making me feel that others were there; I could just sense their spirited presence, so I knew we were undermanned; because we had left so abruptly that the rest of the Deepwater Daredevils were nowhere to be found when we began our spur of the moment trek. We were currently sitting at the brim of this Neanderthals dwelling and our instincts were on automatic still waiting and anticipating a wicked and evil discovery. As we all eyed the puzzling entrance to the train car, we could see cobwebs swinging from the overhead door track like a broken sunset of horrible woven networks that didn't quite have that child's appeal to make a lasting impression on this hideous scene of deadly devotions and wistful desires. I was anxiously trying to conceal my second thoughts of this muddled situation, but my unusual strength of curiosity was like Neptune's spear being driven into the Earth causing its tines to vibrate with rhythm, getting me worked up to enjoy and treasure the thrill of this dance while persistently pursuing our prey. Kevin and I had grabbed the sides of the door, so that we could sneakily swing our heads around the corner to get a better view of the inside, when we noticed what looked like Demonic Languages written on the inner walls in overrated penmanship; mostly hidden by the dark but still clear enough to see that someone had been influenced by monsters with dark and unsettling covert activities. Without delay, Kevin quickly jumped onto the side of this dreadful den of danger and heedfully stepped through the doorway, as I paused for a brief moment and then made an immediate turn to follow. Rene and the other girls stayed behind while keeping an eye on the surrounding area from their secured hiding places, as Kevin and I moved further and further into the endless darkness approaching cautiously, and stealthily while making our way around the challenging objects that cluttered this substantial room. I felt like we would find lifeless bodies sprawled everywhere, as scared as I was, because we could sense an iciness that was cutting deep from the suffering that lingered like settled- in stench hugging the musky damp air; never to let go. I stood there with the wind to my back, exhilarating as it was; absorbing the true things that define you at that specific moment giving me fresh vision, and strength while rinsing and cleansing my inner being to be prepared for this world or any other that would challenge my mastery of survival. We noticed in the back far corner of the train car that there were wooden crates stacked neatly like a barrier that was built on purpose to conceal the unknown, while protecting the inhabitant that lay in a slumber state behind this wondrous unpredictability, and leaving us not knowing that we were closing in on our unsuspecting quarry that had become like a ghost with no settled place as if he had suffered a Napoleon's fate of isolation. We could also see a distinct circular light projecting from an object in the opposite corner of these wooden depleted crates as we drew nearly even with our objective, causing Kevin to gingerly reach into his back pocket and release his slayer of a slingshot while simultaneous digging into his left front pocket to grab his stone pointed ammunition; getting ready for a battle with a means to an end. Seeing that my brave cousin was ready to pounce, I nervously grabbed my nightstick from my fully packed knapsack that seemed like a ton of bricks planting my posture into a Praying Mantis attack stance. After every step we inched closer, I could hear the floorboards creaking, and crumbling beneath our feet sending out an unwanted warning to this unsophisticated individual known as a mysterious myth that we had heard so much about; letting him know that we were there and ready, with no time to communicate our soldiers journal of feelings. When suddenly, out of the pitch black came an obscure, sinister figure that lurched from the floor like a cat surprised by an annoying, playful dog. Tightly grasped in his left hand was a miniature pickaxe with an extremely sharp looking point at one end, and a serrated biting blade at the other with a hook and capture, snag-grab, for accomplishing his tasks. It looked like a butcher's perfect slaughter device for undressing the insides of its lewd lab rats making their way through a maze of mistaken country miles, while adamantly reaching out for new solutions of escape. Sacman was now rapidly approaching our position, as he urgently knelt down grabbing at the light coming from the adjacent corner he had bolted from; which actually turned out to be a miner's helmet with true light projecting from its center front which seemed much more like a ragged, spirited head armor used by warriors in the Art of War. It was a jaunty lid for such an alarming Mr. Hyde that had finally come to animation, as we thought to play him like a fiddle with an entrancing tune that would calm this savage beast; but that ship had sailed because we had no idea that we were on the grandest stage of all: "Unfinished Business in these unfamiliar killing fields of unmerciful attacks!" We had entered this dark world of peril like sand pebbles drifting downward slowly but suddenly, to eventually blossom into these primitive outlawed punishments that were being prescribed by this evil doctor of heart break and take; that had no ambivalence of remorse, or the slightest touch of vigilance about the spirits of the faultless that he had so easily taken as slaughter, and used as "tokens of kill" for his mantel of retribution; and only through his eyes of glory and gratification, he would wangle his own desires of scorned compensation for the betrayal of his past, and his near future. It was as if we had heard the words of "Eat crow, talk turkey, or shake a leg when you're scared, but it sounded like the day was just beginning without the sunrise if we happen to fall apart at this crucial juncture. This devious, terrorizing body that loomed and zipped through this hell of a hole had hungering, glowing yellow snake eyes; and with his quick turn movements made a hissing sound as his body swayed in the shifting dark, looking sharp while maneuvering his way toward us to pounce like a starving alienated bear fresh out of hibernation. It was like he had one smile at a time while glaring his evil stare, as we were automatically overwhelmed with hard decisions that clouded our judgments like a rocky path that's not safe; but we were encountering a once in a lifetime achievement where things seemed impossible, so naming our price seemed to excessive for this intimidating stranger. Kevin surprisingly shouted, "Every man for himself!" As we clumsily back pedaled toward the entrance of the train, my sixth-sense instantaneously noticed that there were rays of rugged light spiraling through a square vent in the roof that hung like a loophole of "Praising the Lord" for hope. I cautiously glanced back to pinpoint our persistent pursuer, when I saw this cunning creature of a brute reaching upward to yank a well hidden rope that hung from the corner of the ceiling; so I quickly accelerated my pace to escape, because I felt something bad was about to occur. In the mix of all the drama that was unfolding, Kevin was rapidly and militarily loading his slingshot in the course of retreating toward the door, as he fired his first shot for victory. The semi-heavy rock object whizzed through the air gracefully striking Sacman in the corner of his temple right below his protective head gear, causing the large hideous giant to stumble as he awkwardly fell toward the twisted fibers of rope. Kevin continued running with all his might as he frantically fled for freedom, not noticing that his shirt had gotten snagged on a "where ever it came from" metal yard decoration that cluttered this maze of a monstrous mansion. Off balance and confused, Sacman had finally tugged his hidden lever of rope, which caused the train door to violently slam shut behind me as I cannon balled onto the soft mud terrain that laid very forgiving on the comforts of the outside. I landed as if there's always silence before a kill; while quickly noticing that Kevin wasn't behind me, making me feel like I was reaching out to someone who had become very distant, although slightly being out of sight and out of mind. Kevin had been shook to the roots, despite the fact that he was a hothead on a mission for respect; he was now trapped and ambushed with nowhere to run like a mouse with its tail caught in a primitive man-made snare. The fear was so overwhelming that I started to run knowing that jeopardy was his jailer, as the love I felt for my cousin started making me feel angry inside causing me too defiantly grasp the inner strength that sat like an anchor deep inside of my being; "To stop and fight!" I was now James the son of a soldier, the son of a hero, who was about to withstand the unimaginable stages of this enduring nightmare that left an eerie stench in this jumbled atmosphere easily consumed, "As soon to disappear." I heroically gazed at the frightened girls in their hiding spots with their faces appearing so cold and without emotion; it was like looking into an empty mirror with no reflection to give its true feeling. Even Rene was in a world of fear while squatting behind a massive oak tree motionless but trembling a hard to believe sight I had never seen before on my daring sister's face. Finally, the lost words that were seeking to be found uttered from her mouth as we made eye contact when she eventually said, "Save him Jayme! Please save him!" The shock in her panicky voice set off an alarm, triggering my legs to start running back toward the train car to reclaim my cousin; quietly climbing the ladder on left front side of this thoughtless hideaway where I was to plan my next attack. I immediately made a beeline toward the vent in the ceiling of the train that I had observed when escaping the clutches of his startling monstrosities, instantly peering inside like a polecat ready to ambush these immediate issues that had my life floating upside down. I could see the trails of light from Sacman's helmet zoomed in on Kevin, backing him further and further into a corner of the train away from the sealed tight entrance door. The scene was a vision of Samson and Goliath fighting their epic battle in an oversized chamber, where respect was everything. I dreadfully wanted to avoid this situation like a catastrophe; because it would be like trying to save a frightened kid trapped in a Gorilla cage at the local zoo. My courage had finally reached its acme as I hurled my tense body from the rooftop like a stone Gargoyle, jumping through the ceiling vent that was set for me to meet such a scarce Legend, while rapidly descending and simultaneously whacking Sacman across the back of his neck with my "Spinks defeater "nightstick as I crash landed like a sledge hammer on the train floor. The huge man stumbled over one of the concealing crates and tumbled to the fragile surface causing the floor to release an agonizing scream of pain, as Kevin nervously sat in a crab like position reaching out for my hand to speedily help him to his feet as he searched hysterically for his faithful slingshot. Sacman had now recovered and looked madder than ever; it was like he was freezing us in time from the awe of this massive giant's presence causing us to barely be able to move or think in a clear mind frame. When all of a sudden, I heard the breaking of the floor boards shattering beneath Kevin's feet as he quickly grabbed a corner of a board to keep from collapsing into this pitfall of a hole. At first as he looked below, he could only hear the hissing of vengeful reptiles that awaited his arrival and as he looked closer toward the bottom of the darkness blinding this decayed cavity, his focus was noticing objects moving in a circular S like pattern making their numbers countless to his naked eye. The gaseous fumes that were being released seemed non-toxic but very pungent, and alluring concerning my sensitive allergies that were at its heightened peak of agitation. I couldn't control an overwhelming sneeze that seemed to dampen this Devil's task, but he was resilient in continuing his "blood on the tracks" attack! I just so happen to have a vial of my special angel dust which was a mixture of pepper, garlic powder, and saw dust readily caressed in my left hand and as I spun to protect myself from his onslaught, I flipped the lid to the container and threw it vigorously into Sacman's face and within that single precise motion temporarily blinded him causing him to wither to the shattering floor. As he laid helpless in a fetal position, I glanced back toward Kevin to see that his grasp was slipping, and he was about to fall like Humpty Dumpty hanging from a wall. So, I darted over to him as fast as I could sliding down to my knees, when I noticed that the creatures inside this black hole were becoming more visible from the daylight shining through the large opening in the ceiling. I could see that it was filled with huge Copper Heads with demands for a festive meal that would satisfy their hunger of bite and ask questions later. I continuously searched the gaping hole looking for an escape route for my overzealous compadre and me, but there was only about a three foot gap between the train bottom and the hole; leaving us just enough room to Spiderman our way underneath the train to reach safe ground. I grabbed my cousin's hand tightly and slightly started swinging him side to side above the opening as

I told him that on the count of three, I was going to let go after building enough momentum to toss him to a secure surface below. I patiently let go at the count of three, as Kevin stealthily landed like an agile Panther automatically reaching back with his paw of a hand trying to release me from my scariest of trepidations. His hand snugly clasped my hand, as I held onto the broken flooring of the train trying to position my body for this bungee of a jump. My concentration was mainly on escape, when suddenly out of the corner of my eye, I saw a ghostly dark shadow hovering above my head like a broken halo where sudden loss diminishes the gleam in a person's soul causing light to dissipate slowly toward being lost forever. Kevin tugged and pulled me with a jerking motion toward him to elude the venomous vipers below, as Sacman cleverly clawed at my situation with his sluggish, scarred hands trying to get a hold of my swaying, dangling body. Kevin finally yanked me so hard like a rag doll hanging flimsy and loose; that my upper body hit the soft dirt before my legs had a chance to adjust to the severity of this underhanded evasion. When I landed, Kevin swiftly tugged and rolled our bodies toward the front of the train where safety was sure but not guaranteed. We courageously crawled from beneath this haunted house, as if the ghouls and demons inside were not welcoming, but very much vindictive about us trying to see what we could find. Dusk was moving upon us at a snail's pace, as we scanned back at the horizon as if it spoke a warning of words saying, "You got what you deserved, but your punishment has not been quite handed down." I instantly thought I could hear the music of Heaven parading, as the colossal train door flew crashing to an ambiguous outset with Sacman standing in the doorway with a sinister posture of "Please come again." We started running toward our bicycles like we were in a chariot race of violent reactions as we began yelling to the girls, "Run for your lives! The monster has been provoked like a sleeping giant with no remorse." Our Deepwater Daredevils were now in an accelerated retreat, where looking back could cost us capture or instant death from the insanity that protected this crazy house of a crocodiles pit. Lucifer's favorite demon had been summoned; rudely awakened to destroy everything in sight or anything that reminded him of his devastating past where hearts were truly broken. Athena's father Zeus couldn't have brought such a wartime offense, as we glanced up the winding path leading from this certainty of "sweet misery"; where amazingly appearing were all the other Deepwater Daredevils rushing toward us with Walter Smith(the oldest of our team), blowing his rusty bugle as if he were leading a Calvary of trained militia. I also witnessed Charlie Crowder with his two sisters Serena and Tammy forming a smooth squadron of go-getters that were amped up for the action that ensued, while following close behind was little Thomas Radford charging with outstanding bravery with the faint glare of the sun glistening from all their hardened faces. This was a perfect time for relief because I knew we would be known as the ones that got away like we had posted bail, and avoided the bounty that was laid on our precious heads. Walter and the rest of the Daredevils had formed a "leading the way" line with their bicycles, and one by one slid them sideways to a screeching halt to make a so-called "Dustbowl of Diversion" to protect us from this unspeakable wrath. The massive dust cloud from the dirt path rose with blinding agitation as if smoke signals were being sent to cover this frozen moment in time as well as my mind, even as we followed the tempo that had been set; that was so cunning and alluring even to the most masterful of naughty and notorious schemes. This Deepwater clean- up crew had entered a situation where rules were meant to be broken, but there were no more playing games since Sacman had put a new twist in an old snake, where he thrived on the panic and mayhem as if he were the emperor of "Eternal Evil." He was a prime example of a dangerous shark in shallow water where none lives to tell the tale, bringing its fatalities familiar to the depths of premeditated punishment in uncharted territory, where exploration was heavily denied. We knew that by pressing our luck we might get caught red handed; but as we all turned suddenly to combat this uncivilized "Sham Artist of Surprise", it seemed that he had disappeared like a ghost through a wagered wall with a conservative price only to reappear later when least expected. Our team of want-to-bee's, was relentlessly surveying the area but there was no trace of this sinister figure; whereas Kevin was still in silent mode not saying a word like this traumatic fear had shattered the lining of his insides causing heavy uncertainty to loiter on his mind. So I finally spoke up, now knowing that my soul had a unique purpose as I confidently said, "Guys, we need to think of a better strategy for conquering this Emperor of never-ending evil, but we'll need time to carve a sculpture of unified success with this tremendous burden that has been laid like a prolonged attack." "Let's just head home with our new found confidence and take a good look within our hearts and regroup, while we get everything organized at the Radford's carport and sit down to pray; because you all know that Jesus calls!" With one more extended stare at this perilous habitat, we all slowly pedaled away wondering if our free spirits were lucky, or was it fate that helped us escape this unpredictable opponent known for horror, and hazardously horsing around. We were jubilantly making our way home with the noiseless sun beaming dull rays of hope on our backs, and still not a word was spoken; only confused glances and the strain of exhaustion were implanted on our completely non-telling faces like poker was our main agenda for justly speaking our thoughts clearly. Presently, over the horizon we could see the Radford's carport nearing our line of focus as the other boys and I began to pedal faster, and faster. I guess it was a manly challenge for us to see who would lead the troops into battle for our next raid to capture this enemy that we were so crazy about clobbering, while doing more to protect the clueless community that more than always often turned the other cheek. My adrenaline was still running excessively high, but somehow the courage I embraced in myself had me taking off full speed toward the carport gripping tightly on my left hand brake, causing the bike to jackknife on its front tire while flipping lightly with my body to make the bike spin in a 360 degree turn, and then land violently but adamantly on its rear tire. Everyone started chanting, "Deepwater Daredevils, Deepwater Daredevils, Deepwater Daredevils," as we all made our way to the picnic tables centered underneath this "Mountain home for various walks of life. Throughout the entire clamor, rejoicing, and celebrating; somehow I was able to go to a place in my mind where I was alone and away from being hurried into this present day of Indiana Jones liveliness. I gradually perceived each and every child's face that had disappeared begging for someone to free their souls from limbo, by extinguishing the cold hearted flames that burned eternally in Sacman's soulless unforgiving frame. It was like I heard Pow-wow drums as I was shaken out of my daydream, of just a little dream of me state, while crossing the threshold of deeper dimensions of destiny. As I became fully focused to the situation; I observed that everyone was sitting on the picnic tables disputing back and forth of when we should go back to Sacman's lair to have a rematch in his "No Man's Land." We were like rats scurrying out of the dark, but a new choice of man or mouse had been formed, having us willing to become more than just young men and women but champions through this demanding ordeal. We still had the appearance of timid Gazelles at a watering hole being vulnerable to attack; but with enough precision of planning we might make it to see the next soul-soothing sunrise. Behind the scene, Kevin and Charlie were already plotting another incursion, where they wanted to infiltrate "The Lost One's" hideaway at nighttime to conceal our approach and to plant traps around his camp to hopefully be able to capture him without any confrontation. Time quickly passed like a childhood hour as we traveled down this same old road; but constant faith and loving someone with all your heart made our journey so strong that any opposition wouldn't be able to break the bond we shared. When out of the blue, Serena surprisingly stood on the picnic table and started talking loudly toward Kevin and Charlie's secret session they were having as she said, "You two so-called Supermen are just setting yourselves up to be permanent clowns with magic bubbles coming out of your rears; it's like you're pulling rainbow scarves out of your Dumbo ears." "I want ya'll to remember that we're part of this team too, so don't try to destroy our sense of unity!" Rene started snickering lightly with still that gleam of alarm in her eyes, as she innocently stood on the table top beside her. You could tell by the flutter in her voice when she spoke, that the big sister who exemplified the world of bold had somehow been depleted; and now stood there as just an ordinary girl with a mother's protectiveness in her welcoming heart. Her body swayed off-beat from the nervous atmosphere causing her to speak with a low tone, while dragging her words hesitatingly; that were made somewhat clear when she finally said, "Listen carefully my Daredevil Danger Seekers!" Her voice had that strange flicker of hope of an entrancing lure, with her dialogue being pin-point projected toward us as she stood there like Caesar orating to a forum of his concerned colleagues. She continued her speech of "letting us know"; as her words became stronger having a more aggressive tone while proudly saying, "We are on the verge of destruction; and I can see the monster happily destroying us one by one if we pursue this outrageous venture of bravery. "I could actually feel that he was easily turned wicked from righteous, and he's just not looking for that spiritual road back home." "He see's through a vindictive mind's eye that seems untouchable and unapproachable by any mortal being that doesn't have that true connection with our Lord and Savior Jesus Christ." "Our escape was luck at its finest; but the odds all speak death as an outcome if our faith and belief isn't right in our hearts; so I caringly cry, because this is a life worth living for all the sentimental memories that are bounded in time like a last breath." "Walter and I are the oldest, and guys I've seen too much stressful intensity today to make me agree with your simple decisions." If I have to protect you all; I'll go tell Uncle Bobby and Aunt Brenda, only to save each and every one of your souls; so remember hearts is what this demon dwells on, and loss of family is a cost I'm not willing to pay to honor our bravery, or to honor our undetermined fates." "I just love you all..." as she broke down weeping with her voice clogged with mournful mumbles of distress gaspingly saying, "Deepwater Daredevils Forever!" Everyone was in awe and deeply inspired by her speech, especially the girls who were a tight knit group; and all of them had weighty tears that uncontrollably dripped down their reserved faces, but for some reason the boys were a high-strung, peculiar bunch that were bent on proving that what was going on here in our community could be, and would be stopped; it's just the nature of pride. Our emotions were running thin like the gravity causing them to pull in multiple directions, as I inadvertently noticed the well kept shrubbery around the carport trembling from the gust of the night wind like it too had run up against this new troublemaker of terror. Rene and Serena both nodded at each other in silent agreement with the wind ferociously picking up more, as they stepped down from the tabletop like run-way models with stately concerns. Walter automatically sprung from his sitting position like an agile acrobat performing his most eye- catching fete; standing on his hands from the seat portion of the bench, and then walking on them while reaching the tabletop quickly and directly snapping his legs in a violent donkey kick to end up in an erect standing position, posing with his hands laid across his chest letting everyone know that he was the man, and that he was the big dog loose from its chain. He immediately started to talk saying, "My young brothers and sisters, I say sometimes a cigar is just a cigar but gallantry is commitment, honor to defend, and protect what your hearts season to believe in with its entire core." "This courted dance of death has me fully aware that we can surely dominate, by working as a unit with unusual powers that would ignite like a blaze of glory running amok through this mountainous countryside; where all we are asking for is a chance to stop the robbing of our young children's souls." "Will we sink, or will we swim is the question?" "I guess we'll find out in a matter of time, but telling anybody should be forbidden; because as I lead you down that lonely path where dark clouds align the horizon, we will steamroll our way, all day to victory!" "So don't be scared or let this fastidious fear overwhelm your true caliber that simmers to severity through your gracious veins." "Stand tall in the face of peril and use your minds to out think, and outwit this evil dastardly do-dirty who preys on defenseless innocence, as I ask you all to continue to advance with every breath, even your last one, while reaching for that victorious climax where we can embrace that final lasting hour together with the Deepwater Daredevils sublime in God's eyes." "I say heed young children of craftiness and creativity, because I have envisioned the burnt and broken shells of previous heroes who have stepped up for the challenge and tragically failed, but this is truly a blessing where our spirits can soar to find that so-called unreachable peace while being tremendously thankful to our All Knowing Almighty." "This savage beast has no calm in his repertoire but he can't outrun his past, and I really don't know why he does these God awful things, but I actually felt a malicious chill run through my body as we approached you guys at his hidden lair that told me that your unexpected raid was very productive, and it was a step closer to learning the infamous mystery of this unforgettable Sacman." He ended his extraordinary speech by saying, "Honor and Respect can be found on the battlefield of the mind with goals and objectives being set, can you trust yourselves to face this target and honestly say, "I can't lose, and I will not lose"; that is the question only you guys can answer, Daredevils unite!" Walter enthusiastically jumped from the tabletop pounding his chest and running around in circles underneath the sturdy safe guarding apple tree that made our cheering, and jubilation reach enormous heights like a rousing night at Mardi Gras. Night time had quietly fallen, as we all continued to debate over ideas that would help us complete the task that we had set out to accomplish; capture Sacman and try to find the missing children from the community, or to reclaim their deserted bodies. We were determined to overcome even though our time was running short, but we were already thinking of ways for this weekend visit to last for at least another week. So, we sent Lia and Nece to talk to

Uncle Bobby and Aunt Brenda, because they had those daughter ways of getting what they wanted from their parents without a lot of questions. While they were gone pleading our desperate case, my mind began to wander again as if I heard the staff of Moses touch the ground with burning pages from an ordained scripture crumbling, and then evaporating into mid-air. I could feel the enticing wind caressing my body as I heard Falling Angels with their wings flapping uncontrollably trying to regain their stability with their flagrant flutters seeming almost a shadow length away. The two speeches that we had just heard were so mind awakening that it thrust my memory further into the past, where I could remember my Father telling me that speeches were given to motivate, and unite the masses; and my Mother informing me that lectures were given to touch a person's mind and heart to make them feel that they belong, and are accepted by the things the orator is speaking so dearly about for witness. It was linked advice that had served so well for me because both portions of information were unique, and honest for my train of thought. My psyche was so obscure from my Sacman recollections that his offensive purchase of children's livelihoods cast a sinister scenario that left my heart in a solemn place. So, I said Lord please break it to me gently when you say I love you, and Father protect us from all the evil we may encounter, as I respectfully kneel for your embrace of acceptance when my time grows still. For Father we have a huge task at hand and without your guidance we will surely fail; but what I've seen from our encounter with this creature thus far, is that he's trying to say that we didn't truly know his story; so Lord give him a chance to plead his case, and tell it through his witness, Amen.

CHAPTER II

Papa's got a new bag

Legends are painted through story or passed down folklore that captures the thoughts of those on a journey for knowledge, while waiting to excite the curiosities that dwell deep in their state of minds. Every myth has a beginning, but can we truly say that they always come crashing to a consequential end. Some of these Tales are unusual and just can't be explained, but let me try to clarify the resurrection of this Bed Time Villain that had masses of youth trembling in the safety of their own bedrooms. It was like a Fitzgerald story; "The man who could have everything but love, while knowing that love was nothing but heartbreak and disappointment; he was set on demolishing everything that had crushed his endearment of existence." It was one year prior to the first Sacman sighting in Deepwater, West Virginia; that this tale originated, and was actually being born with "rings of deceit" hurling through the air of this small plant district of Rand, West Virginia which was located twenty-five miles down the Kanawha River, just a Buck's ear away from the States capital of Charleston West Virginia. It was a place where many metaphorical masks had consumed the fumes from its substantial Carbide plant that left a rotten egg smell seemingly everlasting throughout this diminutive locality that pungently withered their nasal hairs; but was so beautiful to the natural order of things. It was like a wild animal had been trapped in a cage; where it had to prove its maturity at an early age, making this fair town seem sinister in its efforts to cling to the brutality of the physical world. As time went by; a lonely path of alcoholism would be a looking glass into other worlds of how he found the strength to try to decipher between Death and a non-seen transition of Rebirth. Time alone would tell if this Sacman phenomenon really had a good reason to rise in this "knowing your limits; as they say time heals the heart" vagueness. This man with a weighty chip on his shoulder was see-sawing back and forth patiently while juggling the insanity inside of himself, trying to figure out if he should be there terrorizing this unsuspecting community of Deepwater, or should he just go away without living beyond the prospects of hope. It was like a rocket housing waiting to eject its final resolve with wish granters disappearing into thin air without a hint or clue; causing a tragic abomination of his cursed, guilty conscience to evolve while earnestly trying to settle a score that had no reflection of the games being played; so let his story be told. Thomas Wolfe was a local coalminer with three beautiful children and a harlot of a wife caught up in his everyday life of work, and the secret shame of his family's unknown home shenanigans. Collusion provoked this trusting man, who was too scared to notice the truth to finally unleash a hidden side of his self; like asking for some one's canteen in the desert, where Thomas was a symbol of thirst in their weary eyes but he had seen the madness of tragedy like he was grasping at desperation to finally reach that unavoidable conclusion. Thomas actually thought he had a perfect life with a gorgeous wife named Sara, a loving daughter that was eighteen years old named Jenny, who had dropped out of high school her junior year but had managed to save faith in her Father's eyes. He also had two sons, Thomas Jr. who was fifteen years old and was an avid hunter, and fisherman while his youngest son Squirt was seven years old and was considered by many as a "Daddy's Boy" who wanted to be just like his Dad. Thomas was a generation Coalminer, and Squirt loved everything about his father exploring the underground worlds that he encountered; like he was discovering new territory with interesting artifacts. It was young Squirt's fascination of finding shiny, black coal rocks that he collected and treasured, while keeping the ones that shined the brightest like the stars in the depths of space. Squirt would often climb into his tree house at night and gaze for hours at the untouchable elements that seemed to float like fire fly's illuminating the secrecy of the skies. He would daydream about being an astronaut that investigated the vast dark regions of space in search of an unlimited supply of shiny coal. He even purchased a coal sack with his allowance he received every week, getting it inscribed saying, "Papa's Bag" in the top right corner where his dad would see it and think of him every time he opened his gracious gift. Thomas would always take it to work and bring home the shiniest of "black gold" which was a nickname that Squirt gave the founded coal, because of the value it instilled in his priceless soul. Thomas's wife owned a hair salon right beside a local bar called "Fire in the Belly", which left the cupboard door wide open to corrupt the heart of a not yet awakened monster. His daughter Jenny also owned a salon, but her shop was located on the other side of the Kanawha River in a tiny, quaint town called Chesapeake, West Virginia. Thomas knew by buying her a business, it would keep the young lass out of trouble, and make her feel like she could make it in this brutal world; but he would find out later that he was sadly mistaken. Now pay attention closely as Thomas's life takes a spiraling nose dive into a pool of misconception; leading him down that lonely deep end road where the power of vindications were lame at its very best. There was bad news to distribute as he sleepily made his way to his pickup truck departing for his early morning shift in the adventure seeking mines, with his "Papa's got a new bag" Squirt had given him clinched tightly in his hand as he threw it over his right shoulder. He was looking up uncomfortably at the mountains confining his home that had been turned into coalmine barren lands with no growth on their flat crown surfaces, which left him with the thought of demons that dwell in the darkness of morality letting him know that relevancy, had a chance to stand out. As his eyes wandered from the mountain tops, his attention was now being drawn to a white envelope placed like a poorly laid Easter egg for a child to easily discover: seemingly simple and elementary for an unsuspecting reliable soul. His eyes were now wide open like a bat out of hell, but he was feeling confused like being lost in the middle of a thought, as he silently asked himself was he in the mood for this early morning, ice chilling intrigue. Thomas disturbingly started to read this "Curious George" letter that was warning him of seduction and betrayal as his heart started to thump like a taught Tom-Tom drum. What seemed at first so faultless, and innocent immediately sparked his emotions into a raging storm of questions that had him wondering why this was being done to him. He asked himself again, and again "Where in the world was the time of grace" while his thoughts were being uniquely unanchored leaving him in a state of being caught up in the moment with no answers or solutions.

The letter read: "Dear Mr. Trusting and confused, I'm not impressed with your wife and daughters sexual favors for my hard earned money; so it's kind of idiotic how clueless you really are when it comes to belief and being true to yourself." "For the past six months my friends and I have exploited their sexual prowess to our brutal advantage." "They're just dishonest, hometown call girls that are being prostituted out of the businesses you paid for; so that has to make you the dumbest Johnny riding off into the sunset, Billy bad ass with a deep breath of bitter bygones, sucker ass fool on this side of lunacy." "I say to you that Time will determine how it will all end, so I actually do feel grief for your situation because you were just an unavoidable victim of circumstance." "Sincere regrets, from a friend you never had!" "Like they say in the game of chess, a pawn is just a minimal asset, where its loss doesn't sting influence as much when addressing a strategic issue early, and often." "Always remember this Tommy boy, always remember!" As Thomas finished reading his "Dear John" letter, tears of pain slowly trickled down his face dripping Reaper repercussions on the neatly folded paper that had slightly crumbled from the tension and the newly added pressure throbbing panicky through his hands. Startled and apprehensive, he exhaustedly made his way into the driver's seat of now his lonely "Fortress of Great Awakening" with the unforgiving Heavens chanting "A man alone is against all odds", which sounded like broken bells that were out of tune chiming through the seemingly "out of the light" valley. He went to start the truck using precautionary measures as he gently turned the key to the ignition not knowing what to expect next. It was like he had spent the whole night awake, where you don't forget about tomorrow but regret that you survived another night of rage, and paranoia standing in the shadows of the unstrung powers of revenge. The turbulent Saturday morning winds surrounded his misery as if to say, "Silence is sometimes soothing, but in this case leaning heavily toward the border line of over the limit." His heart had been destroyed by the rancor that was so radical, that he was lost in a battle of wills where you have your worst nightmare but can't seem to make it stop. Someone had to be held responsible as he searched through his thoughts impatiently to himself; but he had to fulfill his obligations and go to his dangerous job in the mines with his judgments soaring like the hawks searching for prey in the heavenly mountains of Hawks Nest, West Virginia. Thomas contemplated about what the future held for him but all he could envision were scattered shambles and tattered tragedies engulfed by the brutalities of man. He couldn't believe their insolence, but a history of deceit and jealousy had plagued the Wolfe men for generations and now his time had finally come. Thomas didn't spend his whole life of making precious memories and working so hard to have it all end in this "getting closer to the truth" web of Mad House mystery. "To God be the glory and may he have mercy on my soul," as he prayed with his head bowed soothingly resting in the palms of his hands. Now, as he slowly opened his eyes looking toward the house he saw Squirt waving from the second floor window with a piece of coal held above his head with an enormous smile on his artless face. If you could see the stolen moments in his eyes, it was like a Titan straddling good and evil wondering how could God leave him here in this situation all alone, or was being deserted and making his own way by being betrayed the grand plan to delve into the darker aspects of faith and fortune. Thomas was distraught like a blackthorn had pricked his finger with the blood flowing endlessly; where a bandage would only conceal the power that endures the infliction. His home, where he used to hang his hat was on the cutting edge of all work and no play while giving everything he'd ever had, like the first soldier being put through the fields of war with time displaying past and angry spirits waiting for more conflict, danger, and challenges that were speedily on their way. He could hear a convincing voice blaring through his head that he should approach this crazy condition by being completely upfront, while simply giving up the whole lot as this journey through life seemed pointless at the present, leaving him suicidal and reckless. Some men fear the unknown, and some men fear the night, where their dark pasts are full of fuming mobs with a will to choose if they can advance further than anyone had ever dreamed. At the moment his pride was noble but never tearful in saying his last goodbyes that seemed impossible but somehow Thomas's full focus was on Sqirt and the sentimental value of his "Papa's got a new bag" tucked neatly by his side. He gradually backed his way down the gravel driveway still with his attentions on the shadow of his son fading slowly from the window like a shooting star blending into the immense after death of outer space. Thomas knew his concentration had been shaken and working underground today would be like the falling skies taking his breath away, but somehow, someway he had to maintain and continue to provide like he had done for many years. He had the worst feeling of being betrayed by someone close to him, because he finally realized that their masked love was all just a well played lie. As he leaned away from the sunlit cab window he felt nothing but pure darkness corrupting his purpose, and his passions were delirious like he had been injected with a huge dose of suspense or was severely punctured by a runaway train waiting on a chain reaction of catastrophe. It was a lot more to Thomas that met the naked eye and it would be just a matter of time before his true hand would be forced to be revealed. It seemed that his soul was totally removed from the present and the rules of this mystery had key issues that were formidable for any adversary overlooking the vital points. Karma was tauntingly prodding his memories and exposing them to a great deal of risks where failure would be fatal, but with a little bit of luck his heart would be convinced by the distinctive markings left on a glorified coalminer where he simply couldn't help himself to justification. Understanding what he was trying to achieve had to be torture for him; more than you could imagine! What would you plan to do if foul play had you stopped cold like hell had frozen over and you had so many questions with no answers; would you just continue to ask? Would you care to explain why we all have some kind of ability of human perception that remembers those special moments forever but can't seem to block out the pains and agonies that curse our hearts as if we live them over and over just to balance out the two ways of thought. In the meanwhile Thomas had instantaneously come sliding out of his collection of mental consumptions like a third base runner trying to make it to that home plate of safe and sound. He had finally arrived at the half dirt, half gravel winding roads of Robson, West Virginia that lead further up into the mountains where the mine entrance was located. Thomas suddenly felt the ground shake from the charges of dynamite that were being set off in a staggered pattern, I guess to open up a second entrance into the mine where he worked. It was like God had handed him the keys to a castle, where he didn't have a choice of breaking this positive pattern of prevailing, and it was actually a breath of fresh air to escape the turmoil of his everyday home life where sh** had hit the fan. In the good old days he would work all day and all night, but when he got off work all he could do was sleep and have his dreams take him anywhere his mind felt the joys of peace. You can only go so far when you've been blind- sided by confusion, but Thomas knew all about time and where you find a lot of magic out there like skin walker's casting a spell of hell. He was wading through these murky obscurities to eventually find his way home to that fascinating old town of Rand, like a night of the coyote where his visions were racing desperately to the moon to escape the slipping away sensations that had gathered like a whole flock of vultures. He thought that these bold birds of prey waited till you were dead before they started picking at your bones, but with a little motion of fear such as a shiver or quiver could get you eaten alive like a piranha on dry land. Thomas's pickup truck gradually made its way to the employee parking entrance, when he observed his supervisor standing on a makeshift platform with about fifty to sixty coal miners anchored around him with an inquisitive way about all of them. The scene was artistically set as an image of banded brothers like nomads gathered at a scarce oasis where the desert had them greeting the day with caution, and a great respect for the unknown. When Thomas had finally made his way from the parking lot and joined the grim-faced onlookers that had inquiring expressions spread deeply across their faces, he instantly noticed his friend Collus sitting on his lunch pail with a half eaten egg sandwich and a thermos full of hot coffee resting like a pleasantry in his gigantic hands. Collus perceptively looked up, while smiling like he had happy clown's makeup spread flawlessly across his face as Thomas nonchalantly neared when he said, "Look what the wind blew in! A big sack of donkey manure with the stench of an aggravated Elephants a** flapping like a flag in the wind." Thomas and Collus both started laughing hysterically like Johnny Carson or Don Rickles had told the funniest joke they had ever heard. Thomas cracked backed like he was recoiling a whip to zing it aggressively back at his "words of play partner of Para-phrases and punch in the face." He easily replied with a "spunk of spice come back "as he sportily said, "It looks like your trying to cure an explosive case of diarrhea by shoving that metal box of a plug up your lose lips of an a**, you cock-a-doddle-doo-doo face caveman." Now this was always their normal greeting of hello, as Collus sprang up quickly from his lunch pail like a jack rabbit about to leap over a burning bush of magicians screaming painful moans of "Abra-ka- dabra" or "Presto" to finalize an impressive feat. The two jokesters both had smiles on their faces a mile wide, as they gave each other a brotherly hug and a hearty handshake; while still laughing and patting each other on the back. Collus was a giant of a man as was Thomas, and both were drawn to one another immediately when they met fifteen years ago on their first day of work at the Robson mine. Thomas said, "Thank you Collus for making me laugh because I've got a lot dragging me down today and ribbing with you has made me feel like I should own the rest of the day." Collus gave an amusing and concerned response by saying, "Tom my bighead brother, this mine is our ship of salvation and somehow it creates dreams of immortality by surviving our dangerous feats that we encounter in these pits of tortuous torment." "I wish I could explain, but you and I are still breathing and kicking so that's all that counts! We are definitely what historians would call "true survivors." As they gave each other another "believe in me" handshake, the loud speaker started to roar and whine like it was walking noisily through the most sensitive of eardrums to get an alarming point across by shocking their attentions into a stand-still. John Clark the mine supervisor (who everyone called JC for short) was about to give his morning "rally the troops" speech and now all ears were tuned in to his bravado broadcast. John shouted, "Good morning Local Fifty-one! The mighty sun is glaring over our precious heads today, and our zest for life has been activated to the "adapt and endure instincts" that are passing amid worries through the gateway rays of light, while gradually opening like corridors leading our souls victoriously over the biggest hurdles; where painted pictures of yester year line the incomparable hallways like fine carved tapestries." "It's like the birth of a tornado, where old secrets come to light while gradually spreading like bright flowers such as romantic roses and tranquil tulips with close irreplaceable bonds; but somehow blatantly blind to the odds stacked against them." "I say safety is our goal!" "Safety is our jobs!" "My good friends, I say safety is our life!" "So let's get to work, and remember safety is waiting patiently for all of us to return tomorrow just as our families expect us to come home." "Safety lingers as if it were sulking angrily for us to keep it flourishing in our home away from home and may God keep us safe!" "Stand tall my Local Fifty-one and protect what you love; I say protect your brothers and sisters in this underground whimsical of a world; today and everyday!" Everyone knew JC was power playing the positives, and his speech was like a thousand words of "hoopla" and "rah rah"; but they all had the same meaning as before. He had made it all so clear like a lion tamer; where you have to be aggressive in your approach as you journey through these extreme cases of life's unknown dangers and mysteries. As Thomas suddenly turned to walk toward the mine entrance an eerie feeling flowed through his insides for a brief shocking moment like two tons of sand grains were seething through a narrow opening leaving a spotty trail of evidence to its climatic cause of "Beware!" When out of the calmness of the reformed unity that now graced their spirits to achieve; the loud speaker once again wailed a tune of attraction drawing everyone's attention back toward the center stage. JC held the microphone tensely by his side while he was in a heated discussion with his trusted underlings, Jeff and Carl Edward the mines Foremen and Shift Safety Coordinators. All the miners had stopped cold in their tracks clueless to the rough patch of distress that was about to unfold. It seemed that everyone was heading for the skies and if they got lost in it, it would be off into the wild while being barely out of time like a shattered one armed clock. It was like looking at the Sun that you couldn't touch but prayed for dreams to come true when you're dancing around the obvious when the so-called constants have fallen apart. John was now waving his hand in the air frantically signaling everyone to gather around once again. He finally spoke after conferring with his two specialists as he said, "Attention, Attention Local Fifty-one; Code Black!" (Which meant the mine was unsafe to enter and that every miner from the previous shift and the one starting at 7:00 A.M. had to be accounted for with no discrepancies?) He cautiously continued by saying, "The explosives set off earlier has weakened the foundation leading into the initial mine entrance, causing a major cave-in." "When all hell breaks loose, we still have to stand and deliver!" "So I ask each and every one of you to cooperate with the Safety Staff that's ready to take a head count to speed up this process of search and recovery." "Please give your Crew Shift Leads name, followed by your name, and the shift that you are assigned to work." "As it stands now the mine was clear of any crews still operating in the mine, but urgency is a must to make sure our whole family is safe." "Rescue Teams have been dispatched to the scene just in case our advisory of miner's still in the mine is inaccurate, and to be set in place and ready if anymore problems arise." "We have set up five tables near the mobile cafeteria to give the protocol that we have requested." "So at this time, I ask that you all form lines at the tables and give our Safety Team the necessary information that they will need to conduct the mines policies and procedures to a Tee!" "When you are finished with your needed "punctual efficiencies" (which were big words for information, that JC loved throwing around to show his scholarly side of his West Virginia backwoods upbringings); you will be considered on stand-by, meaning do not leave the site and be ready to continue work once the mine has been cleared of all dangers that are detrimental to our safety." "Make sure all of you sign the time sheets so that you get paid, and please hang tight for hourly updates that will be transmitted through the mines loud speakers." "God Bless us all!" After JC finished his announcement, everyone started forming lines at the designated tables to quickly help with the process of pinpointing all employees' whereabouts, whether it was above ground or still located in the mine. Collus earnestly filled out the Safety Teams sheets and briskly started walking straight toward Thomas, who had finally made his way to the front of one of the lines. Collus, with no thought or care started shouting in his enthusiastic voice that he always communicated in, which was "loud and proud"; "Tom!" "Tommy!" "Let me catch some Z's in the back of your truck man, so I can feel like I'm sleeping on the dock of the bay waiting on that quiet midnight hour." Thomas started laughing like a hyena in heat, as he was finishing the forms needed for compliance with the mines safety standards. He gave a semi-concealed chuckle as he said, "Pre (which was short for Collus's last name Preatta.)" "It's sitting on the dock of the bay big brother; but I have to admit your word play can't be matched." "It's as if you're plucking a web guitar while making that funky music dance like a hula girl that's seducing the most celibate of ears." "God's speed, my Lion like maestro of laziness!" "Go do your perfected imitation of Slacker Joe browsing through the candy store, taking a guided tour knowing he's coming back for more; laid back like a fat cat rubbing his belly waiting on that mouse to mature into that rat of all rats." "So quit licking your chops and go setup shop Big Bro, and here are the keys to the lock box in the back of my truck." "Make sure you grab the sleeping bags and the beach umbrella, and I'll be there in a minute to parade around the boundaries of paradise while listening to beautiful music like little angels that's important to the past." Now with a sense of pressing importance, Thomas speedily completed his paperwork and briskly started walking toward the mobile cafeteria to grab his radio that he had left sitting in the bay window the day before while taking his last break. After retrieving his handy radio, Tom headed toward the employee parking lot full of gust; like a violent windstorm sweeping a path of "get out of my way, here I come, … dumb ditty dumb." He automatically acted like he didn't notice Collus hard working on their cabana of comfort for kings, because discretion was like a session with a Psychiatrist… "Shh, Don't tell know body." Pre had gotten everything perfectly set in place, and the only things missing were the music and the relaxing drinks to soothe even the longest nights or just simply to take the edge off the shortest of stand-still days. Collus lackadaisically looked up and saw Thomas approaching causing his emotions to quickly reach a state of anxiousness as he said, "Hot damn man!" and simultaneously jumped out of the back of the truck with a sprinter's trot heading directly for the trunk of his car as he abruptly came to screeching halt. It seemed Pre was in relentless pursuit like a posse, as he scavenged through his trunk for what looked like a bright red suitcase that was definitely dripping moisture on the gravel beneath the bumper of his car, letting you know something cold and captivating was chilling nicely within its contents. He enthusiastically shouted back at Tom saying, "The good doctor has prescribed the best medicine in the world, Melma's hit-the-spot old fashioned Home Brew!"(A savory wine that his great grandmother Melma Carter had taught him how to make at an early age with black berries and lots of love.) Pre continued to boast as he said, "Four for me and one for you my giant of a brother, and please forgive my greediness but you know I have to fend for myself and since you've supplied us with these fantastic accommodations, I'm willing to split this "miracle working" medication with you two and a half a piece." Thomas was loving this "haven of here say" as he laid back lounging in the back of his truck, where the skies seemed like they should be "Donita Diamond" unrolled and placed on a canvass for future fantasies. He started slipping little by little into a sober dream state with half moons and bottomless lagoons with tiger sharks dressed in Armani suits surrounded by seven Angels with golden halos playing harmonic flutes accompanied by an image of Good Luck Charlie perplexing his isolated roots. About three to five minutes had passed as Thomas leisurely started coming out of his fantasy fraise as he confusingly replied, "I'm glad we see eye-to-eye but you know there's always a price to pay for our pleasure." It seemed like Tom had been betrayed his whole life, but he had found a great friend in Collus while sensing that particular times had changed, he always continued to hang on to hope. Thomas knew never to make deals with the devil because it was like having a rattle snake in the house, but more importantly you should never keep God waiting and yet we only ask that he would defend us in battle against Satan's minions that unleash chaos, and an abandonment of belief. As Tom's thoughts illuminated with wonderment, Collus had their magnificent oasis appearing like the greatness of distant galaxies looked at through artistic eyes of a Goddess that formed their man-cave into an untouchable, iron clad haven beyond the imagination. The two colossal men were finally restful and at peace; occasionally toasting their jars of ice cold homebrew, and listening to everlasting melodies correlating from Thomas's radio. They were feverishly floating on a high premium of feelings, where there's just life and a pinnacle of providence intertwined with their love of coal mining flowing sternly through the core of their hearts with its rapid beats never ignoring their new found gracious awakening. Some have said that enormous things have insignificant developments, and the most frightening thing in the world is nothing but as serious as the mine's situation was there would always be an end to an ending, and a beginning to a beginning where the smoke finally clears and the only thing that remained was filtered transparencies. The music was blaring in the background and playing a tune that revealed verses of vision, as "the two brothers from another mother" reeled in some aggressive rays, with Collus observing how the music mesmerized Thomas into a trance like it was his beauty of passion with an alluring arrow shooting through his heart. Factual thoughts were actually bracing this "on the rise" tale that would soon unfold uncommon emotions of explosive flashes that will ultimately occur, but somehow not knowing what your destiny holds should hopefully have a peaceful presence on the memory and oblivion; which goes hand and foot like a tug of war between rationality and lunacy. Pre and Thomas were thoroughly relaxed and enjoying a moment in time, where dark forces remained and waited like a fixed reaction with sarcastic tones of harshness from the unassuming surroundings, quickly igniting a spinning out of control storm that could carry away the bliss and cause it to disappear into a swarthy mist; followed by heavy tears of pain. The violent storm was coming and nothing in the Dawn of Humanity could stop the Fallen Angels of discarded Light to call out as if to summon the Devil himself, stating that evil is back like the Diabolical Diablo a.k.a. Lucifer (Mayhem's favorite fiend). Open minds were now being forced to encounter drastic measures that were diligently working hard on its imagination of security, as if it were surrendering a "shoulder height" of secrets. The two miners were waiting on the ripples from the skipped rocks in their minds to transcend the birds flying high overhead that carried the meaning to life as they silently delved into their simple gratifications. Suddenly, the Rescue Team approached the mine like an arrogant air raid with their sirens unbound, while everything else was just simply waiting, and waiting. It seemed that life was full of surprises with fearless roots turning back the potential dangers that followed along the traveled path carrying you to the brink where some deep scars aren't visible; but are vaguely hidden in the days before shadows of the indefinite. The Emergency vehicles congested the gravel road leading to the main entrance of the mine interrupting Thomas's and Collus's fiesta, causing wreak less tensions to be set off where they might have liked a little trouble, but they really despised chaos. Collus looked at Tom with his platonic theoretical smirk on his face and said, "It's us against the world Tom my brother, and I see that we live in a different heavenly body of existence than others." "We must leave no stone unturned while looking for the hidden answers; and the answer I'm looking for today, is why in the hell can't we find peace that lasts?" "I wish we could stay here in our "forever land" until the end of time being filled with tranquility; or is that just out of the question?" Thomas responded, "Pre, I think you are nine times infinity kind of crazy, and I think those times have gone by my friend, but sometimes you have to get your <u>hands dirty</u> searching for those diamond treasures that we call serenity." The Emergency Teams were now on sight and already activating their game plan to search, locate, and recover any missing miners whether they be on Pluto or under a rock in the back creeks of "met your match" Powellton, West Virginia known for its shiny coal and wasted years of secret shame that left their deceased at a state of unrest whispering, "Why is torment often overrated?" They would be looking through (put to an end and save your breath) eyes that should judge harshly while steadily being misconceived, causing their lost souls to behave coldly where their own reflections were corrupted into something unrecognizable with trepidation trespassing on spiritual morality. The Heavens were secretly conjuring beautiful spirits that had a hint of rage like a temper, whose claws are out of reach but still having an unconscious mind with infinite patience where all bets were called off when the pain of sacrifice performs like a symphony orchestra coming together as if they're skilled in the art of deception. Even if they spoke to us from beyond as the days are gone, the flaws of one would be the strengths of another as they search from behind a mystic's veil ordering soldiers to a standstill, where intimidation was a pastime while raising pools of dreamers and also noticing that temperaments are different; but willingly embracing the victims that were affected. As they gratefully prayed to the skies above they would also offer encouraging, forgiving words such as "you're a lucky soul" and "keep fighting", because there's always a chance when you obsessively think about it. They would honestly be observing confident men that cherished the bluish-gray skies, where the sun sat like a restless and out of breath fixed point of attention emitting an immaculate pressure to prevail, that the darkest days had labeled a star. Certainty was being very truthful as it started to set in like it was sent there to calculate the theorems of their hallucination stages, and perform a "Bizzaro" to their worlds by making adjustments to ease their "dream real" transition. Now what seemed like its final answer was actually a hypnotizing hypothesis eager to reach out and draw their focus back to what was occurring in the "here and now". After hours of their staring into the heavens above, the skies suddenly opened wide unleashing a swirling, circular motion with a rare twirling noise; where the flutter from the windswept a path of curious chaos with pertinent questions that now had to be answered. The commotion was heading straight for the mine compound with a great sense of urgency; yet off in the distance, but seemingly up close and to the point of being direct. It was like listening to wild animals being very expressive causing the world to rush in, and if you stand far enough back you could truly witness the path of destruction from the soon to be misguided anger in the mist of asking God to forgive your tortured soul. So I'll catch up with you later when you're lost in the frigid forests of the night, and when that lust for vengeance comes a calling you'll actually be no different than the rest of them that couldn't maintain. Collus unexpectedly sat up like a Cobra with its back against the wall staring aggressively toward the clouds, wondering when the voice of the voiceless speaks it's something awareness has to heed or be forced to hear the whispers of corroded corpses from deadly defiance. As probing questions slipped through the cracks of inquiry and wild thoughts that were overtaking their greatest of fears, only unwanted replies were dangling from the longevity of life lines in the palms of their hands. The aircraft that had summoned such simple purpose of interest from its intruding approach had landed in an open field near the road leading to the mine. Three men in Police uniforms departed from the helicopters side door sprinting toward the mines office compound uniquely postured as if importance was camouflaging an unforgettable emptiness, where you instantly dropped to your knees and prayed for sermons on the great mount, and family suppers that would last. JC and Carl Edward were standing by the mobile cafeteria with looks of bewilderment as the officers approached them with courteous greetings, exchanging introductory handshakes. The men were in deep discussion over something that seemed very critical because of the serious expressions chiseled on their stone but sullen faces. Thomas and Pre were still relaxing in the back of Tom's truck but keeping a close eye on the verbal exchanges between their supervisors and the officers. Tom finally broke the silence between the two men as he spontaneously said, "Pre, Big Bro my Spidey sense is tingling like crazy, and I can't stop these frantic thoughts from racing through my mind like its closing time at the Apollo of sorrow!" Collus responded, "I know what you mean Tom, but I'm thinking there must be some miners still trapped in the mine for all this unusual activity." Collus and Thomas were steady in the face of compliance with a slight touch of defiance, as they noticed the five men making their way to the supervisor's offices while Carl Edward was showing them paperwork he had neatly stacked in folders underneath his arm. The men were deep into their conversation as they slowly disappeared into JC's office where higher causes for the Troopers arrival were in continual talks behind closed doors. A half hour had passed, and it was no sign of anyone entering or leaving JC's and Carl Edward's office; when out of the blue the office door swung open like a saloon entrance exited by riff-raff being thrown out into the dusty streets of a waiting, clamoring mob. There were about twenty to thirty miners standing outside the supervisor's office entrance when JC and one of the officers came out like Butch Cassidy and the Sundance Kid making their final determined effort. Times of reflection were atrocious, and if you could touch the face of God while singing your heart a sentimental song you would believe everything was going to be Ok as if summoning deeper relationships between recognizing and doubt. The miner's immediately started asking questions; "What's going on JC?", "Are there miners still trapped in the mine?" JC was like a stranger at the door, where his words were used as armor awakening too many regrets to mention as he calmly said, "The situation at hand is personal, and I do respect your concern; but privacy and sufficient sensitivity will help us deal better with this matter that's been placed on our hearts today." "Every miner has been accounted for; and like I said privacy is my lead." "So please feel at ease about the safety of our brethren, but remember a little rain must fall and misfortune can appear in all forms when its least expected." "Compassion in our hearts will help us as a team and as a family my Local Fifty-one!" "So I graciously ask, please no more questions." Tom and Collus saw the two men walking away from the curious crowd and heading straight toward the employee parking lot at a steadfast pace still exhibiting a "mystique of unassuming consequences." Tom continued to stare intently at JC and the officer approaching; and at times it seemed like they were moving in slow motion while being cautious as if they were crossing a bridge over distressed circumstances. As the men drew closer and closer, Pre and Tom put their jars of homebrew back in the cooler that Pre had retrieved from his car earlier to keep their "playground pleasantries" fresh, and cool. By the time JC and the officer reached the edge of the parking lot, the two giant men had stood up in the back of Tom's truck like soldiers standing at attention that regrettably had to leave their relaxing state to a standstill. Pre aggressively started pounding his chest and said, "Fe-Fi-Fo-Fum! I smell the scent of some inquisitive ones." JC would usually come back with one of his snippy wisecracks, but he had the most serious look on his face like a gunfighter trying to intimidate his opponent into indefinite submission. Urgently and respectfully as if he could lift the anchors of truth JC compassionately said, "Thomas would you please come with Officer Givens and I to the supervisors office, because we have received vital information pertaining to your family and I think confidentiality would be more appropriate." Thomas couldn't immediately respond verbally but he nodded his head in agreement, while trying to accept every single moment as if everlasting couldn't exist. They say the powers of persuasion are an endowment, but filling in the pieces to the puzzle would be malignant and intense to what blessedness really stands for when an avalanche is suddenly about to occur. Thomas started to remember when things would go wrong; he would often feel weary and sick of trying while crying himself to sleep where his failure to communicate had his situation of awareness incapable of sorting through the lies and what was actually authentic. He was looking into the open fields of tomorrow where men of peace have an astonishing exit strategy easily balancing reactions of fate, and at the same time eagerly trying to regain their footing toward the mountaintop. It would seem the Founding Fathers of wrong and right would have noticed the difference between cheap imitations of work, and fatal errors of judgment when reaching the age of barely knowing; in the midst of standing toe to toe with the unknown. Collus alarmingly spoke with his boisterous tone startling the three men as they made their way back toward the offices, causing them to stop in mid stride like Pre had opened the starting gate, and the time was now for a healing touch of words. He said, "Tom when life seems hard and merciless you must counter it with stability and self control; that's a must my brother!" "So if you need anything bro, just call on me to be your anchor because I will never let the eclipses of existence darken the path of such a gracious and memorable friend." He encouragingly continued by saying, "Hearts are forever Tom; and you don't know what it can endure until it's faced with misfortune causing you to find out what you really have deep inside of yourself!" "I promise I'll be by your house tomorrow to bring you your truck; so I'll just use the spare key that you gave me and head over early in the morning to make sure you're okay; just remember that I'm with you bro and I'll always be there for you!" Thomas looked back with the saddest of eyes that would only blink if the tears that were being held inside were easier to comprehend. He gave a short disappointed wave to his concerned friend as the gentle giant of a man turned as if he were raising a shield to protect himself from this jungle of misery that's most always cut and dry. It seemed to be a long and tortuous walk for Tom, but once upon a time these journeys that seemed so physically incapable would often have the wind articulate; sounding like a whisper rustling its way through the most sensitive parts of your thoughts.

It would calmly say, "The world isn't what it seems sometimes, it just gets bleaker and bleaker while draining your elements as they approach the Rapid River of past journals that explain the messages that were left for you and why the world can't just simply hold you back." "Time is like a fluid as it narrows its way down where momentous decisions are initially betrayed by the uncertain outcomes of life", but for Thomas it was like he was looking into a mirror that had two faces where his mind had lost its keen edge of recognition. Now by the time Tom and the two men had reached and entered the supervisor's office, Carl Edward and the other officers were huddled at his desk like a cluster of tamed chimpanzee's scratching their heads over the unbelievable paperwork the officers had displayed causing their expressions to be somber and surprised at the same time. When they looked up and saw Tom, JC, and Officer Givens enter the room their eyes looked like deer in headlights as they quickly focused their vision toward the floor trying not to make eye contact with the presence of the men. One of the officers cautiously began to speak introducing everyone as he said, "Thomas my name is Staff Sergeant Honeycutt coordinating through the Rand and Chesapeake Police Departments; you've already met Officer Givens of the Rand Homicide Special Crime Unit, and the officer standing by the desk is Agent Tolliver of the FBI who is working diligently with our offices to solve this unfortunate dilemma." "Mr. Wolfe sir, I regretfully have sorrowful news that your son William Squirt Wolfe was instantaneously killed at the train yard near your house at approximately 9:00 A.M. this morning." "As the officers on sight combed for answers to your son's death, an on-going investigation of your wife Sara and your daughter Jenny for prostitution was being played out with our task force raiding the two businesses that's in your name "Clear and Cut", and "Heavens Radical Rave." "The joint coordination between Rand, Chesapeake, and the FBI has turned up multiple counts of solicitation for prostitution; and the hair salon ran by your daughter in Chesapeake had drugs and cash money stashed in a back office totaling twenty thousand dollars with a journal of suspected clients credit card numbers and the amounts they had paid to your daughter posted in a ledger with asterisks stating in highlights "Sex for Cash or Credit." "Bail will be set tomorrow morning; and you're free to post bond for your family but Mr. Wolfe, Tom; we feel the agony churning inside of you and our deepest sympathies go out to you for the loss of your precious son." "Please sir, I know this information is catastrophic and this type of nightmare can damage the strongest of men, but we ask that you call this number on this card." The officer reached out sorrowfully handing Tom a "last resort" business card as he continued to lay out the facts. "Thomas, her name is Miriam Jackson a local psychiatrist located in Rand to help you deal with the trauma that's been placed on your soul today." "Now Mr. Wolfe we're going to fly you immediately to the hospital; so sir if you would please come with the other officers and I, we can avoid any delay in dealing with these severe sensitive issues." Tom slowly stood up trying to maintain his composure while feeling weak in the knees and extremely nauseous, but still facing these uncertain times much stronger than he had prayed to do. JC and Carl Edward headed toward the office door ahead of the others with heavy hurt on their hearts, gently patting Tom on his back with compassionate brotherly taps as they passed by him to clear the entrance to the office of any prying miners outside. JC turned solemnly as he reached for the door knob and said, "Tom, I regret that I can't find the words to express my condolences; but you know you're a big part of our family and we'll do everything we possibly can to help you; and I mean anything at all to get you through these tortuous tunnels of consequence." "So, please stay in touch with Carl Edward or myself to let us know that you are okay." "You'll definitely be on our hearts and minds, and I can only say God bless you and your loved ones." As JC opened the door, Carl Edward and he started clearing the miners back from the office door and the gravel road that lead to where the helicopter had landed. Thomas started walking out of the office like his life was seeping from his soul while walking heavy like a two ton elephant trying to make his way upstream in a gushing, flooded river of pain and suffering. If only he could conjure up a spell to change his fate, as he grimaced over the out dated pictures that were traumatized by horror running through his mind; he would sell his soul to Lucifer himself to change his pitiless outcome. Natural explanations were being tranquil as the four men made their way down the gravel road, when Tom finally lifted his vision from the ground looking wondrously to where he had left his faithful friend. He could see Pre still standing in the back of his truck like a Gargoyle statue protecting the inner sanctity of friendship to a tee. As he continued to look around the surrounding area, Thomas knew their faces but the names were a blur to his recognition because the turmoil was tearing apart his insides like a Lion making notable memories while being trapped inside the belly of his easiest prey. The demons within his brain were clouding the journey of his destination where the sudden perceptions of him were getting closer to causing "I remember feelings"; meaning to explore two places at once with guilty pleasures and perfect understandings while blindly entering a place that didn't exist. His lonely led dreams and everything that came with them had Thomas encountering a bad back lash that was offering no explanations and had mysteriously left him close to almost no one. It seemed like he was being made to suffer, easily deleting his strength that protected what truly mattered most to him; "always offering a heart for the world." As the four men boarded the helicopter and began to gradually lift off from the open field, burden was like a herd of elephants trampling and plodding on Tom's mind as the sound of the powerful propellers deafened the voices of communication within the aircraft leaving the men to fly in verbal silence. Hand signals and head nods were the language conferred between the heralded hoverers over hills and hallelujahs; abandoning Thomas's imagination to wander with no forgotten aversely visions that could conjure distinctive times, where he had a choice of romancing hope as it faded away while never looking back for options. A new chapter of his life would soon begin where you thought he was finished; but was actually set on proving that a man's got to go his own way when times are just too hard to strive for memorable moments. His life was accelerating toward being a legendary hell raiser as the unique and sleek helicopter zigzagged through the sun lit sky making its way to where the nights of celebration was no more, causing family drama to be a value of being patient; yet far beyond him and what would eventually come for him toward the end. It was like he was a fighter with no fear where he had to ask for help and it finally made its way lifting him to overshadow his thinking by spilling his gut feelings with vibrant sensations as if he were a peasant before a Queen; bowing to the normalcy while graciously expressing the truths that no one could imagine, which only made it seem so "Royal!" Thomas was desperately trying to contain the untamable frustrations boiling inside of him after receiving this urgent information that instantly killed his will on impact; making death a complicated matter because he couldn't slay death and death had nothing to fear while inhaling love as if it were written, but in the true light of things there's no such thing as an "honorable death!" He thought to himself that there would be no more sunset walks or father and son talks, leaving just a mother who deceived her son's young curious mind as if she were making him eat dinner with a spoon where the main entrée being served were tenderloin delusions. Thomas's mind was still racing with smash and crash feelings as the helicopter approached its landing on the hospital roof in Charleston W.V. just fifteen minutes from his destination of walking in the footsteps of a monster. The top of the trees were being weighed down by the turbulence from the machete like propellers plowing its way through the empty feeling air while having a sharper focus on rejoicing in the Lord's turbulent winds to quiet storms. It was like the breath was being sucked out of Tom's lungs while having a fragile grip on reality, which was comparable to a web that was about to break hanging on for dear life screaming "defying the elements!" The ugly darkness inside of him was simmering under the cloudiness of the sky like a caterpillar changing into a butterfly on its one-way flight beyond Hell. Now being so many light years from understanding sanity but drastically trying to help him to happiness, life's biggest questions could see right through him; making things very interesting and causing Tom to open his eyes to the loneliness starting to build up in his soul like the end of the world; but far from the end of this drastic and thunderous sounding tale. The sinister shadows cascading from the rigid rooftop were playing ghostly games as if he were about to leap before he looked; but it was a faithful leap of knowing that his decisions were being guided for a special cause while being enlightened by nature, easily summoning a higher purpose of redemption and justification to call on his inner strength when something terrible was waiting for him, deviously grinning like a fat cat chasing tiny terrors of mice that are enthusiastic with fright. The punishing pressure was straddling heavily on Thomas's brawny shoulders as he found the courage to smirk as if he were reinventing new directions of perfection for his soul that took so long to finally come home. The smile that crept so unbearably upon his face wasn't expecting everything that he thought was true to be a hindrance of getting ahead of the situation; but it was like he was being ambushed by a dreamless sleep where the constant thought of bleeding hearts could never make him feel sorry enough. Even the vivid pictures of this menacing scenario could hold no water to the grief that could sometimes cause crazy things to occur as he followed his heart, where making rash judgments could honestly be a sorrowful thing. He was opening a whole new world, knowing that instincts never change; where he had wasted enough time fighting angry spirits that didn't blink from a dead man's splattered blood, causing him to allude methodical captivity as his mentality journeyed through the looking glass of life where there were no exits. It was like coming in from the cold as the Officers and Tom seemed like a group of banded brothers slowly walking down the desolate Hospital stairwell leading from the roof headed straight to the basement floor, where the morgue was eerily and cynically located. Special Officer Givens broke the icy silence between the men by informing Thomas that Dr. Jim Edinger would need him to identify the deceased, so that the proper paper work could be conducted for little William's body to be released for burial. Tom quietly turned in acknowledgement and gave the Officers a half focused nod as they continued to scale the "wearing you down" flight of steps that exerted Thomas's ability to fully comprehend the atrocious view his eyes would soon witness; leaving him with no sense of shades of gray. As the men steadily continued on their endeavor, they finally walked through a squeaking, dreadful doorway that led into a huge Morgue chamber with rasps of chilly wind ricocheting off the metal enclosed drawers that encompassed this tear ridden room. Far off in the corner of this "past and present" area of humaneness there was a lanky, slender man deeply concentrating his attention on a body lying under a white blood stained sheet that seemed to have him stressfully searching for answers. Staff Sgt. Honeycutt called out to the scrawny, frail man so engrossed in his work that he didn't hear the men enter this massive space consumed with soulless bodies. "Jim, Jim ", shouted Sgt. Honeycutt as he sounded out trying to draw the doctors concentration toward their presence. The young Doctor shockingly spun around from his task of tedious "Tomb Engraver", seemingly being drenched with compelling cases that cemented his superiority with a dutiful response, "Yes, yes Sergeant I will be right with you gentlemen, just give me a moment to wrap things up." The serious and spirited Doctor stood there with blood dripping from his gloved hands, where the tears of children couldn't express the heartache that repeatedly bounced off the walls of infinite wisdom to describe this memorable, gruesome scene. Tom started to think that this unfolding of gloom was like entering a time machine, where real problems still existed but the tempo of its expediency was flawless in its pursuit of exactness; never being blindsided by the mirage of torment causing him to walk around helpless and lost in his own valued recollections. Dr. Edinger had concluded his extreme examination of the bloodied corpse, as he slowly and admiringly pulled the white sheet back over the mutilated corpse while diligently trying to conceal what was already known to the assuming and imaginative mind. He started walking easily like a predator of "praise and pounce" toward the Officers and Thomas, innocently disposing of his latex gloves in a nearby trash can as he approached the men with a honest and concerned look plastered like a wall hanging of "MOTHER" on his face. The Doctor's voice came across like a whiny child begging for attention; but his words were so articulate and soothing that they caressed the lost secrets hidden in Tom's own subconscious. "Mr. Wolfe" he said, nonchalantly adjusting his posture as he continued to try and understand the "orchestrating like a maestro" of pain that had been inflicted on such an undeserving casualty; soon to be caught in the moment where life was taking its own course of "stranded on the way side of heaven." Dr. Edinger was a concerned and caring man, who was always trying to solve the solution to a problem that more than likely had a "stronger to weaker" resolution. He just stood there straddled across a burning bridge with a span too wide to leap toward sensitivity, as his words continued to flow like a scalpel cutting a severed wound of regret. His voice hesitated, and then heightened as it finally found the courage to continue on by saying, "Sympathy is an understatement to the tragic and terrible "swing of the hammer" that has knocked the wind out of you today sir, but we have to continue down the path laid by everyday existence without fear, as we seek out the answers toward closure to relieve your saddened soul." "The officers called me from the mine to let me know that the four of you were on route to the hospital for identification of the body Tom, so I need you to be prepared for a rude awakening that will definitely swallow your destiny and spit it out with no flesh, leaving only remnants of remorse." "I regrettably must say, for I am a father myself my friend, that your son William "Squirt" Wolfe was instantaneously killed this morning at the train yard near your home with a puncture wound through his aorta causing a horrific death." "After rescue teams reached the scene, your son was pronounced dead on arrival and the deceased was immediately brought here to my office where I performed a thorough autopsy determining your son's cause of death." "In simpler terms it would be what I call "Arteriovenous destruction", where the main artery (aorta) is demolished by a thunderous penetrating impact causing the ducts and walls of the artery to collapse from extreme shock having the victim go into cardiac failure, and bleed to death immediately." "Now, Tom please maintain your walk "steady and secure" because I will need you to identify your son's body, and I know it'll be the hardest thing you've ever done but hold strong and brace your heartache for the unsuspected wonders of "time reminisce!" Dr. Edinger hesitantly turned and headed toward the metal drawers against the walls of the morgue with numbers and handles on each individual square stacked two high for conservative space. The doctor reached onto a metal tray while grabbing some paperwork attached to a clipboard that had been sitting neatly atop of some folders and other miscellaneous files also wanting to be examined with expediency. As Jim started to scan through a few pages, he instantly headed over to a dreary drawer that was lettered and numbered SACMN-13; a sequence Thomas would never forget or ever want to remember. He slowly started to open the drawer where young Squirts body rest in peace which seemed to take an eternity for the rolling encasement to come to a complete chalk screeching halt. Dr. Edinger reached for the white sheet that respectfully covered Tom's son, and with a gentle tug he revealed his Angelic-like corpse. Thomas's eyes went from completely wide open to traumatically being clinched shut, while never overlooking the similar circumstances that surrounded his being. It seemed that he had at last been dealt a "dead man's hand", as he made his lonesome stand where twists of fate were like Aces and Eights, and the price he was paying would never be enough to savor his faith if ever forward toward the Pearly Gates. He was now the enemy of his enemy, who had made his self known with no good deeds, while being led through a foxhole full of surprises where he could only picture hearts that would revengefully bleed. Tom was trying to hold on to what was real but he could sense a storm was coming with a slight twinkle in the sky, where he would be standing all alone in the depths of a secluded mine with uncontrollable anger vibrating viscously through his mind. He could already hear the horrific noises that sounded so terrible and severe, erratically trying to make its presence out of the dark; but there was no more light on this particular night when his conscience was slowly shredding and tearing him apart. He was in a strategic struggle trying to make life as his own, but at this provocative point if he could only manufacture love he would finally find his way back to the comforts of home. Thomas thought that he had mistakenly stepped into the realms of hell and hate, where his nightmare was like suffering from a quiet desperation of soon to be alienation, because his frantic screams of agony drew no precise signs of recognition from the hollowness of this realistic dream. Dr. Edinger noticed that Tom was in a state of defiance and delirium as he respectfully handed him the release forms that would make Ruby red seem like nothing compared to the bloodshed that was fuming on the frustrations of Tom's fanatic fantasies. Tom reached into his front shirt pocket and grabbed a pen as he sluggishly began to sign the paperwork with unstoppable tears flowing from his eyes; and then like a disturbed and agitated grasshopper he sprang from his seat without a word or eye contact as he solemnly walked away. As he distanced himself from the other men his hands clasps his brow in disbelief with his onlookers watching his every step; they were wondering how to reach this man, who just had the world drop a hemisphere of hard knocks upon his tense and distraught soul. The signs of wonders were steadily defending life with a clear vision; while a sudden spark of a message had been secretly delivered leaving no one to notice the signature on the dotted line where Thomas had strategically signed; "Sacman Wolfe!" (He had driven a strong wedge of secrecy, while leaving a clever and readable solution that the beast was now awakened, alert, and ready for the here and now.) The Officers stealthily and gingerly started to follow Tom, while relaying encouraging and consoling words, but the horror of heartbreak had him too vulnerable to share his feelings to any sentiment of human compassion. Staff Sergeant Honeycutt spoke with a soft and trusting voice as he delicately said, "Mr. Wolfe sir, that's all we have for you at this particular time, but I only ask that you please go home and attempt to get some rest." "Now Tom I know that seems impossible, but serenity can be found if you truly believe in the concept of faith!" Thomas just responded to the officers "hoorah-hoorah with a slight huff and a puff, as if he were waking up in clouds of misty smoke with a fatalistic outlook of "blowing down the house" when he finally said, "I guess I have no choice sergeant, do I?" Tom did believe one thing though; is that you finish what you start when your spirit rules your judgments and reality constantly beats you down, but as you dangle your feet in the freezing waters near the base of an iceberg, you simply just; "relax"! Thomas's thoughts and words were blindly beginning to surface as he spoke with favoring verbiage by saying, "Officers, I only ask that while I am willing and able, that if you gentlemen would please take me to where my wife and daughter are being held so that I can feel if heaven is as close as they beyond of a doubt would say." He was urgently trying to zero in on the things that were important, while waiting to hear his loved-ones somber admissions to the faults that were more shocking and heated than multiple revolutions around the scorching sun. Tom with an exhausted and inquisitive look on his face freely said, "All I need is that one last good-bye to satisfy my imagination, because they actually thought they could try me; and all I want to know is, how did they really think this would end?" The unnatural look in Tom's eyes were like razor blades making a jagged, cutting statement filled with crazy ideas of a human wrecking machine scratching and clawing his way back into the fringes of fear. Special Officer Givens looked at Thomas with an intense and iron cast face as he helpfully said, "Okay, no problem Tom but you do know some things aren't meant to be changed, and while reaching out with open arms shows that you still have faith, you should never try to overshadow the benefits of time." "Time is an unacceptable medication for the healing process, but it's the only way to control the unthinkable nightmares that are sure to come from the clever crevices of chaos." As he cautiously continued to lecture, he said, "Agent Tolliver's car is just outside in the hospital parking lot, and we'll respectfully take you to where your family is being held." "Earlier today Mr. Wolfe they were taken to the Rand County Jail, but have recently been transported to the Women's Correctional Institution in Dunbar, West Virginia (less than twenty minutes away)." "So, if you would please come with us, we should arrive at the Institutions Intake in just a short while, but I'll call ahead to let them know that we're on our way." The men stood in silent agreement and steadily exited the lobby of the hospital making their way quickly to Agent Tolliver's car as they loaded into the vehicle with complete serious sequence on route to the Correctional Center. The ride seemed like time without end, but they arrived at their destination within a brief principle of hope, as if they were walking into a new life. Tom wasn't questioning the aura of destroyed lives that swam like piranha with "bone biting brilliance", where there were still glimmers of anticipation with furious desires of creative endeavors. He just patiently followed the Officers into a huge maze like structure, where building a bridge would have seemed like a cake-walk compared to climbing in and out of the multiple endless tunnels as if he were pulling the wings off of insects just to make it to a recognizable destination. The four men finally entered a massive room where heroes of culture honored loyalty, and certain eye witness accounts would often take advantage of what's wrong in society today, knowing that evil is never satisfied, but still wandering the "last mountain" like facing choices has made it this way. It was nothing like Thomas had expected, while Swan diving into the day and never giving up, looking over past promises where fire filled his lungs until they were swallowed by hallowed flames crowding in on his passage of fear, while being careful of "what not to know". They had finally reached an area of the facility that had a large glass window with Intake embellished on the wall above its eye catching mystique of reflection and "I can see you" allure, causing Tom to anticipate and accept the prowess of pain that he was about to endure. He knew deep in his heart, that if you suffered mercilessly by the hands of hardhearted individuals, and if you could somehow summon that last hurrah while living on course with victory in your grace, God and all the forgiving Angels would be understanding to the struggles through these tests of time. Whether it be as Thomas Wolfe, or the mythological Sacman; he thought what is truly in a name, because when you're spiraling out of the darkness there always comes light for a bright, new day as Mother Nature and her perfect passions scream, "Behold"! It was as if he were genuinely being an artist with somewhat flawed gaffes of logic and rules of thumb, to reach that unforgettable masterpiece as he walked in the word, but somehow basked in the rigid rays of recognition. Thomas started to slowly, and silently escape his burdensome fancies when the Officers approached the large glass window with their ID's flashed like nudists at a public beach, while waiting on a welcoming and wishful response from their diligent comrades on duty. The heavily fortified prison overshadowed Tom's overwhelming, but deadly dreams of taking revenge on those who betrayed him in such a discreet and do-dirtily way, which was unacceptable in the confounds of the secrets of war. He just couldn't resist a challenge, because intellectual defiance's were like playing chess to Tom; calling out moves like rook to B8, bishop to C4 and in response queen to D8, with the dominant adversary retreating his bishop back to C4; and then finally check mate. He loved throwing out elaborate diversions while playing this game that had more responsibilities and delicate matters than a relationship between a ring of fire and a pale of precisely weighted water. Thomas's thoughts were viciously being torn apart by the slender but tender passions that had a bit of absent mindedness, when encountering scary situations that was like crossing a bridge of dragons while desperately trying to reach out to his family. It was the equivalent of being stuck in the same day over and over in his mind, where time was never on his side with visions of picturesque moments that couldn't be touched, while he constantly tripped over numerous stumbling blocks in his sight towards the truth. Even though shocking secrets hung like slanted pictures on a wall's random song that remained the same, rational analysis couldn't focus on the evil deeds that would soon be carried out. It was as if he were listening to fantastic tales with tactical traitors in the midst, trying to figure out how many devilish disguises roamed in the realms of their safe keep, while inducing his visions of perils from entombment and surviving the gruesome grips from his gloomy and vain marriage. Strongly stepping forth was a "if I stay" Legend with fanatic acts of courage, offering no forgiveness or silver tongued slogans to seduce and synchronize the main speed of this spiraling downfall. The sunken-in sun glare from the high ceiling windows were introducing a new and nostalgic presence, as the security door adjacent to the Intake window opened like a highly compressed can of Styrofoam snakes. The slithery surprise abruptly set off an awakening alarm that rudely interrupted Thomas's dog dumb regrets, where he actually felt like he was planet rocking on Pluto; while being so far away and couldn't return even if Neil Armstrong himself journeyed to retrieve his insoluble piteous "onward into the storm" body. It was identical and simple as entering a glass house, where his countless steps were shocking like the truths of sensitivity; fragile but stern in its footed finesse. Although his new journey would be very rigorous with a hairs touch of leniency, his mind wasn't totally prepared for the fatigue caused by the fornicated fallout of trust and his marital failures. The alarm that was blaring so boastfully and blasé had finally come to a silent halt, slowly releasing his mental clarities, but as time went by his refocus had trusted him to deal with his unpolished situation. An Officer standing at the "starting gate" of a door attentively motioned the men to enter with an unsympathetic wave of his arm that seemed scary-happy, but inviting at the same time. The three Officers and Thomas made their way through the entrance of the Intake while noticing uncommon men and women working diligently at their ebony-opal desks. As they surveyed the hollow hallways that echoed of heinous violations and considerable pain; it seemed the walls had honest questions while asking, "Where is this sad song going?" Tom had traveled a long way from Heaven to Hell and was finally coming face to face with the tragedies of hard luck, as the valuable lessons from the truths of God's words had him steadily navigating through the difficulties of life. Even though his world had been shattered after learning of his wife's infidelities through the blood, lies and alibis; only proved that nothing could bring his family back from the over abundance of falsehoods falling from the shallow in the deep skies. He was crying out of control over his son's tragic death with laminated bustling tears, and praying to never die of fright while eternalizing his unshakeable fears; but he stood like a warranted warrior with a hollow hole in his "someone like you" heart! Thomas's Lion-colored soul was slowly rotting like a carcass in a bright desert sun as the nonchalant Officer led them into an outlandish chamber where writings of lonely soldiers were plastered on the walls with written reminders placed in plain's eye view of their many accomplishments of service. While perfectly positioned to their left like a pack of "dead to right" wolves was a control room that looked like a NASA launch facility; where there was no room for error, while having total management of the steel confinements that caused stranded societies to be robbed of your love and commitment sometimes. The robotic like Officer that led their way, discreetly signaled to one of his co-workers behind a glass encasement, as if to tell them to bring out someone that was hidden behind the astute fortress walls of this complicated compound. The group of men continued to walk straight ahead stopping at a glass window with a telephone attached to the side of the sitting area directly adjacent to this Fortune Teller's transparent structure. It was as if they were patiently waiting on understandings of the universe to suddenly appear in this square-like crystal ball, where the strongest of the strong were slowly broken down to fall to a creep and a crawl. Thomas painfully looked through the glass with the babyish of eyes as if the sun had tears; hypnotized by the mysterious, mighty steel door behind the holding area that was like looking through muddied waters as it slowly but surely opened. Even though it was an extreme change in the game, his wife and daughter guilt ridden and humiliated shamefully appeared from behind the negative walls looking like two depleted whores with nothing else to give but a life's long third-hand resentment. All the words that couldn't come to mind; where being on the other side seemed strange and remote caused Tom to abandon his plan of questioning the two women but instead, he held up the sack Squirt had given him and placed it forcefully against the glass window that "sure enough" separated them. Tom then slowly picked up the receiver on the phone that was mounted on the wall below the glass divider, and as he thought to speak plainly his heart was overflowing with confusion causing him to serve a "calculated elimination", as he gently placed the receiver on the table and instantly walked away. He could hear the muffles of his wife's and daughter's voices tearing at his suppressed forgiveness, as pleads seemed to revel and coax their way through the phone as if their words or yearning didn't want to be like the Forgotten; where they wondered over yonder years never reaching the ears of a deserted Dog that could never again obey that sudden whistle, which brought him multiple tears. All he could hear was: ("Tom, Tom, please come back!"; "Daddy, don't leave us here!"; "Please come back, we're so sorry!" and finally, "We beg you, please don't go!"). Thomas knew it was time for him to leave because his emotional entanglements were just a step away from lunacy, as he seriously thought about the lies they would tell, he also felt like a prisoner himself in the "don'ts of the do's". Although he would always hold his wife and daughter dear to his heart where life changing decisions, and the understanding of those risks that had his courage and sacrifice excepting no more monkey business; Tom was fiercely done! He continued to walk away to escape the drama as the officers quickly followed him like lost puppies waiting for a sudden reaction; but none was given. Thomas seemed to be on a mission of a "maddened monster" as he reached the Officers car sitting intently in the Correctional Center parking lot. He was tragically mourning his son's death like being at the sacred grounds of the Haliwa-Saponi tribe, where

"Faith" will always be thinking of someone else; protecting them and bringing sunshine when there is a storm of grief that throws off your balance while journeying through life. Tom silently prayed to the Kingdom of Heaven as his insides wailed with remorse, and his words uttered like a trembling tree branch as he solemnly said, "Oh hear my cries dear Lord for I have a vengeful quest, as if I was an agent of retribution with critical ambivalence stirring in outrage like I was sulking in a high dungeon with not a cloud in the sky." "Father I ask that you please forgive me if I should stray from the path, so that I won't be smothered by these subsequent discoveries as I topple obstacles with a fresh start of belief with no doubts ever crossing my mind, because there is no getting back from making a mistake of trusting the unforgivable." "So, I choose mayhem before chivalry as I enter explorations of wrong doings which could only be seen through my eyes; and Father my only request is to please let time stop because I can't suppress the pain that drives me out of control, have mercy on my soul." It truly felt like Thomas had a massive hole in his body separating his heart from the pits of his gut, as one of the Officers unlocked the backdoor to the car where the will of Heaven was unafraid to let him know to keep moving, and to never look back. I've heard passion, lust, and anger sometimes eats at your scars and marks causing windows of opportunities to slam close like a vault door to a safe that catches you by surprise; sort of like an Irish curse where the Heart of Anger is an apex predator making nature have you ask, "Why do leaves fall?" So keep up with the Spirit, because when the viper attacks it slithers out of trouble into a unique position of triumph with its sense of danger and awareness of judgment. They say, "If you don't learn from History, it's doomed to repeat," Like taking your first step or running into a brick wall "face first, hands down!" It's just unpredictable when the Sun is throwing so many shadows that you can't contemplate the truth through these secret lives of loved ones with no soulful looks from the methodical styles in this circle of obliteration and isolation. He could sense murderous events like Roman Priests that couldn't orate "that perfect speech" to keep him from falling into this awesome abyss with no recovery, and neither could the Officers that were driving him home; because they kept coming up empty with their words of encouragement and bringing value to life. They were witnessing a different animal all together where profound anger had enthralled a big expressionless monster with a lust for reparations seeping from his soul like a whiplash of gash and stab; slowly one by one. The Officers car eventually pulled into Thomas's driveway like tranquility on that travel to paradise; asking him to embrace the moment as the voices were getting closer, but still seemed so far away. Failure to communicate throughout this passage had Tom set on doing this all alone, asking himself, "what did he sign on for?" He knew Death wouldn't be cheated, but still his emotional growth was limited to personal self indulgence and hiding the killing secrets that are always the worst in a man; just an ordinary man. As the journey continued, Agent Tolliver's car came to an unsettling halt as a Panther colored black cat the size of a Lynx crossed their path with anchored paws that looked dishonest in its powerful steps it took; to quickly disappear into the murky woods nestled tightly to the side of Thomas's house. Officer Givens was riding in the front seat as his hands were slammed against the dashboard from the force of the cars discontinued motion, as he immediately started to swear, "Damn Tolli, you couldn't see that nine live ferocious feline crossing the driveway in enormous fashion?" Agent Tolliver responded with a "flipping of the bird, while thinning of the herd clarity comeback in his words" by saying, "OG! Mr. Front-Back seat driver; A red sky at night could cause a malaise Redwood to fall, but my vision was consumed by the malevolent darkness and the bellows of frigid fog; so do us all a favor and cross an "X" on the windshield to make sure there's no Ancient evil with the Devil's breath that awaits our arrival." Officer Givens was shell-shockingly amused, and just gave him a high eyebrow look as their collision of wits and know how quickly evaporated, it seemed into thin air. It was pushing close to a little after 9:00pm, when the men pulled up to Tom's lethargic House-hold after a long day of uncomfortable, emotional beatings that caused an aftermath of after thoughts; where Thomas's travels were long, all-knowing that he wouldn't be able to sleep through these darkest of times. As He somberly looked out into the vivid colored night, he barely noticed his sister's mini-van sitting near the driveway, backed up to the front door of the house. He immediately felt like a little weight was being lifted off of his shoulders, because he knew he would have to send his oldest son Tommy to live with his sister Linda and her husband Larry Turner in Huntington, WV. Tom had regrettably recognized that his days were done, and his time was over as a Father, and Family man fixed on a feasible future. It was now Hell in a cell trying to contain the Sacman that dwelt deep in his "spirit of fire and flame" that wouldn't be extinguished with just a simple explanation or apology. It was as if Island flowers and Forbidden fruits had smiles of charm, but old mistakes had gradual goodbye hugs that could never rectify the pain of dishonesty, that had erected an opinionated drifter into a smarter breed of Boogeyman; where his costliest endeavors were like <u>Elba</u>. As Thomas parted ways with the Officers with calm handshakes and conceived respect, he felt like he was crossing the golden sands of an Egyptian peninsula with untold centuries, and symbols of love that reminded him of rough waters and rabid rapids sparking waves of violence; while knowing that he was clearly hiding behind a smoke screen of discretion and wonderment, never again to find his common ground. Tom was emotionally in tune with his barbaric poetry as he gently closed the door to the back of the Officer's car, and his mixed emotions were like reading the last page of an epic story; where guilt is sometimes too simple to justify a complex situation as he clearly heard lost voices with soft rustling sounds saying, "survive and thrive!" Love is really crazy, I guess? You don't miss what you don't remember, but if you do readily reminisce; no Earthly possessions or beautiful disasters could administer a sidewalk slam to put the fire out of a cold desperation for passion. It was identical to a brightly lit Ferris wheel spinning sporadically at a Carnival, making hearts flutter with a childish joy of infatuation, where everything you know is pulled from the core. Left stranded and abandoned while strongly feeling that revenge solves everything from a once in a lifetime tale of treachery, when there's never enough time; as you stand "for still" with the worst odds ever eagerly trying to connect the broken pieces to the puzzle. Thomas sought, and sensed that the walls were coming down brutally like a battering ram over his head as he sluggishly made his way toward his sister's van parked at the front of his door. Linda was calmly coming around the back of the van with boxes and bags packed in her strained arms, while looking heartbroken from all of the events that had recently occurred. Tom made direct and penetrating eye contact with her; and it was as if she was looking directly into evil's eyes with disturbing visions of the Devil, "That you know!" Now there's been a lot of songs that's been sung by the best, and something's are actually older than spirits, but a dance with Death

54

goes over and over through your mind like a Medieval Madman on the run from horrendous points of view about life, while facing the greater of truths; simply cutting you off from experiencing the blessedness of vitality. Linda softly spoke like a whispering ghost, as if her voice was coming from light years away barely reaching the feelings of Deaths touch that had flooded Thomas's affections like a sadistic stranger sworn to secrecy in the interest of clearness. Linda hesitantly spoke up as she said, "Tom! I'm so sorry, but Big Bro you know that you have to be strong, because it's time to move on." He couldn't foresee or except a resolution, because in his heart he was still begging for precious minutes like a dried out leaf turning and blowing agreeing with the wind; while he was desperately trying to connect with God. His recollections were vague, but there was one final piece of his true identity, where radical therapy and hard hitting questions were just barely enough to help him cross this desert full of snares and pitfalls. Linda reached out with wide open arms and gave her Big brother a sincere hug that had his uptight feelings inside his body finally relax; and release some of the built up tension that plagued his masculine frame. Linda reassuringly and gently whispered in his inviting and good grasp of an ear by saying, "There are Angels working from the skies, as I am working from here to help you get through this uncompromising grief, that's engulfed in the middle of a cyclonic problem with a potential risk of elimination." "I will take care of Tommy like he was my own, and you know he will always have a family with us while you try to deal with this unbearable pain." "I am going to take him home with me tonight, but we'll all return soon for Squirt's funeral and commencement of final goodbyes." "I've already set up arrangements with the local Funeral Home to contact you with all the times, and dates for the order of services for our young "Guardian of the Gates" that will lead us home one day, when there's a final dance with the dead." "So please Tom, hang in there for Tommy and me!" "I know you're a great Father and sometimes it seems hopeless at finding the answers you're looking for, but try to stay ahead of the moment, because these next few days will be crucial steps while struggling to bridge this "shadow of a doubt" gap. Now on the contrary, there was "weeping Tom" with thoughts of Vietnam, although calm for the moment was like a ticking time bomb where toxic techniques had him devastated with a false sense of security battling his way through Destiny and Time, while clasping his sweaty palms with "all is lost" memories of his dear departed son. His mind was spinning in a thousand different directions, and it was just too cloudy; as if he were being blinded by the renegade rays from the Sun for him to serenade the Moon on this silent confessional night. Instead, he responded with a make every moment count retort as he honestly stated, "Father is just another name for a protector or a guide while your children are in search for wisdom; but sometimes love takes the wind out of your lungs when strong opinions meet sneaky suspicions, and manipulative personalities." "Love can leave you in a lonely place by making a long journey seem short and narrow, while trying to hold back a barrage of unstoppable tears that leaves you in a state of bleak depression." "I can only say Baby Sis is that I have a darkness festering inside of me under these sinister skies, and I'm plainly afraid of the dark as I'm asking to be let out; but it's taking so much out of me like entering hopeless ventures that's causing me to be mentally unhinged, while living this tortured life and being taunted by conniving scavengers throwing fire that could actually make bloodhounds loose the scent from false, pretense hugs; and then there's sudden silence like sshhhh!" "I know wild hearts are opposite from hearts made of glass because they can't be broken, but they can be scarred internally leaving a mark of destruction; although not common, however very off balance from pushing the envelope; and I also know that I've never quite formed a family tree, yet I'm still atoning for past trusts while there are private conversations sounding like bagpipes that are so eerie, but there could be a second chance for happiness because we all know solitude is a secluded place to die." "Right now I'm just being haunted by the gruesome truth, where the structure of the whitish gems reverberates like the highest level of ghostly noises calling, and seducing me readily rolling out the red carpet for me to just tuck tail and walk away." "I mean, unbreakable bonds with Devil horns are the last thing you think to see, causing you to tell yourself that the end is near; where the vastness of the mighty oceans roll waves of slow tensions with sluggish terrors while entering the fields of honor, causing you to have doubt in the promises you need to keep." The moon was steadily rising with a hundred stories to tell like unwritten rules had Tom's heart shipwrecked like castaways in the eye of this mysterious and remote storm, but the daunting tasks that lay ahead was a one-man war with no win scenarios. Time was too late, and actually seemed like it was slipping backwards as Linda once again grabbed her brother and embraced him, showing the intensity of her openness where she had nothing to hide from her passionate love. As the two siblings stood in somber relief and justified grief, young Tommy came out of the front door like he was swinging open a fearless fence that was approaching a fragile grip on reality with agonizing tears dripping heavily from his distraught stricken face. He slowly walked toward his Father and Aunt slightly looking downward as he reached out throwing his arms around them like a spirit that had been broken while trying to make its way through a terrible and "in too deep" transition. They were all homing in on their new identities, because now there was a new family in town feeling the pressure of massive problems that was creeping through the walls of vapors and fog; while hiding riddles in disguise that crushed the dignity of innocent bystanders. Although Linda was poised on the surface with just a thimble full of choices, young Tommy and her encumbered their disheartened bodies into the front seat of her minivan as she looked out at Thomas with those concerned and concentrating eyes that was typical when you're fighting a saddened soul. Their stares of anguish drew a line straight threw Tom's caring attitude, cutting it in half to never be reconnected like being lost and by no means being found. With a gaze of guilt and guidance, Linda gingerly stepped on the gas pedal to depart; as Tom stood like a compulsion of "for better or for worse", fully wide eyed with childhood slights and explosive discoveries summoning whispers of death, while hiding in the shadows where life is still people who are sometimes difficult to understand leaving the challenging question of "Aren't we all on our way of creating a little chaos?" Thomas held his hand in the air with an old-style goodbye wave, like he was trying to retrieve a falling star that was summer- salting through the clouds of mist struggling to find an alternative to human companionship. As Linda's car faded into the mournful night, Tom was still positioned like a pine tree in the driveway with his vision engrossed upwards at the fully unveiled moon, wearing a dumb-founded howling look on his common but cinematic face. He had regrets of remorse resurfacing from under the knots in his abdomen, where the hardships would shortly provoke his evil traits to ignite like a Roman candle very much alluring and illuminating. The world Tom knew was long gone, and shell shocked like a war inflicted veteran barely surviving and unaware of all his tactless surroundings, never imagining it could take everything from him; although he knew there was always a reason for everything. His feelings of guilt left him valiantly about-faced with an incredible strength that was fully equipped in his heart, to desert his former life like jumping from a neglected voyage at mid-sea, because he was left with no other choice but to abandon thy ship of outcome. He could feel the tension mounting as he went inside and locked the front door while aggressively surveying the inner layout of his once comfortable domain that had since recently given him a sense of shameful sentiments. Tom was crossing paths, and acquiring a fire that was looking for a mission of mercy as he turned off all the lights in the house except in the family den located near the front of the house. He mysteriously made his way over to an ancient radio sitting on a table near his favorite recliner chair, and started tuning in to his favorite radio station; because we all know that love hurts sometimes, and music has you take everything in; no matter where you are, even if it's on the battlefields in this arrogant arena of life. He finally collapsed in his "ten cents of a chance chair" after the music started projecting through the speakers, as if he was in the front row of the Apollo with an array of musical talents for his listening pleasure. Thomas had at last gotten his diminished body to a stable and relaxing state, where he could focus and enjoy the lyrical tunes singing soul touching harmonies through his "face to face" of a radio. He listened intently to the words that flowed from the taming telegraphy that could make hardened criminals stop and meditate. The fluidness of its saving stream challenged his demeanor of inner emptiness, while clearing his head to open minded views, and self sufficient perseverance to please his primeval accomplishments. Tom's eyelids were growing so heavy that they appeared like they were falling into a spectacular size unaccountable sinkhole; until all of a sudden, he was awakened by a loud noise banging against the inner walls, screaming from the upstairs of the house. Thomas jumped up like a Jack-in-the-box wearing springs that had him dancing in his socks, with his mind running amok like a fully loaded semi truck with no brakes, displaying plates of past gone; flared like bait, wondering and anticipating escaping this dreadful fate. He immediately grabbed his "trophy" of a pickaxe, firmly mounted on the wall; which was actually given to him as an award for saving one of his co-workers from a cave-in in his first few months on the job. It was made by one of the finest steel workers in the surrounding counties; and Tom treasured it like the sack he held dear little Squirt had given him that he called "treasures are forever a price far above rubies and <u>Red</u>." Thomas slowly and stealthily made his way around the corner of the den and started his ascent up the "breaking the silence" staircase that squeaked and moaned from every step, where charms aren't lucky enough to steal the voices of others. His feet felt like concrete that was secured to the steps leading to the upstairs area with his pickaxe held tightly overhead as he edged his way neared to the top of its structure. When Tom rounded the corner of the hallway heading toward the loud and sudden noises he paused; to notice that a bay window at the end of the hallway was partially open blowing the drapery in a frantic "every which way" motion. A shocking and soldier like gust of wind unexpectedly marched through the house like an Army of "Love conquers Death", forcing the drapes to launch straight to the ceiling; and then there was a surprising bang "squawk boxing full of stone able rocks" coming from behind a door that led to the attic of the house; and then another, and another. Thomas was now a "lethargic listener" with desperate hours of issue, as he noticed that the attic door was partially ajar, but wide enough open to stick his head through to get a glimpse at the unusual disturbance coming from within this complex mystery; which had his protective nature reaching a turning point for his record of truth, to say the least. At what time does the night come, when the moon and the sun share the sky at the same time; where spiritual awakenings will be grasping for responses to the inspired impulses that are oh so powerless, while quickly learning valuable lessons like it's there and then it's gone, but you can't imagine a more cynical synopsis? Tom really couldn't hear the music anymore over the clamorous, sudden sounds echoing down the forlorn and frigid attic stairwell. Indeed, he thought that he had finally succumb to an uncontrollable blood lust, sort of like Dr. Jekyll and Mr. Hyde, but he knew it was only one kind of insanity where losing his memory to take away the pain was like being the most deadliest man alive with a sadistic destructive force inside the noxious clandestine of his warped and withering mind. He fiercely fired off from the rumble of juice peculating in his veins, by keeping his head down as he swung open the door and ran up the attic stairs yelling brutally like he was playing with fire that was lighting the flames to his heartache; as if he were about to slay the mightiest of all dragons. Thomas, like a horse-trade of thorough breeds sprinting for the finish line had speedily reached the crown of the attic stairs, when something large flew by his head like a heat seeking missile missing its target by a fraction of its intended purpose. Tom franticly started swinging his pickaxe like he was trying to cut the head off of a snake while in mid-air; but his efforts were thwarted by the object landing on a rafter on the other side of the attic. He immediately tried to focus his vision to get a clearer look at the evasive intruder, but his view was being blocked by loose insulation and stalactite like spider webs that hung just as loose netting dangling from the masts of an old pirate ship. Thomas could finally see that its dead eyes were ruthless, yet vile and vicious with its glowing unyielding stare featuring certain qualities of a spotted wood owl. His agile mind was now patient, which was the reward at tackling the problem that lay before him, because the greatest fear in a man's heart is the envy of his enemy's intelligence. So if it's truly on, it's on; and I want you to take witness and <u>know that</u>! Tom backed up cautiously toward a window on the other side of the stairwell, re-stepping in his dusty footsteps he had made in his inhuman attack of bombardment with his prized pickaxe. He was watchfully keeping a close eye on his new found adversary, as he opened the window as far as it would go, so he could somehow get the owl to flee the confinements of this unsatisfactory, temporary prison. Thomas, with a brushing- motion of his fully alarmed body moved back toward the stairwell, and with an "I don't really care look" as he stared down this mischief-making crazed owl gradually disappearing from the confrontation with this deadly and deceiving stranger. He two-stepped like a thief, as he curiously stepped back and took a good look at the true beauty of this mystery, while back pedaling down the stairwell and quietly closing the attic door. He now calmly sat on the floor with his back against its frame, as the wind was still heavily bustling through the upstairs hallway with his memory being violently jogged by irony and the distractions from every word of lies that he had ever heard. He thought to himself, "I left my wife and daughter to rot in a hell unknown; but I can somehow find the compassion to abet an outsider to slip away into the friendliness of freedom." How envy can kill a dream, when you can't find the words to make things okay, closely listening to "get at you" voices with a promising touch, but never healing old wounds, and still being weighed down; but somebody holds that "golden key". Thomas stood up firmly holding his pickaxe and clinching it tightly to his side as he approached the open window pushing back the drapery with his free hand, and then resting his elbows on the peaceful but curious window sill. He was gazing into the night air with a full moon that was immense like a fall prey; as he faithfully took his eyes off the prize. Tom glanced to his upward left to notice the owl flying out of the attic window looking down at him with its piercing dark eyes, while performing aerial maneuvers like a moth doing a back spin, and then quickly circling back toward the house. As his rival got closer with every waking moment, it seemed like it had no soul in its risky quest of being acquitted without a trial by jury. The owl headed straight at Thomas with an all out effort to use him as a scapegoat to its graceful caper of escape, never to be late by the colors of hate, that sit and wait; as I had always told my sons to anticipate that moment. It flew within a few feet of his face, and then went into an effortless upward spiral; soaring with a warrior's image, over the woods beside Tom's house and across the lake until it was completely out of sight. Tom backed up respectfully out of the window, closing it tightly as he did the same for the one in the attic; making sure no more trespassers would seek refuge by overstepping their boundaries. Broken and in turmoil, he exhaustedly made his way back to the den and his favorite chair; where he felt like he was turned inside out, but hearing the music again was soothing to the rage that had consumed his soul. He couldn't help the feelings that had inflamed and drained his brain, as he passed by Squirt's room on his recon mission to expel the troublesome owl that for now, was an enigma of "wow"! Thomas was still trying to regain his self control and fill the hollow cold cavity that surrounded his unforgiving heart, beating like a bass drum; Dum-ditty-Dum-ditty-Dum-ditty-Dum! The rhythm felt quite right as he quietly sat and soaked in the therapeutic sounds, as he once again dozed off into a dreamland of dilemma, where he was in the face of waves of terror and sinister agendas; but also hearing mysterious messages from his deceased son saying; "Dad, don't leave me yet, I have more to tell." "The owl in the attic was me!" "I know it's hard to understand, but I think deep in your heart that you knew it was me the moment you looked into its eyes." "I never got to say goodbye, that's why I returned to show you how much I really missed you." "I flew for you, Dad!" "I flew for you!" "To let you know that I'm okay and that you don't have to worry about me suffering or being in pain." "My soul is truly fulfilled and free!" "I thank you for loving me so much, and I know that I'll find that same love here, where I am." "Remember me forever, and I'll always love and watch over you, because you are the true essence of the word, <u>Father</u>!" Thomas continued to dream; the dream of the most unique, and artful recollections that made him have close awareness to the spirit-filled signs; because this was his day of witness. It was as if he had a self awakening of growing beliefs that were efficient, and resourceful, yet heart-rending to the Sacman that dwelt in his blood; someone, no one knew thus far. He continued to journey through his mental pictures, while now wading across a rumbling creek to soon be standing in a field of grazing cows all huddled in a circle. As Tom cautiously approached the brotherhood of bovine with his hands currently held above his head as if he were waving presidentially; but the herd of animals shunned his advance; nonetheless slowly started to move apart, opening a small gap for him to walk through. It seemed like he had intruded onto sacred grounds, as he continued to edge forward on the path they had set. Looking slightly toward the sky he caught a glimpse of huge, soul-stealing Buzzards circling the crumbling clouds longing to barrel down on the haunting realities that had met their grisly ends. Thomas continued to move to the center of the herd, suspiciously noticing that the green meadow grass was rapidly converting into piles of bloody mangled bodies laying in disorder and delusional disarray. His brain was becoming unhinged and scrambling to focus, but he still remembered what his Dad used to say, "If you see a snake laying in the grass don't "miss-snake" it for a rabbit; Got that Jack?" It was if he was trying to reconnect or capture the reins to this evolving nightmare, so that he could once again find comfort from his song-after-song gently whispering in his ears. Instead, the dauntless possibilities were only getting worse; because his view was being summoned by a sculpture of a black skull with ruby, red eyes sitting like a crow atop of the hideous carcasses sprawled inside the wagon train of cattle. The wicked images Tom was witnessing were so bona fide that it made the kill spots inside a lion's den seem like a walk in the park; so fetch Rover, fetch and don't you dare bark or bite, there's so much evil to destroy before things can get right. He wanted to get out, but he was afraid of waking up in hell, where looking back to his youth would still have him facing a losing battle against the keeper of this insane domain. Thomas was shaking with goose bumps, frozen like a four leaf clover with no luck from withdrawal, as he looked into the blood like eyes of the sculpture with everyday circumstances seeming dishonest and disobedient; preventing a hasty escape to reach a higher path to evade their inaccurate inceptions of life. He was traveling through the eye of a hurricane hopelessly trying to awake; when out of the blue he could hear a voice calling out, "Bro, Bro, let me in; Come on Tom, please let me in!" As Tom concentrated on the voice beckoning for him to return, his eyes were being filled with a shining, bright light like a giant star bouncing its luminous gases off the rings of Saturn. He vigilantly looked behind him, to see a field full of bodies, with now strange totems placed in five positions encompassing their idiosyncrasies. Thomas's eyes quickly started to flutter like butter dripping off a knife, with a vision of a humbled Humming birds wings releasing a spirit from a hapless, reckless past and future; and then suddenly he was awake. He swiftly, and squeamishly sat up in his chair with the music still blaring; surprisingly being interrupted by the repeated knocking at his front door. A voice came echoing through the bay window like a rollercoaster, roaring through a mountain tunnel, "Big head bro, come on and let me in man; Tom it's me, Pre!" Thomas didn't promptly respond to Collus's calls, because he had left little pieces of his soul with exuberant trails of mayhem floating like a stranded ship wounded by dread; in his wild and reluctant imagination. Something amazing had been stirred inside of him like poking at a Beehive, where the Pyramids of despair had let the universe provide the eternal flames with nameless faces, to get him to change his views on his guilt ridden, fragile circumstances. Tom would not waver though, as he hesitantly made his way to the front door with what seemed like a "Mighty Joe Young" monkey on his back, whose actual name should have been "Nervous Breakdown"; but he steadily continued to press on by any means necessary. Determined and stern to his ways, it seemed that he was destined for disaster as he softly opened up the door with the look of a Mythic Warmonger trying to break the chains of his psychological limits; but he wasn't who he thought he was while needlessly looking to the future, where he would take matters into his own hands. Pre was hysterically standing on the front porch with the glare of the sun cascading over his shoulders with the intense rays of light rolling off deep questions for the conundrums that surrounded. Thomas was being placed with passion; where the end begins, and the beginning starts to mend from the infliction of sin and the no-win, from loss; trying to figure out the exact cost of pleasing his alter-ego of a "new boss". Collus was overly curious and slack-jawed as he anxiously said, "Tom, I've been worried about you all night bro!" "Are you okay?" "Please tell me what's going on, because I've been going plumb crazy trying to figure out how I can help you my mule headed brother." Thomas's emotions were distant and disillusioned, as if he were on the brink of collapsing from these major life changes that had him consumed with an obsession for vindictiveness. He could barely look up at Pre with his heavy, sullen eyes that had an appearance of spiritual doubt from the strains and pains plastered across his face as he mumbled out only one word, "Life"! As Tom continued to walk onto the porch while slowing down his momentum, where Collus was waiting, and determined to come to terms with his best friends grief; he leisurely reached into his front pocket and pulled out the letter he had found on his truck the day before, and sheepishly handed it to Pre like he was passing nitro glycerin to a buttered finger receiver with a hot potato "problema" for the drop-sies. Collus was now expressionless, but tremendously curious about the unflinching climatic events that were unfolding right before his eyes; leaving him mesmerized, and challenged from the points unknown. Before reading the "letting it stand as it is" letter his heart broken brother had given him, Pre reached out and hugged Tom like the good graces that held together the moon and the stars; where uncovering chilling discoveries and the sharing of somber secrets had the two men racing through time toward a vast amount of unforeseen complications. Collus eventually spoke up with a trace of a quivering tone that exerted a high voltage of vitality rumbling deep from his vocal chords. "Bro, I would have been here earlier, but I had to go by the mine to pick up your truck, fill out some more information for the new mine guidelines, and get copies of my medical benefits from Carl Edward." "I had my crazy cousin Cliff Combs, the Bob Villa of the "sticks and the ebony colored like bricks" follow me here; but he's at the hardware store picking up some lumber for his so-called renovations to his house." "Old boy said once he finishes he'll swing back by to pick me up, so that you can get some well deserved rest." Thomas depressingly replied, "Rest won't do me any good Collus!" "I feel like I've been left without purpose; because my baby boy Squirt was killed yesterday playing on a train car, and fell off puncturing his heart; they killed my baby's heart Pre!" "Bro, he didn't have a chance while tragically being captured by the hour of death; and it didn't even matter that coal was his stone of destiny, the Reaper was still lying in wait to take my baby boy away from me." The wind was presently leaving its simple and spirited print on their faces as it franticly blew, but Thomas continued to unfold more monstrous consequences that left him breathless; exhibiting a fragile interior from the impact of this free-for-all hard landing of his endless sky fall. His voice continued to shake as though it were being blown from the wind, but the built up tension that had his spirit being tortured forever, had finally released his emotions to speak again. Tom had torn between tears in his eyes as he delayed; like he had no more love in his heart as he could barely see the shadowy darkness of the Sun, but had words that were chilling and willing to breeze onto the scene like a crisp "can't get enough" collar jerker; so pay attention you know what I mean? He solemnly said, "Pre I don't know how I can go on bro, it seems that my life is an "in living color" charade." "I mean, yesterday my son dies, and on the same day my wife and daughter get arrested for a prostitution ring they were running out of their hair salons." "Please Collus, I beg you bro; read the letter and try to help me understand these active creations of lunacy that plague my deepest of thoughts; please my friend!" Collus had no clue of the false and true, as he unfolded the letter with streams of sorrow trickling down his cheeks as he began to read the mind boggling quick turns of this twisted, but true account of a cheating wife's plot to cover up her lies that were unquestionably exhausting; leaving you where you have a lot to learn about old-time oaths that had been shattered like glass; trying to reach unattainable levels, barely eluding the ruthlessness of deceit. It was like reading a fantastic tale with tragic outcomes, making the days seem hopeless and full of difficulties; where judgments were being called into question in the thrill of the hunt for impossible escapes from controversial and inadvertently entangled plans. Pre continued to scan the letter, while sinister storm clouds were briskly gathering over the treeless mountain tops that were aligned in a dark and dreary background for this time of day. He could only stare angrily from the audacity of this piece of news; with its unassuming, yet direct approach of leaving clues of cardinal sins; where anyone would want to throw in the towel, while asking; why did I ever fall love? All of a sudden it was like a light bulb had been illuminated in his understanding, while seemingly narrowing in on the distance; as he finally blurted out an erupting volcano of words. "I be damn Tom, this letter looks exactly like Carl Edwards hand writing man!" "I'm a hundred percent positive; come here and take a look at my copy of the new mine guide lines that was added on from the forms we signed yesterday." Tom was still trying to eradicate those undead demons, while sitting and listening to God's plan, but now the cat was out of the bag as he looked over the add-on that was hand written, and about six paragraphs long. He held the "Dear John" letter in one hand as he compared it to the guideline add-on in the other, feeling like a dog chasing its tail; although the proof lay right before his very eyes. Thomas was glimmering with humor and haste as he chuckled out loud, and then burst into a hysterical, menacing laughter with his eyes swollen from crazed, crocodile tears. He wasn't afraid to learn the truth; knowing he should always question their motives, but the loneliness had him now cornered, and trapped by "Sweet Misery!" Totally surrounded with whirlwinds of the most challenging, eerie reminders swirling violently through his disturbing visions; showing unbalanced pictures of the anatomy of the monster within him, battling with self-containment. Tom ragingly said, "I'll kill that fat Tom Cat mother f*****!" "I'm going to rip his heart out, and eat it piece by piece with his blood grotesquely dripping down my face; I swear to everything wicked and cruel, that I'm going to slaughter his "whole world!" Thus, a psychopath for revenge had evolved, while being lost in this hopeless and helpless place where the Stairway to Heaven was being blocked by the horrors of humanity. Pre was in utter disbelief, as he stood there with a discouraged grimace spread across his face while having grave concerns for the stability of his friend, who with his outrage of words scared the rationality right out of him; and sent it packing, to be locked in the depths of the prisons of a scorching Hell layered with piles of ash remains. He could see the raging fires burning eternally in Thomas's eyes, where traditional sayings may have made things different across time; but dealing with intense relationships and their actions, were forcing Pre to barely just adapt and survive. Although the inclement weather was freakishly unraveling and locking horns with madness and virtue, Tom's past sufferings had finally caught up with him and giving "hush-hush" hints of his dark-side, while causing blood thirsty, teeth chattering fear to be whisked through the trenches of heartfelt desires. Pre cautiously chose his words before confronting the mammoth of a man that had been pushed to the limit; because sometimes things don't go as planned, although struggling with horrifying memories that were drawing a one-of-a-kind line in the sand; which was a fine line between laughter and tears. As Collus pondered over his old and very befuddled friend, he seemed doomed to failure in his ageless approach of "wait and see", and "let things settle" before you try to play "Malcolm in the middle." Tom was exhibiting the self reflection of a madman with distinct features of anguish that would grasp your attention immediately to the ultimate sacrifices that were inflicting, and wreaking havoc on his unsettled psyche. He had without a doubt begun the "dance of death", where the steps and movements indicated war in every conceivable way, but no one had seen the warning signs until this dimly lit candle of an unforgettable day. Tom's dreams had seemed meek and timid to Pre before, but now they were deranged and violent, reframing these unexpected situations; sort of like a run- away train that escalates with no possible end, but is destined for destruction and ruin when the journey finally comes to a "Whoa, <u>Trigger</u>" halting end. Collus's eyes were now fixed on Tom like a magnet on metal, as he paced back and forth across the front porch looking like a fuming fire-cracker ready to explode from the intensity of pressure building up inside of him. His personal demons were magically attracting the clouds to roll in so heavy and heated, that it looked like the sky was closing in from its anchored position steadily blending and mending together to form the stage for this epic encounter between a broken man and his devoted, and caring "Brother in Arms"; but you'll know the real when it boils over into saving the last one. Pre began to speak in a stern voice as he said, "Tom your imagination can affect everything you do man, so if you want the blunt truth of how to learn life's lessons you have to relax and focus your energy on our Lord and Savior Jesus Christ." "Then think about what you're saying Bro, Its pure madness!" "I know your heart is in a great amount of pain, and how you must feel lost; but you're traveling alone where there's dark fields, with broken flowers; and as you can see there's no growth in it." It seemed as if he was preaching to appease his prized pupil, by letting him know to think ahead and not be overly spontaneous about the evidence that had been presented before him. He continued with his words of wisdom by saying, "Let me do some investigating for you; and I promise I'll find the answers you're looking for, but it's going to take a little time." "So, be patient and please calm down and you'll have the proof you need to call the authorities and let them handle this shady, back stabbing phony." "Bro, I tell you life can be worst than imagined, with no light in the tunnel where cold souls have shadows that are silent; and memorable moments erode without a trace in the visibly cold casings of this "take no- prisoners hour glass." "Yes, my friend the playing field isn't even, especially when the deck's been stacked against you; but I know you can turn things around by toughing it out as we piece together these new clues." "Now is the time we have to be meticulous, to avoid a final confrontation, because the smiles and smirks of evil await; bringing a unique "Thunder and Rain" to flood your man of the house way of life." "I know from experience that grieving is just a speak-easy word for isolation; which causes lost time by bringing the world crashing down on you without fear or consequence." "So, reality is tremendously hard my life-long friend!" "Actually, it's common knowledge that raising hell is like fighting a fight that really doesn't matter, because you'll be living the same day over and over in your mind on your one way journey to embrace Satan." "I warn you Tom! Don't find out the hard way, because it would be a lonely place to die, while mysterious noises repeatedly echo the names of your countless victims; forever and forever." "Bro, I'm telling you it's Okay to show anger, but please take control of the helm and steer this crippled ship back on course, because the Captain doesn't always have to go down with it; you Bullheaded land lubber!" Tom, with guilt written all over his face looked like a simple child chastised by a guiding Father, who was only trying to lead him back to the safety of stability. His eyebrows were now arched high, as if he were curious or intrigued by the hundreds of words his friend had laid on the passage for his "heart and soul" walk of wisdom. Thomas was like a ticking time bomb with a searching for a miracle spirit, forced to be presently made of ice that contained deep origins of monstrosity; and from his grave betrayals, he was only playing out his thoughts that had come unglued from his frustrating struggles. He was witnessing lines that should never be crossed while profusely bleeding, and lying feeble from the bold moves of the devious; quietly surrounded by gentle breezes that were causing Dark Times to prevail. He knew adversity established character but it seemed he didn't have a choice; and living this lie that was flowing back and forth in time like make believe, made revenge for the fallen seem like vintage magic in the air. This voyage of validity that he walked, like starved Lions and Tigers had him feeling a soulless emptiness; because no one could hear the discreet summons making him absent-minded, and vulnerable from the death that had touched his life in such a devastating and destructive way. Tom was lost in thought and heartbroken with a switching outlook intense face, as he ultimately decided to lead with his heart while slowly gathering himself to express his inner most feelings as seen through his eyes. "Thank you, bro" he said with a new tone in his voice like the ringing of church bells attracting its congregation, to come and rejoice. He was being hit with a flicker of belief, as he continued to say, "Damn! I thought Pre was short for Preatta not Preacher; Mr. Reverend Righteous, and Renowned." They both gave humongous, humorous laughs that were followed by charismatic chuckles as they smiled ear to ear like here-after had arrived. "Man, you could've shaken the walls to the Kingdom of Heaven the way you expressed those overseeing views so eloquently." "Bro, I'm touched by your rare gift of commitment and wishful thinking, but a tempest is coming and my hands are visually full like a blistering inferno with cursed cries in the wind, devastatingly followed by billowing smoke from the entering into the unknown of a tragic aftermath." "I'm just a simple man that now walks in defiance, while being left with unresolved questions; and as the Puppet Master, mean-spirited as he is schemes and waits to entice the condemned to suffer, and face difficult decisions set by his artistry of psychological limits; I have to stand my ground even though calmness has set in, because I feel I know who's to blame." "I can't promise you a scrubbed mission or that my rage will dissipate, but I have a gut wrenching feeling that there's going to be a dramatic outcome where I'm wandering aimlessly with no emotional goodbyes, while being unaware of the pivotal symbols of life from my belligerent bitterness toward a fierce, and fate less Kiss of Death." "Pre, my feathers are ruffled like I've been debuted in a cock fight with a mistaken identity of Thomas Wolfe, that's leaving something precious behind; but I'm asking can fortunes change?" "No more proof is necessary from where I stand my friend because I can see the varied messages in the letter, and the closer I get to answers, there's just sudden silence; and then the unquiet dead start reflecting the depths of this jilted face-down." "If you want to continue to find more confirmation, you go right ahead, because you'll be racing against time and I'm so far beyond time that I'm a shallow and barren nothing!" "Nothing as in, nothing left, nothing will stand in my way, and nothing and I mean nothing will change my trapped forever foul mood." "I'm deeply sorry, but that's all I can offer and that's all I can give; so once again, I thank you for always being there as a devoted friend and a beneficial Big Brother." "I know that you're ashamed because I let you down, but I've been robbed of my senses that have lost its luster and it just can't be undone." "In my eyes there is "no days" after this, and it's clearly and easily seen; maybe far-fetched from sight, but the breaking dawn and its rays of light shine dead center with its lucrative positions that are giving me flashbacks of changing memories that are quickly crossing paths with these sparking tensions, which appear to be difficult to ignore and complicated to circumvent." "It seems that I have fallen into the realm of ancient worlds, where failure to communicate is my agonizing demise and I accept this wretchedness; why can't you understand, bro?" Collus was now alarmingly aware to Tom's needs as he replied with a coaxing comfort that would make a cat stuck in a tree, agree to flee with open arms as he softly said, "I do understand, Tom." "If I were in your shoes, I honestly don't know what I would do." "Ultimately, I couldn't come to terms in the wake of these harrowing events, nor would anyone ever forget from here to ever after, my relentless roll of the dice rage." "I truly do understand; but I also know that the wilderness sometimes seems like it has mirrors making you take a good look at yourself, and what you see is what you get, plain and simple my friend." The two men stood there with "cold questions" fiddling and riddling through their minds, like messages in a bottle being washed ashore, only never to be answered. The drastically uncommon looks on their faces while struggling through the thick of things that had recently passed, and the things that will inevitably come, were like something of value; rare, but torn between priceless and uniquely unforgettable. With his heart on the line and a haunting feeling of "how in the Hell" ripping through his edgy, swept off its feet torso; Thomas wondered could there be a different approach for a gratifying explanation; but nothing came at once, or twice while being frozen like a Caveman constant in captivity. Tom's edge to edge sentiments were prematurely interrupted by the sound of Cliff's truck barreling recklessly up the gravel driveway, like he was being chased by an Army of abducting ghost trying to recruit his soul for a deliberate deal of his destiny; with brainwashing banter saying, "Just sign on the dotted line." When the truck finally came to a rumbling halt it gave off a thunderous backfire that sounded like a Fourth of July finale of fireworks that caused Tom and Pre to quickly duck, as if someone had fired the first shot for **FREEDOM**! Pre angrily snapped at Cliff with a "rant of restraint", but it was meant to clearly get his point across as he yelled, "Cuz, what hellhole were you running out that's got the Devil with his pitch-fork burning holes in your britches as if slow your a** down never crossed your mind, you big knuckleheaded Neanderthal!" "I'm so sorry fellows," Cliff promptly said, "but NASCAR Nellie got away from me believe it or not, and all I was doing was smacking her on the rear and saying, Giddy up Nellie!" Tom and Pre looked at each other simultaneously and wanted to laugh, but their amusement was in a remote area with deep hidden canyons consumed by darkness, where the wind constantly whispered; "ain't a damn thing funny anymore." Pre was amused by his crazy cousins wittiness, as he graciously ask Cliff to give him just a few minutes, and he would be ready to go; and by the odd looks on the two giants faces, he knew something serious was going on; so he just gave Pre a courteous nod and patiently waited in the truck for his favorite cousin. Now, when the two men turned toward one another to continue their conversation, you could tell by the sincerity in Collus's eyes that he was desperately trying to fight for the moment; to bring his friend back to a peaceful place, where pointed out matters bore a strong resemblance to "slivery" silver and "gloom gifted" gold that had taken Tom far below the fiery pits and depths of despair, that Hell had to offer. So, Pre swiftly started to speak with the wit of a Wiseman, willing to tell a story of blessedness to calm the mood, but all that could come to his mind was to talk about the antics of "Cool A** Cliff Combs." He said, "Bro I love my first cousin to death and I know he's a little untamed, but he's a Professional "Jack of all Trades"; and I really admire his "Go-Getter" spunk." "That Old Fitful, Faithful Fool always tells me that he was a former Evangelist, and a former Pimp; but now he says that he's been converted into a modern day bullsh****." "He's straight out of a box of

Lucky Charms with his swaying arms, fishing for a four leaf clover, over the honeydew residue that layers the well kept grass; while spitting a Bucket List of manure that isn't sure if it should be shoveled or cocked back, and thrown like a pass." Thomas was a very troubled man that was listening intently, but was instantly elated by the humor of his Big Bro; which brought a little peek at the sunshine that was glaring on the other side of his "hunt down and sharp tongue words for revenge." It was quickly approaching 12:00pm in the afternoon and their discussion was see-sawing back and forth; but at times seemed to have found common ground with a brief sparkle of legitimate acceptance. Pre slowly started to down shift his approach, as he told Tom to please think about the things they had talked about, and to please stay in contact with him; steadily reassuring his sizeable student that he would keep him in his thoughts and prayers. He promised him that he would attend young Squirt's wake and funeral; and for him to contact him with the times and dates. Thomas reached out with his massive hand, giving Pre a grateful handshake, as if to thank him for everything he had ever done to help him out. They both started walking down the stairs of the front porch at a snail's pace, still exchanging pleasantries and advice; before Pre gallantly climbed his immense, drained body from his unfettered discussion with Tom into the passenger seat of Cliff's truck. Although through all the preaching and all the lights that danced across the water on the nearby lake that contemplated a calming mood; Thomas was still a bitter and broken man, like an egg shell not ready to be hatched, just yet! The balanced, meticulous movements that Pre waged had fell on deaf ears, because Tom was stranded in a hopeless place, where flights of fancy were very difficult to deal with; and like a pebble compared to a boulder, the inconsistencies simply explains itself. Standing all alone and abandoned with hard decisions to filter; Thomas suddenly waved at the two men as they eased out of the driveway and made their way back to the main road, while acceptingly returning their good-byes with boisterous blasts from "Cool Cliff's" attention grabbing, harmonious horn. Tom with his limited and unexplained visions, still somehow knew he would soon be living in a different world, and the long odds of serenity were extremely slim, with his slight glimpses of Heaven; which seemed eons away. He suddenly spun, and turned in a whimsical way, as he could barely hear the repeating ringing coming from within the house, that was tugging his bewilderment, and causing him to break into a brisk walk toward the front door. He flung open the screen door and hurried into the breeze way where the phone was neatly resting on an antique table beside an exquisite ottoman, as he finally let himself embrace the comforts of his simple treasures. Tom was at last relieved as he sat on the soothing sofa, and answered the phone with a quick, and quirky; Hello. The static on the phone came through like a Morse code of distress as the voice on the other end of the line sounded grief-stricken, yet sympathetic in their tone which sounded unfamiliar at first, but as they continued to converse the more recognizable it became. It was Linda, calling to let Thomas know that she had made burial arrangements for Squirt, and that the processions would be held on Friday, and Saturday of this week at 11:00a.m. She also informed him that Sara's brother Donny had stopped by their house earlier this morning, to let her know that he was heading to the Magistrates office to post bail for Sara and Jenny; so they would be able to attend Squirt's funeral service, and get things organized for their future court proceedings. Tom was aware that Linda would never choose between affections; and like a revolving door there were different means to avoid the myriad of problems that had taken them by surprise, and now existed as an obstacle in Thomas's grieving process. The current news was making life extremely difficult, as Goodness had a chance to grow by taming the wild; and although barely visible there might have been a possibility of achievement. He was within moments of mass hysteria as his past behaviors were exceeding his grasp, but he was still true to his roots as he asked Linda if she would please contact Pre and let him know when, and where the funeral would be held. He was swiftly being blinded by the fear inside himself, as if he were entering a "terror trap"; where he was scared of the animalistic fury that had forged internally, and formed a personal connection with his fragile state of reason. When the revealing cold comes around hoisting the "revenge rule" on its mighty shoulders, they say Hell's ferocity can't compare to the over kill thrill situation that miraculously meditates like a guilt sensation through the deepest cores of risks and chances. Linda persisted to make sure that her brother was doing well, but somehow knew there was no easing the pain of his severe loneliness. She reluctantly told him that the "**family**" and she would arrive at his house on Thursday morning, because family and friends would be gathering for a "memorial of memories" of young Squirts short, but very interesting life at around 6:00p.m.; so she wanted enough time to make the proper preparations. Linda also told him that Tommy was adjusting well to his new surroundings and that she was going to register him in school soon, but she didn't want to rush his progress in establishing a secure frame of mind. She promised Tom that she would call Pre tonight when they got home to let him know of all the arrangements, and ask him would he come to support the family at this sorrowful time. Thomas was very thankful; however, he had foreseen a different path, although it may be a tragic course, he perceived what he had to do; almost like a prisoners dilemma of wanting to be un-caged by slipping away through the shadows of his past. Even though Linda had her own thoughts about the occurrences that had unfolded, she had to bite her tongue with a "sorry, not sorry" attitude and try to remain neutral on the matters at hand. She wouldn't even comment on the activities of her sister-in-law and niece, but just told Tom that he had a strong foundation, and to take care of himself; and that they would see him in a few days. Thomas told her goodbye as if yesterdays didn't exist anymore, and it actually made perfect sense for him to ponder leaving; because "sweet nothings" couldn't heal the internal frictions bent on reprisal lingering like a stench inside of him that were so moving, and intense. As he cordially hung up the phone with Linda, all he could think about was being let down by his once trusted loved ones, when he mildly muttered a few words that were complicated to comprehend but to the most sensitive of ears it sounded like he said, "I guess they love the way they live, Mr. Friend I never had!" Tom was tip toeing on the edge of explanation, while desperately trying not to descend into the treacherous labyrinth of chaos, where striking a balance was impossible from all of the unpredictability that had fallen into his lap. Through all the intolerable cruelties, and eternal damnation that he faced, Thomas was now full of load as he rose to his feet and feverishly made his way to the kitchen, while reaching under the sink where he had stored his "Pre, get you tore up from the floor up homebrew", which had been getting more potent with the long derivations of time. Even though the guidance he had received was pure magnificence, he was still facing the new nightmares that were cleverly unmasked; which left him with invisible wounds never-before-seen, but were felt from the hardened pulls of his inner agonies screaming for help.

It simply wasn't what he expected, as he was rushing to make quick decisions from the swift changes that depraved human impact; sort of like a rocky start of being on the cusp of entering a passage way, where he would face many nights of fury that would destroy the bond of what he once loved, while shedding a leading light on the difference between the myth, and the truth in his search for never being a forgotten man. His life had been shattered and smashed, and it was no more savoring the music like the last tango where eventually the music stops, but the ceaseless voices still persuasively spoke; letting him know that final tasks must be accomplished as they said, "handle what you must, by rooting out the main source of these possessive problems!" Tom started walking as if he were on a military mission; from the kitchen back onto the front porch, and strategically sat down in the swing hanging from the ceiling with his "medicine" secured tightly in his lap as the swing slowly started to rock back and forth trying to release his caged heat that had burnt, and branded his presence of peace. The moment was very common, as his next few hours were spent devising plans and honoring proposed solutions; but his mind was already made up and there was no more time for compelling words. Tom just sat gulping his intoxicating brew, and burnishing his pick axe that he had grabbed from beside his favorite chair on his way out the front door. He was hesitant at glancing toward the sky, knowing that Father was upset with his feeble faith; while neatly being sketched on the horizon he could see a flock of geese flying in an exact "V" pattern, as if they were clashing with the wind beneath their groundless wings looking more graceful as they moved further away fading into the comfort of the clouds. Thomas was steadily drowning his sorrows in the large cask of spirits that occupied his lap, but continued to admire the optimum beauty the world still endured on this eve of madness, while the tales of Elusive Legends, and Black Magic broke bread heavily with the Devil that he knew. When out of the blue, Tom let out an eerie, but alleviating wail that resonated down the barren road leading from his house, and carried across the lustrous lake that caused vast concerns to arise from the sudden outcry of an outcast with no one to witness the darkness of his heart, and its desperate cry of distress. He had finally come to a conclusion as he was closing in on their secrets, but the curiosity of not knowing was eating his insides like a starving parasite; where he had to act soon or be devoured by the deep seriousness of broader moments soon to arise. Thomas was beyond the fringe, while being immediately surrounded by the unexpected that was running rampant as he was finding more strength in his taken aback strife's, and unreachable long desired dreams that were causing a memorable, but somber departure. It was getting riskier with whatever chance that he took, but he was on the verge of eliminating his evils; which was daring exploits for even an ex-prisoner of love and more notably an invisible executioner that would vanish and never be found when the smoke eventually cleared. The occasion was flying by like a shooting star guiding its way through the galaxy at light speed, while Tom continued to drink his self into a blurry, staggering, and mouth-gaping crisis as the serious moonlight reflected heavily from the bloody moon that sat like a fat smiling cat with a masquerade for his sinister, sly tricks. He was suffering unyieldingly from his identity crisis that was causing just another lonely day, fragile as clay, but for keeps or forsake; Thomas decided to play. He was due to inhabit a new world with his eyes flickering quickly open and shut, before crossing into a fresh threshold of hope, that was embarking on a journey while finally figuring out the concealed, shady shadows of smoke, sparking a fire with reasonable approach; that left his heart swelling with violence thrust into silence until it snapped like a twig and finally broke. Tom was now drifting somewhere far away in a tiresome and draining half-way slumber while falling with no limitations into despair; where his understandings were vulnerable, and easily being penetrated with veiled threats that were very cumbersome until tranquility invaded, causing a chilling reception. As he made his way into the house and collapsed in his favorite chair, he was feeling cold and bitter while being pressed for time and facing a matter of perspective at dawn. Thomas knew he had an unfinished life with missing components, but he was poised for growth while seeing things anew; when out of the shadows of subconscious and every crevice of humanity, he was now sharing nature with his alter self; (SACMAN). Tom alarmingly woke up with an empty house horror jutting off his mystified and wryly face, as the wee hours of the morning snuck up on him and shouted, "Boo!" Startled and confused, he was like a kid going camping for the first time as he impatiently started packing his prized possessions in the large sack Squirt had given him to collect coal, while never realizing it would be used for a more cruel and wicked purpose of storing the hearts of his countless victims. After Thomas hurriedly gathered his things, he took his last survey of the interior of the house, turned off all the lights, and briskly shut the front door trying to flee the pinnacles of pain that wandered freely like a horror show that caused a toxic presence for his battle of wills. A violent and sudden storm was ripping through the area as Tom started down the front steps while throwing the hood to his poncho over his highly emotional head, as he continued to reflect on the story of his departure like a vague matter beyond the here-and-now. He had swallowed a lot of anger lately, and he didn't see anything wrong with his repute for revenge, so it was no reason to actually re-think his decisions. Thomas just pitilessly made his way down the heavy soaked road with small wind-toppled trees aligning the skirts of its muddy and tributary passage. It was an hour of darkness to watch for while in the midst of all his troubles, and everything around him now was a mystery with unknown tones, sounding like baritones, and massacring moans. He had been morphed into something bigger and smarter with unpredictable elements ruling the panoramas of his life that set the mood of these final moments, before his huge physique blended in with the wee hour sky and like a wraith with an empty life; he vanished into the awaiting wild wilderness. Thursday morning had finally come but felt like the distant past as family and close friends started gathering at the Wolfe's house to coordinate, clean, and capture the reminisces of such a precocious young boy that had the world of a promising future which was unfortunately cut short by the horrible, and heinous hands of time, where you had never heard of such a thing so sorrowful and surreal. The Clan of mourners unloaded and swarmed on the house like scavengers on a hunt for history and hypothesis as the darkness of its inner realms stood up and greeted the intruders with a "reign over me", hello. As Tom's kin and friends filtered throughout the house, the women eventually started gathering in the kitchen preparing sandwiches, and small snacks for after the ceremony; while the men were all huddled like a miss-match football team in the den, reminiscing about days past and juggling between intense conversations with underlying problems from unforgettable humorous activities of different family members, that left their stomachs in twisted knots from the hysterical laughter. Even though the house was filled with solemn expressions, the flashbacks of such antics were like restful colors;

and the family with their friends was pretending not to see the baffling questions being asked, or the terrifying experiences that had reframed their melancholy situations. They were all feeling the warmth from the crowdedness, while being jammed together like sardines with a crisis of faith and bleak outlooks as they waited for Reverend Kinney to arrive to instill spirit back into their mask-less souls that were slowly burning and going down in flames, because some weren't willing to face or understand the unbending implications. Linda and the other women had at last put the finishing touches on the refreshments as she stealthily navigated her way from the kitchen and pass the den, slightly tapping Collus on the shoulder while motioning for him to meet her on the front porch. Pre stood up as if he were wishing upon a star eagerly anticipating if his aspirations would lead a way forward to help bring his broken friend back home again. As he made his way through the crowded room he playfully patted Tommy on the head, who had the look as if one of his mother's secrets had crept into his bones; where the price of resolution proved to be too high, which made it very hard for him to hold his head high anymore. Everyone's eyes were closely focused on Linda and Pre, and their mysterious concealment; causing uncomfortable silence to encompass the room, as Collus hedged his way toward the door steering his main attention on the shadows that were playing games with the lights radiating from the inside like three bad signs of: death, destruction, and nothing but pure and absolute darkness. The screen door made a wailing, crying for help sound as Pre nonchalantly pushed it open with a glint of finding an end to the sadness and sorrow we all face when the unexpectedness of loss walk hand and hand while trying to avoid the turbulent road to Hell. Steam was streaming out of the kitchen as curiosity had crept inside of Sara, who was still making finishing touches to the food preparations while trying to avoid the many questions that lay on the tips of everyone's tongues. She was like a chameleon creeping behind the contentment's of camouflage, as she came out of the kitchen while sharply noticing that Pre and Linda were standing on the porch in a deceptively simple "I tell, you tell" of conversation. Sara had already heard the whispers floating around the room about their unusual circumstances, so she knew they were talking about Thomas; and like a vindictive goddess with a partially clean slate looking less than half-way erased she made a major effort to see what they were discussing, as she quietly positioned herself by the corridor of the front door. She pretended to entertain while striking up informative gibber-jabber with the clueless but "sniffing it out" crowd, but her main concentrations were centered on the activity developing outside the partially ajar glass screen door. Meanwhile, Linda had just ask Collus had he heard from Thomas; and Pre like a messenger of the multitudes swung his words fluently like his tongue was Excalibur fueled by passion, truth, and a hint of grief's darkness. He calmly replied, "Linda, I haven't heard from him directly but I feel he was vulnerable enough to be responsible for the reckless behavior that has left four men dead; and one of them being Carl Edward our Plant Supervisor." Pre told her about the last talk he had with Tom and the evidence in the handwriting they had discovered; that sent him into a "killer within" state of mind releasing his recent transformation, and more than likely the reason for his sudden disappearance. He looked pale and ghostly as if he had just risen from the grave as he continued to tell the tale of the widespread panic where unsuspecting lives hung in the balance like airless spaces in time with their last breath actually being their last whistle for Dixie. Collus continued to inform Linda as he said, "The Deepwater Gazette reported that early Wednesday morning they found four bodies in Carl Edwards workshop that had been tortured for hours with their hearts hacked right out of their chest cavities, as if someone was digging a new and shorter passage to China." "There were no clues of forced-entry and the only evidence they could gather were their human remains and the deep "replacing a cluttered closet" of holes that were laid on thick through their sternums; because ain't no love in killing softly!" Pre proceeded to flap gab the juice, as if he were listening to a magic flute with eight golden voices singing like a canary chirping classically about his friend who he pictured saying, "Catch me if you can for I am hopelessly out of control." "My revenge was served stoical, and I'll never stop, because my depth of anger is inexplicable, and keeping their hearts was like a journal of death; well written and outlined for a timely demise of those who with their circle of lies crossed their last line." "So, please pardon my future and the new identity I have established, because I had to go with my feelings for the sake of the sins of the Father, the Husband, and the Brother toeing the cliffs edge with evil lurking closely behind converging with my unsettled soul; forgive and fear me in the same thought, for I am real!" Linda spoke up as if she knew her brother better than anyone as her words were to protect Tom's image as she said, "my brother is good-natured at heart and not like what you are saying or seeing." "We have to gather together and find him because he's walking into big problems, and we shouldn't overreact or come to any conclusions without any positive confirmation." Pre honestly agreed as he sympathetically replied, "Your right Linda, and I know we have different perspectives but I'm reading between the lines and I wouldn't dare try to sway the situation in the direction I witnessed, but I'm a lot like Tom and I have to go with my strong sensibilities." "For one, Thomas is gone with no clue of his whereabouts, and the only things taken from the house were his pick axe, the sack Squirt gave him and his antique record player you have to wind up to play; so all in all, they were his most prized possessions and I ask you what else could make holes in a body like that besides his finely, honed pick axe?" Before Linda had a chance to repudiate Pre's, "what seemed to be private thoughts", a large black sedan resembling a hearse was making critical maneuvers up the driveway trying to avoid all the parked vehicles that sidelined the narrow gravel road. Sara was watching their every movement, while still being hidden within the screen door with her ears locked intently on the battle of minds on the porch as they scrambled for answers. She couldn't hold back her curiosities any longer, as she surprisingly pushed open the screen door and quickly said, "Is that Reverend Kinney finally making an eloquent entrance?" Linda seemed startled by Sara appearing from out of nowhere, and her intuition was telling her that she had been hanging around the front door gathering bits and pieces of information to sooth her tarnished ego. Linda eventually replied, "Damn girl! Yes, he finally arrived but it seems that you've been waiting to make an emergence since Collus and I started our little discussion, Miss Peek-a-boo." Sara was slightly embarrassed as she turned a bright red and rolled her eyes like a pair of dice with snake eyes showing on its decisive tumble for everyone to see. Pre immediately started to laugh while smacking himself on the legs like a joke of "gotcha" had been executed and delivered with the most prolific of timing. He continued to chuckle with his monstrous laugh, as the Reverend began gathering a few items from the back of his car and briskly started walking at a hectic pace toward the three onlookers. Reverend Kinney spoke out with a boisterous greeting as he said, "Hear my sermon, my faithful flock. The word has found its way home; even though sometimes the road taken seems to be unfamiliar, it's still a glorious path, a learning path, and an arduous path for the believers who were sent beforehand with songs of the mountains echoing a healing for thy soul, like Wading in the water, or Kumbaya; God here's your call my children, God here's your call, Amen!" He continued with, "Good evening everyone and I do apologize for my tardiness." "They say that "patience is a virtue", and that "absence makes the heart grow fonder", but when expressing all emotions through a very intense matter it can make the rain often come down hard and unflinching; while seeing that every rose has its own thorn where no kindness is too small, when much of life is missing, and wandering in its wits." "I ask that you accept this as whispered advice, yet forthright and direct, it will somehow challenge your thoughts on the harsh realities of life." "Long ago, I was told that when death comes it rides a determined and unyielding horse bringing unwelcome obligations with sincere elements of confusion." "So, I beg you my children please listen to your inner voice as it sits on the edge of sorrow and love, forced to exhibit a different mindset; consistently helping you to see past the obvious, while attempting to keep this ghastly, grave-sitter preoccupied." "The cold truth is heartbreaking but invigorating contemplating death as an end, or is it a beginning; because it's said, just to follow the light; to me the light being the stars on the other end of the universe transported by a black hole that hurls your soul through time as it enters embracing, and trusting while trying to find its way home." "God, I say the sky's the limit with lasting impressions striving together with your strong efforts of envisioned Heaven; spiritually seeking God's will and his foundation of blissful wisdom, constantly receiving insights about your approach; because sometimes you stand alone while evil is afoot, but let us gather in harmony today to find our Paradise for a calming spirit such as young Squirt." "May it be so?" The three fruitful onlookers stood as Three Wise men in awe of the spirit bestowed upon them while being sensed as distant men hitting a roadblock with clarity, compassion, and hard facts manifesting their desires of growth, like a tree's anchor that's everlasting and emblazoned with stable and strengthened roots shielded from the dark and gory faces of others that are hidden for only a moment from the echoing attacks of Sadism. The speech of Reverend Kinney was cognizant, and immediately ensued by the warm welcoming of handshakes and hugs as the stout, dark-rimmed eyed man made his way cordially around the greeting party of opposing viewpoints that were posted like stop signs on the front porch. Pre politely held open the front door as the four ushered inside to commence an uplifting tribute, and expressions of condolences for the deceased, William "Squirt" Wolfe. As the night had passed by with tears and sad comments of natural outcomes, with "out of the past rejoicing", and "way back when" commemorations of their precious unforgettable love; time seemed to be neatly nestled in the moment of reconciliation, followed by powerful strides to a successful coping of their irreplaceable loss. The morning had crept in like a deceitful teenager breaking their curfew, disrespectfully late and sneakily furtive in its vast approach of shedding light on the questions of, "What is paradise, exactly where is it located, and when do things that really matter start to peak into a legendary reckoning of raged retribution?" Sparking our curiosities to also ask, "Does a Dawn horse running free and wild with no seen rider harnessing a blazing saddle of lava like fire exist; or is it just a rush into the first option of beyond and never understanding the rebellious, uncontrollable penchant of passion?" Unfortunately, leaving a man to make a fast exit, where enough was enough; who was said to have been chased away by a deceitful family, now lingers on the outskirts of nowhere never stopping to take a look at the big picture, where he's already started to sink in a puddle of his dark desires, that seem thick as mud. As the wake for young Squirt was rapidly approaching, all thoughts were wondering, how could a Father who loved his son so much be absent from this closure of saying his last goodbyes, and laying his baby boy's remains to its final resting place here on Earth? The pain he's carrying must be pure anguish, with a frigid like ice weight of guilt being on overload afflicting his thoughts, and rash judgments with a not at this point answer to the intervention of interrogators wondering, why, where, and how? Meanwhile, as the day flew on, the parking lot to the funeral home was starting to fill at a gradual pace as multiple quivers of light reflected from atop of the overshadowing mountain that towered the terrain, and seemingly floated over the wondering eyes of the congregation below. Lo and Behold, it was Thomas sitting on a ridge overlooking the funeral home as he stealthily watched the proceedings from afar through a pair of Squirt's old Boy scout binoculars, as he intensely thought to himself, while contemplating his next moves. "Oh I pray to the

Heavens of clouds of gray, and I say Momma was such a vigil light, witnessed as a breath of fresh air; always was honest with her particular talks of openness and to the point candor while having the sweetness of an apple with its irresistible flair." "Dad was a soldier, and you Mom were the smolder in the smoke that lifted father to the unforeseen levels in the minds of folks, as you pointed out the things that were the best of any given man." "With his kindness, generosity, and his forgiveness of the clan that alienated his progress to be an integral and vital part, where he always wanted to receive their joyous love in return, but it was just no place in their stubbornness of hearts." "Negativity and Faults were their weapons to keep an outsider wanting to be an insider yearning and at bay; no one wanted anything to do with you because they couldn't see that alcohol was soothing for your ways." "Now they both are gone and left me lost and confused; with only love for my own and a limited tolerance of betrayal with no more beating around the bush, I was set up to fail." "They sneakily played against the rules and warranted me the chosen fool, while solitude seemed like Eden, what else was I to do?" "So, as today and hereafter I struggle to be relevant like an elephant in the jungle of life; looking for water at the oasis of reminisces, while asking you to feel the concepts of my heart, to be more precise." "I'm just a simple and ordinary man turned into a monster it seems like almost overnight; as my reticence disappeared quickly without the slightest of trace, but I could still see the quaking trees and dangerous curves on this hard road home to paradise." "Even though I'm love sick like the Blues with painted visions of longing to leave strapped with desired results of unfinished lessons, I left howling hysterically, undeterred and spinning free while responding improperly to the crash course shaping of my new found essence." As Thomas attempted to steer his focus back to the new realities that lay before hand in the valley below, he noticed that all his close friends that had slipped away from his "circle of care" were now gathering in the greeting area of the building, before going over to the ceremony for the wake of his greatest love. It was a matter of chance that Sara and Linda walked out of the assembly room door of the funeral home following Reverend Kinney over to the viewing area to make sure that everything was presentable and honorable for the difficult, but enlightening farewells. On their way down the well groomed sidewalk, they could notice the flickers of light coming from above, while Reverend

Kinney held open the door for the two women as they graciously walked into the huge room adorned with bouquet after bouquet of exotic flower arrangements. Nevertheless, Sara was staying direct in her approach toward the "beauty of divine" casket in the awaiting candle lit, majestic chamber; when she noticed an envelope and a large piece of coal placed on top of its secure sleek design like a veil of confusion; where understanding would soon evolve, if the message was received and taken in strides as seismic shimmers, with peals of thunder causing this day to move; and eventually your intuitiveness turns on like a scavenging search light. She inquisitively opened the envelope with cunning and extremely uncontrollable eagerness for the unexpected that would never be recreated, like the first impact of each startle of shock that granted her this uncomfortable situation of fate. Sara started to read, as if she was awaiting a message of judgment, or simply an understanding of the new portraits wondering in her thoughts of a vanishing and unsuspecting world. It read, "Had a wife name Sara and I tried to give her the world, blessed my empty soul with a beautiful baby girl." "Added two sons, my little soldiers; but now I'm all alone so how do I still live, with my soul, my heart, and my life God, is all that I can give." "For my treasures that's been given, I graciously praise the Lord, I feel like Sir Lancelot trying to pull out the mightiest of all swords." "From the stone that encases its truest and rarest of essence, I learned from betrayal and death that my life is just a whirlwind of lessons." "Didn't want to have to flip the switch for annihilation or destruction, but I feel I can't function without payback and the security of insane corruption." "How do I continue looking out that desolate window without a family to help me up that ladder for a man to steadily grow, because all I see is solitude as I allude when they pursue, while hoping that my dreams of happiness and forgiveness come true; be it so." "Yes, I'll always continue to search, to seek, to find while being temporary adrift and tumbling like a stone in the mysteries and intrigue of my sinister mind." "As moving forth emerges, I dedicate and leave this last clue for you: If I was a bird flying without a care destined for nowhere, and then I suddenly disappear before a cherishing of yearning stares; somehow I'll always appear like a twinkle in the sky, largely unseen and very seldom noticed but I'll always be there!" Sara, after a pause of recollection dropped the letter like a falling leaf to the grass in the middle of the edifice, as she frantically started to run toward the entrance of the viewing area. She might have thought possible, for the impossible because her resourcefulness was exhausted and shocked; but she still didn't have a clue to face to satisfy her need for knowing, so we all wait wonderingly asking was her fidelity faithful or faithless? As she stood there pondering all dolled up and fallow in the middle of the courtyard looking far back in time where thin excuses were like a work of art, something intuitively drew her direct focus to laser onto the mountain top that was giving alms to the intellectual conversations and challenges that were, and might not have been, if it wasn't for the willingness to look for a different route. The gleam of efforts that might have paid off in the past were like the luck of the draw as Sara and Thomas were now staring eye to eye it seemed; but actually only glimpses of secrets that ran astray were willingly and vibrantly searching to bask in this eternal sunshine. Tom was starting over from scratch and presently writing a new beginning for his creativity of calculated killing, with adventures hurling toward the future as his mind jettisoned his worries and fears while never repeating his patterns throughout time, because the world had never met anyone like him, as an impresario of an evil nuisance. It was like an old-time revival as Thomas stood on top of the mountain as a visual spectacle of revenge being doled out through appropriate boundaries; thinking to himself that he must reside before he could shine, because beforehand he'll be lighting up the night sky's as a problematic professor of knee-jerk responses barbarically shouting, "**HEARTS ARE FOREVER!**"

CHAPTER III

Up Yonder and a Graveyard away

As the season shifted from late spring deep into early summer, Thomas walked off that mountain top on the most somber of days and through all his pain and suffering he had endured all alone; actually caused the withdrawal of his association to be more undead than that sick sense of nomadic denial latching like claws onto the pit of his stomach, which was causing his intellectual powers to beat severely like an aching heart-break. He was about to pull the ol' switch-a-roo, while playing a ghostly harmonica that sounded like an owl hooting hoo; who goes there foe or fiend looking for an exit plan to this whole puff of smoke that was being blown through a fictional screen. Although his intentions were stern and sound, he would never be able to plant his feet quite firmly on the ground while discovering things about himself that years ago he had already found. He would just watch and patiently wait like a hawk converting the uneasiness of a predatory pariah into a moment of familiarity of acceptance and triumph in his own tortuous twisted way. Yet, days ago Tom had tormented Carl Edward and his co-conspirators into aggressive submission costing them their lives, their hearts, and souls; while retrieving all the information he needed for his critical mission of irresistible urges of finally smothering a dying fire. Thomas swore that their families, friends, and children would pay dearly for their insolence and smooth-tongued arrogance that destroyed the heavenly order of his seemingly "Garden of Eden" life; where love and understanding were like the joyful melodies of river songs serenading them into and endless happiness, that only exists without the puppeteer of evil tampering and disregarding the concepts of the generations of genuine family. Now, briefly toward the condition of the future where this mystery was unraveling and being stripped to the bone by a group of community kids known as the "Deepwater Daredevils", who were still looking for a piece of the action with a willingness to look for danger where a teaching of not to be afraid was being worn like an adornment chivalrously tattooed deep within our brood egos. Time was presently being introduced as a particular period of recollection, as Nece and Lia came suddenly running down the driveway hill like an unhinged rocking cradle swaying a "la a bye" that was sweet to the innocent ears of the waiting, and anticipating of jubilance that was expecting an A-Okay for their Hail Mary of endeavors. Deadly skills with trails of tears lay ahead for the ambitiousness of this "ain't no quit, when we spit and stay loyal to the grit of the grind"; because we see that we have an allusive monster to track and find. The two sisters were a lot of hop, skip, and jump as they approached the backyard full of quickly thrown together shelters, and built up wonderment awaiting the key to the lock; to begin the process of resolving the utter chaos that was hanging on like Grim Death with a conscience that never stopped and listened to him. Everyone was sitting like war hungry Indians craving the crevices of the hunt as we sat in front of our tents with wrapped and dedicated attention as Nece started to shout, "The time is now to strike our blows!" "Mom and Dad said that Jayme and Rene could stay another week, and that they would take them to Grandma Pete's house next Saturday to meet up with Uncle Blushie and Aunt Cil." The shouting and cheering erupted like an active volcano, which made our roars reverberate and rattle the chains that held "Streak" the family German Sheppard, who started growling and pacing his chain links with a ferocious wickedness for protection of the "don't give up" Daredevils; that made Kevin have to calm him down by waving his hand toward the ground firmly, and shouting the command of "Lay" with a stern direct voice to settle this over aggressive defender of loyalty and love. The disillusioned night was steadily growing darker than a shadow of souls, as we braced for trouble that would soon come; where we knew a little mystery went a long way when trying to get back to the basics of whodunit and what for. Now making the most of the moment that we had all just embraced, while discreetly discarding the fragile and broken ones; Walter surprisingly crawled from out of his tent with the look of a General, and commandingly walked up to the caressing campfire with his leather black gloves on to signify "Black Power". Not the Black Power that you might be thinking about, but the type of authority where large numbers, unity, and imaginative capabilities that a group of kids with tears and tantrums were honored by feeling strongly connected to everyone in their circle of Custer-teers, while yearning the early years where it should be the only years of forget me never, and forget me not. Our group of rare minds with endless creativity was heading in a new direction, and we was just beginning to recognize that we couldn't see an end to this war even if by destroying such a fatalistic fable with our new clues to this enigma; where over thinking certain situations could cost us to lose our heads with lonesome echoes chiming in the background while humming in a soft voice saying, "Man is a beast as if a beast is a man, try to stop me, try to stop me if you really understand." We were gruesomely seeing visions of the dead, with chills of combustion chasing our minds-eye view; causing it to catch on fire like an inferno in the evening starlit night, while flawlessly being tortured by the turbulent years that shone bright, where no one really cared for the assumed crazy that was reduced to pure savagery; with no remorse of it being wrong or right. It was a story to die for; because it showed strict, sculptured gardens evenly parted like the Red Sea cut deeply by the fine razors of staggered time, causing an untrusting sense of normalcy while this "locking horns of an instance" was dragging its feet in the face of dying. I once heard that sin never withers or shivers in the cold, but grows very old in souls; and when those who expose their weakest petals of rose, become frozen in time like the swirls of chances that they regrettably chose. While slowing starting to gain momentum like the Maiden Mary of prevail, with a feeling of being Benedicted and ungraciously derailed; scorned and left to die alone with no more stories to tell; easily discarded like there is no learning curve for justice, while living in Hell. The heart of our lives were now being challenged; and often not seen as life, but as strife mixed-up in the wrong place at the right time as Walter summoned our full attentions to gather for a powwow of the youth; that was acting like Wolves with a predatory prowess of Ali in a ring victoriously winning in the jungle of hope and desired dreams, where cheers of "must" were the only answer to the final outcome of things. The boys and I were struggling with our particular sins where we were relying on "believe in me" to forward stride our aggressive braveness in this battle of wills to be a major breakthrough; while competing for this crown we knew as "manhood"! We all started gathering around "the learn to love challenge" of a campfire with our knees to elbows and an accelerated concentration as young warriors, still afar but almost like Indians touching base with the Spirit World where going past boundaries were shown as God's will, leading us to new paths that were needed to be found. As our attentions were centered with little voice, the more time we had to draw up strategies on mini-paper pads and pass them around to the rest of the Daredevils, who were anxious and feeling like Frontiersmen blazing trails with our eagerness and camaraderie; while slightly being shadowed by a hint of the fear that we would soon face. An hour or more had passed, and the final plans for our "cloak and really matter" surveillance was about to be executed; where hesitation was sometimes a flaw, but tonight was being used as who can you trust when your choices still involve concealed deceit, danger, and below the belt do-dirty-isms. We were training for the wars of the damned; damned if you do and damned if you don't, as we innocently invited this five day conflict; which was like an eternity in dog years of nightmares where the mighty Overseer chooses and picks. It was as if looking up at the stars would give us the answers in learning about ourselves, and pulling dusty books off the shelf could truly measure the survival knowledge in a man's wealth. Jeered judgments for how far our last stand was, was "swirly bird tweeting" through our brains as we practiced our talents in the art of tippy-toe, lay low, and don't let the Boogey Man see how many ducks you have lined in a row! It was like a tournament of shadows as the trees swayed with vigor of vibrancies, double- daring us to come out and play in the presence of the latter, and things that actually matter in chance; where you always hear that "pit-a-patter" in idle chatter, which was like a novel of reinvented romance. We were being confronted by Specters of the past, as set it off smoke signals shimmered from the "no going back bitter flames" almost like the air you breathe; which made the scene irresistible, thrilling, and flawless when someone's actually trying to convey information to you; but you're senses weren't taking enough time to listen, when the message should have been captured like "after words". Allusive mysteries were now pulling the strings to us unusually fiery turf warriors, who were trying to roll with the punches, and have it our way; where bypassing certain situations that were unpleasant, and stressing a big deal had a slight touch of cynicism while distorting the story from the heart like an arrow of love. Walter was systematically finishing the final instructions to our master plan, when he focally spoke up and said, "Heed my young Daredevils!" "The plan is set, where we must accomplish a task that seems unlikely, but is very much achievable if we stay committed to our team work, and trust in one another." "I'll stay here at camp with the girls, while you four fearless foot soldiers execute our purpose of pursuit, and peek-a-boo protection to aid in the capture of the reputed to be the obvious choice to prevail, Sacman." "Your only mission is to watch closely, set traps, and gather intelligence for a much broader strategy that should be more direct and easier toward our future sudden advances." Before another word could be spoken, it was like all of a sudden and lightning fast as the ferocious roar of a train came barreling down its aging tracks with bright gold lights looking like an Olympic athlete surging for that dauntless and elusive gold medal; while immediately spawning the thoughts of our group to depart deceptively under the cover of this metaphoric "blackberry smoke", which caused a gritty and very alert approach that seemed somewhat resistant to any discipline, as we really didn't care what the enemy said; here we come! Although we were slightly behind schedule the tempest was raging as we quickly gathered our gear to dart off secretively into the "taken away" midnight darkness, where the scare factors were more tense than frightening. I said, "What in the world?" as I started feeling the pitter pat of heavy rain drumbeating on my arms; and as I glanced toward the lawn of tents, I witnessed the rain tap dancing on top of the seemingly sand sprinkled shelters causing strong reactions to second guess our decision to "move out", but there were no harsh criticisms where sad secrets remained hidden in "the Yonder and a Graveyard away!" I knew that this encounter would be like a showdown with Ike Clanton himself, as I desperately tried to ease everyone's worries with my last minute sparks of insanity rant by saying, "So what about these eggshell elements of side effects that's trying to hamper our obvious choices of think fast and act quick, when we should be asking Jack about jumping over that lit candlestick." Now, my words were chosen uniquely for the moment, and the audience that was ready to accept the unexplained activities of danger on a more simplified risk. So, I spoke louder and louder wanting my words to be felt and to try and drown out the thunder of the train rumbling in the near vicinity. I said, "Snap out of it, stay motivated, and pray for the best; and the best shall come." "We know this is a "make or break" mission, and there's always a song for the ones facing death; so I ask you all to sing and rejoice in our absence and honor that will, by God's will return safely." As my last words crossed the minds of my confused Daredevils like a ticketed time warp, the four of us fled freely toward the North Star; which was the massive locomotive staying visible, but gradually starting to dissipate up the goodnight, goodnight wicked trail for giving cues. I slowly looked back toward our hope and inspiration; to see that the spread of sufferings and sadness were passing by as time like being clocked like Big Ben slowly ticking a torture of persecution on my left behind families seized in the moment faces. We were readily turning back to the task at hand, and it was like the future was transforming right before our eyes fatally painting the big picture; while we faced life's trials and hardships where we could still conjure a smidgen of hope to keep us moving forward! We might not have been sure of our choices for what was heeding and heartfelt, but we would continue to travel down many different avenues. It was an honor of change within us that were being blistered through these fast transformations, while hashing over the old times but being prepared to greet a standoff with the present. Cool breeze whispers that could barely be heard were pulling us further and further into the "chilly mood" of the dark, steadily crossing the threshold of no return which seemed not as important as right here and right now. The hour was belonging to us and us alone as we faded into the powerful, yet vulnerable awareness of possibilities that lie ahead; and then we evaporated like water vanishing out of vision and the pretense of the presence. Meanwhile, back at camp the other Daredevils were settling down for a restful night as Rene and Walter set up guard duty for everyone to be implemented with rotating one hour shifts, so that the person on watch would be more alert to any outside interruptions. Rene said that she would take the first watch, because she felt that no one should be kept alone and drained looking for a way out of "does it matter"; and she knew that everyone would be more productive with the proper rest and reassurance. The two sympathetic leaders of the group were giving them a great sense of direction, while beaming in on the warm heartedness of protection and overseeing, where Kings and Queens would state that they "remember you." For the moment magnificence was manifesting, as the wind started to howl them sweet bed time stories of darkness that was falling rapidly and growing grisly grave suddenly being engulfed by an eerie stench lingering in the muggy, humid air like an excavation with intrigued finders, finding a way to search for the answers of the past even though the task was less than an hourly wage. The Daredevils were simmering down and settling in snugly for the night, but some tensions were still running high and causing a staggering effect on their imaginations; because earlier in the day they had been pushed beyond what they thought they could do, and the thrill of our achievement was uncontrollable. Walter, like the cool cat he portrayed was playing a song on his Close and Play record player by Michael Jackson called "I'll be there", which was propelling our discipline to embrace the words that had a lot to share, words that exemplified "true feelings" expressed with a lot of care; while being extinct to some non believers which made these particular words significantly mighty and rare. Now, in another part of this "vagueness of trap doors" out in the wild yonder, we four marauders were tracking down an unwanted guest in a hostile environment which made us to be easy and potential prey impeding our chosen course of action; but not the same as a lack of a warranted message. However, back at base; flash backs and lightning cracks were forcing mild fears to penetrate the thoughts, and built up barricades of bravery of Rene, who had bunkered in and taken post under the carport like a sentry on a "see it all, and tell all" watch out for the wicked. She was sitting like a squaw, where earlier eternal sunshine was now being followed by serious moonlight which was giving temporary reflections of major shift controls of stability and upper hand rules of thumb. Everyone else was fast asleep even though the excitement and stress was soaking through their veins of vigor causing them to compete for a "sleep tight and don't let the bed bugs bite type of night." In a cat's whisker and at a near distance, lightning was flashing legitimate reasons to be concerned; where shocking repercussions for all mankind forbade them to reconsider their opinions and to desperately hold on to their bitterness and anger, because it was justifying and left their rival at a disadvantage; if that wasn't bold enough! Although the rules may not have changed, Rene was slowly nodding off and being a little less adventuresome than usual; as the beauty in the night like a crystal lined stone was taking her with it, deep into slumber where difficulties weren't meant to be, which honestly lifts you to a new level of understanding. This conscience sight was perfectly set like a mid-summer's nightmare as the "fortified" Daredevils were awakened by the shrill barks of Streak, trying to guard against the gates of Hell that separated the camp of tents and a huge garbage bin that was hiding a shadowy culprit lurking in the hazy rain, causing it to look slippery as an eel to the wonderment of their fatigued eyes, as they were woozy and lackadaisical from their dead tired sweet sensations of "hold me closer and rock me to sleep." Rene was so startled that she instantly rolled backwards out of her Indian seated position with her elbows on her knees and her hands tightly resting on her chin, into a regressive handstand pushing her nimbly into a feline's grace of surprise. Alertly and reflexive to mayhem, Walter came crawling out of his tent like a sprinter taking off out of his starting blocks, coming upright into a full dash like he was a scalded rabbit with his blowgun strapped to his back, and ready for the seething heat of this soaked scenario. Wildly and in a husky suppressed voice Walter yelled, "Daredevils defend!" This meant for everyone to go into counter evasive maneuvers, and to assume a protective position of defense; and in God's eyes, be ready for the "want some, get some" altercation they were about to encounter. "I wish it would rain" smothered their screams that were being bottled, so not to alert Uncle Bobby, Aunt Brenda, and the Radford's; who were just a pebbles toss away of causing ripples to manifest in the rainy puddles that land mined the whole entire backyard. Rene had pulled herself into the rafters of the carport with her bag of rocky-river rocks, known to cause knots on the hard heads with soft a****, eager to swell for the thickening of this plot. The other Daredevils had dug deep into their column safeguards with an Eagles eye on the invader that was ravaging and pillaging the contents within this "safe crackers case of concessions." Streak was going out of his mind and wired like he was screaming, "gimme some more" as Walter came running toward the carport with his eyes set on the ladder that laid like a stairwell to heaven; or even yet like an Angel looking down from the sky at the "hunt or be the hunted" in this world where testimony of triumph was a true treasure. Walter in his nifty effort to leap to the rungs of this helpful wooden structure loudly and instructing said, "Streak play dead!" which was a trick that my Dad and I taught him as a puppy before we had brought him to stay at Uncle Bobby's and Aunt Brenda's house, because our landlord wouldn't let us keep a pet at the "alley shelter" my parents rented in Charleston; so this would be his temporary haven for now. As Streak acted like a dead possum playing "a on the side of the road" parlor trick with his road kill technique; Walter speedily made his way to the top of the carport above the position Rene had secured, who was keeping a close "conceal and kill" watchfulness on the perp with a sleek black sweeping body. They could hear the soft voice of the Little Engine that could words creep through the troubled sky, "I can, I can, I can" as they both witnessed the shadow of this invasive monster which seemed big as an elephant and destructive as a quiet, unpredictable storm. Nece and the rest of the girls were feeling weighed down and over burdened, but in a winsome manner managed to edge their way closer to the activity blossoming outside the fence and about twenty yards inwards from the "discover the truth for yourself" railroad tracks. They were deep in the heart of the game, where a hysterical haze surrounded the situation that was about to occur, even better than talked about while their imaginations wandered freely feeling the steam from the passion; and with a wild manner entered their new challenges that were so overrated but expected, with their fiery personalities truly grasping the unpredictable edge. It didn't make sense that this trespassing disturber of peace was inspiring them to rise, defend, and protect the hard scrabble passages that might have been a disagreeable task, but ended up being an experience of expressing their selves without hesitation or the slightest of thought. Walter was now set in a bird's eye view of the mischief marauder, as he finally got a clear picture of what this menace actually was when he alarmingly shouted like a sound breaking siren, "It's a bear!" The "going to great lengths" creature was maneuvering slowly, but being very much forthcoming in its perception of seeing life in a unique style of acceptance, where his Robin Hood antics of stealing from the fruitful and giving to the messy moans of his belligerent belly was just a following of the recipe to lightning never striking twice; if that wasn't a small enough sign of success. Over the glow glistening moon and with an eye for an eye of the dear hearts that's so consumed, they were being drawn to a cause with vague information while now seeing adventure in a different fashion when approaching others; which only added to the desirability of fighting for a place pictured as just perfect, but it feels so awful to be this correct. The right answers were like well laid smoke screens, as Walter loaded his blow gun to inject "a get out of here quick attitude", which might have been blatantly rude but their boldness was beyond the curve only leaving the wickedness of this after dark, and the horror that had suddenly fallen up on them. Our daring and dazzling Daredevils visuals were overly eclectic; seeming temporarily vacant, but left the mission at hand to appear easier said than done. The smothering shadows had engulfed the massive mammal's monstrous frame like dark gray clouds encompassing the highest peaks of the Himalayas, as the outlaw with a blowgun shot his projectile with "ace of spades" accuracy for his first shot; which rang like the Liberty Bell of prevail, and go to Hell if you don't except respect of a jury; but sometimes it fails. So, feel the fury of the reins being accidentally dropped in their conceptions of their courageous off-the-wall ideas; which immediately created a simple opening to precious desires that reflected their new transformation. There is no right and wrong when it comes to that seductive ringing sound echoing through your mind systematically showing you the way through the weight of hostile surroundings that result in conflict, where courageousness was meant to be heard; making those baffling questions approachable which doesn't seem so elusive anymore. In their stubbornness of hearts it seemed that there was no escape from fear, as Rene started her bombardment of modern day stoning; pelting the large nuisance repeatedly with shot, after shot of death knocking body blows that would have left the fittest of prize fighter's gasping for breath, while Walter simultaneously launched off two more darts into the body of the "scaring them in the dark" intruder, with expert precision and painful, punishing, passion. The startled bear was so surprised by the aggressive assault that it stood on its hind legs waving its front paws, as if it had encountered a bee's hive stinging its presence with continuous, calculated attacks of punishment for only "starving like Marvin"; so whose willing to feed the ones hungry and helpless to the cruel concepts of "survival of the fittest"; leaving a distinct taste in your mouth wondering how can you forgive someone whose really hurt you, when all you wanted was a chance at existing in a struggling, unpredictable world of chaos and catastrophe; is the first question that should be asked? The enraged beast was regretting its special place in this "blame game" hell, where he never quite managed to crash the gates that had rejected its pleas for a quiet dinner, and a peaceful enjoyment of the gratifications of this somewhat tedious conquest. Retreating in a disappointed, defeated manner while trotting off grievingly, this large outsider was looking back at what was pictured as just a simple supper; but turned out to be off limits to unwelcome associations. Walter was still poised on the carport rooftop with his right hand placed in a saluting fashion across his forehead attentively watching the turned away tenacity of this two-toned terrorizer with temerity; who rose abruptly with its toughness and grit, but was turned into a ta-ta, goodbye, goodnight, and don't let this unforgettable flight be a discouragement in plight to doing what's right for the complexity of things; where poetry is timeless in a cruel humanity seen as black and white. There was no immediate celebrating or rejoicing; only relief was glimmering from the "wins over mystique" Daredevils like new light and the clash of trial and triumphs shinning brilliantly on these resilient whipper-snappers. The plan was still pushing ahead at mach speed without any compromise to their foresight of flawless execution, and their hush-hush secrets from the elders was a looking beyond the obvious of disguise and technique. Meanwhile, the chosen warriors were on our mission of different styles of attack and surveillance, but we were hooked on the idea of clawing our way back from out of the past events that left us scared to death and screaming passionately from our inner voices. The rail tracks were still shimmering and vibrating heavily from the rolls of "true thunder", sending wave like echoes bouncing across the deeply altered landscape causing us to flinch and take cover every time an unusual sound ruffled our feathers of fear and frantic antics; where a long hike, and pacing ourselves like worrisome Worry-warts was kind of suspicious shifting through the angry huffs and puffs of the rustling wind. Through a nearby field the inside scoop was wailing toward our situation bordering the tracks where a need to run wasn't far away knowing the predicament was now more serious, and would be too much to take if preparation and determination wasn't a key asset in our central message of staying alive. As we looked up at the sky in wonderment it seemed that there was no twinkle in the sky as the unexpected was lurking with a surprising visit of whose home for the visit of "skinned to the bone." The patient predators that seemed to be lying in wait must have gotten a good whiff of our formidable scent, but we still took a quick breather in a forest clearing, where suddenly an off sounding birds activities had been muffling the approach of "the say over and over again" enemy that was honoring boundaries of confront boldly and thrive second to none. We were going with the moment and feeling very touchy, as Lil Tom noticed yellow glowing eyes like lightning bugs scurrying through the field at a hurried pace closing in on our "I can't tell if hell is our destination, but it will take a diligent effort to send us there" location. Lil Tom was the closest to the sudden incursion, where a brief period of quiet was thundered over by his boyish shouts of, "Wild dogs; wild dogs! Hang fire to the trees!" Which meant, hop to it and take cover in the treetops or get mauled by the Big Bad Wolves zeroing in for a midnight snack that was mouth watering and irresistible to the "can't help loving the hunger" of a "thought to be easy meal", and without even the slightest of a huff or a puff from these crafty, creeping canines with no fear. Everyone came out of their resting postures straight into a "make it snappy" mad dash of darting away, to take cover in nearby treetop refuges like the safety of a nest or an aerie, to survive this bonkers of be ready for battle when the Starters pistol fires and then suddenly harks back for the "feeling off-kilter" of fleeing to commence. The dogs definitely weren't giving up on their hounding pursuit as the wild scavenger's throttled lightly across a little creek to quickly close the gap between us; as we barely reached the base of the trees. My only thought was to say a quick prayer as I closed my eyes and reached out to Father with my faith and fortitude as I silently said to myself; "Oh, Lord getting to first base was like smashing a homerun out of the ballpark, which was very much exhilarating and challenging but extremely necessary for our critical situation; and if there was an evil dead lying in wait like a slice of this gruesome existence, it actually brought forth the true realities of "Glory overcomes Denial"; that I know you've witnessed before." "So, I ask in the name of Jesus Christ that you bring us home safely and unscathed, for we are sheep searching for our Sheppard to fend off our aggressors from this beginning of a deadly confrontation; Lord I pray!" As I quickly looked around, everyone else was speedily ascending up the trees like our lives depended on it; so I immediately followed way like Tarzan or George of the Jungle fighting the depths of grit in their souls to save that still tormented survival instinct that was twisted and knotted in the core of their braveness, where there was no sense of confusion; only God's reasons! We were now exhaustingly towering above, while looking over the new but persistent wrinkles thrown into our game plan like something or someone was about to sink our battleship, and really didn't care if life preservers were being used as floatation devices. While nearby and really needing assistance, Charlie was barely hanging on from a fragile tree limb, begging us with desperate pleas as he hysterically said, "Guys we have to do something fast, my arms can't hold on much longer", as his loosening grip on the branch was dwindling like ashes on a cinder or slightly fading like the focus of a newborn baby trying to understand his last cries. My think-tank output was bursting with hopeless message-triggers; but my fatal instincts thrusting my trembling and unsteady hands into my backpack, nervously reaching for my self-made M-80's, Jumping Jack flashes, and Baby TNT's just waiting to be released like a riddle start of heed, "Death is not an end!" As I witnessed the green grass lying beneath, cursed by the dream to dream winds of sin with a glimmer of moonlight reflecting off mine enemies snarling teeth, I dared to speak with expression while being lead to danger that sparked for control of hopes being crushed. So, we all started assertively shouting and praying, "Don't push where there is no give", because the only thing remaining on our minds was to live; so, it's about that time "to live!" The dances of life were vibrating wise warnings with its texture being fine; as I held my silver butane lighter with a black skull on its face in one hand, and a group of Jumping Jack flashes in the other, strategically igniting them like birthday candles on a cake while mentally thinking "surprise, surprise"; as I made a come true wish of blowing a breath of fresh air through their devious disguises of hide and seek; sort of like Gorillas hidden in the mist. The fire crackers were launched with grenade like astonishment, causing a "combustion in a hole" type effect as they hit the center of their valiant efforts of jumping and clawing at the bottom of the trees; when all of a sudden my "critter control" creations went off simultaneously making the 4th of July proud to now be a witness of similar success. The furthered dreams of our mischievous mission was still intact, striving and surviving in this mid summer's heat sending their whimpering sideshow back across the babbling creek of sneak, sneak, and peak; but tonight there would be no more havoc for them to reap. Heroes and Villains were secrets with a secret in our true inner selves, and these would be "chasing ghosts" attackers were intending to steal the glory from our iron will vitality, but their onslaught was flawed, under estimated, and full of arrogant mistakes that gave our hopes and determination a constant point of no return. Charlie was still hanging by a thread of a Spider's web looking powerless to gravity like he would soon fall to a going under sensation that could only summon a mental fog of tragic defeat in a victorious and particularly gracious scenario. Lil Tom was quick to act like he was breaking in cattle of herd or creating a new word that had never been heard, but his rope of hope that he wielded spoke like a rolled up life-saver that he always carried close for these heightened situations that required a long hand of assist at any risk; where bravery and wise moves were a necessity in this major deviation of a life threatening urgency. Tom tightly secured his grip and started improvising like a dedicated Jarhead, as he swung his lasso with a pushing yourself to the limit technique where a somewhat hollow victory was clamoring to be filled with a heroic feet that Legends and Myths were honored and always remembered in the minds of us Storytellers and many Rulers by virtue of wealth. A dull clang suddenly rang through the "marking your actions" forest from the large deep sea fisherman's hook on the end of the rope that rattled like a reverberating Rattlesnake, while wrapping itself like an Anaconda squeezing severely; where "you can't breathe, you can't scream" as it Mary-go-round latched around the sturdy branch two to three feet above Charlie's head. Kevin swiftly shouted out, "Grab the rope, and hurry Charlie Boy!"; but as his pleas slide through the chilly air with ice skates of shiver and shake, the limb that held Charlie for what seemed like time without end finally snapped, crackled, and dropped from the air, jettisoning the young Daredevil in a sideways descent, as he frantically reached out for remembrance. It was like a picture was being painted like Picasso or Da Vinci, where pure beauty dwells in the mind sort of like learning to crawl or walk as his nimble hands clasped the heavy weighted rope that was slithering through the branches and giving him a ready-made reminder. As stubborn as he was, Charlie was actually coming to grips with this handout success and had full control of his downward freefall when he realized luck wasn't really luck; but a mere blessing chosen by the All Knowing when making time for loved ones, and his children in S-O-S distress. We were all thankful for prayer and belief as ridged results of completing this mission brought tendered thoughts of how some things are important but many are not; where diligent responses are necessary, and when something close to your heart needs to be accomplished it always has more than no value; of all that stands before the Mighty. We were all breaking past conventional thinking, as we climbed out of the trees readily available to make important decisions; while feeling betrayed and still struggling to learn forgiveness, which was very tough when our focus was centered on acceptance, but recognizing that we really should have just let it go. As we eventually reached the ground with caution, and alert awareness of our surroundings, we knew how close we had come to our hopes being crushed by barely controlling this tough, unforeseen encounter of the unknown, but it turned out to be an asset for our "lesson learned" in resolve. I was clutching my Baby TNT's in my hand with the knowledge that we weren't fluid as time, almost like stepping into a liquid of living water or trying to strain water through false fronts with fake pretentions of which way to go; while working through stern problems and hidden agendas that seemed instant and upfront. We had a lot of ground to cover, but we had to shake off the swift change in the wind; where our instincts were guiding us with military instruction past an envisioned beacon of light with flashing red blinding circles through this thought- provoking night. We were now a beginning number that could only add with success, as we moved on with motivation and multitude awareness; it felt like we owed our frightened Community for the gruesome shadows casting mountainous darkness over their lives, so we began to double-time trot toward our destination of known to be "Mr. Walking, Ticking Time Bomb of calm and chaos." Frantic urges from shortcomings were plaguing our minds as Kevin urgently said, "Pride, Greed, Envy, Jealousy and Lust for power all come from within the human heart, and our hearts are on the line tonight; so rise like the Sun my challenged Daredevils, rise like the Sun!" "Our mission is far from over, and I don't want you guys to be intimidated, but we definitely have to cut through the legendary "Spiritualism Cemetery" to make up for lost time, but once we reach the other side it will be an easy exit to reach our dedicated destination." His sudden route change had me scared and on the edge, but I was ready to commence this war of "Trying Times" and move forward to reach that moment of honoring who I was; because every door leads to an individual looking over a steep an unavoidable ledge, but for today and forever, I was willing to walk that fine line for what I faithfully believed in; Amen! So, I began to speak with intense feelings that were flowing through my lanky, frail body like I was breezing through these turbulent currents of courage and heroism that was like a signature signed, sealed and dealt upon my chest. There was no delay, as I lyrically spoke in a poetic "words of Justice" type of tone that was rhythmic and controlled for this last minute problem of circumstance. I said, "My journey may be unpredictable and unstable at times, yet my judgments may slightly fade while forcing my resilience to dig-in deep and guide my shifting absence of mind, but there is no erasing the past when going forward toward a new future of last minute tendencies of standing up for what's right!" I was trying to keep a neutral attitude by patting myself on the back from recurring problems, where wise words were heard from the different facets of this arrogant an utterly miserable night with small changes that can sometimes lead to big benefits, as I pray to the Lord; that I'm free and wild. There was no response to my aggressive rant of "putting the word out" as we continued to roll through these situations in a trance like state that seemed sometimes coming unglued, as we silently pounded our chests, but sounded loud and proud; For we are warriors, so don't get this head-case of suppressed anger misconstrued. We were Daredevils that were true, through the inner sanctums of our cores from dealing with a life of heads and tails; so I begged them to travel with me, my faithful companions; and yet even if we fall or fail, together we'll walk through heavens doors clear, easy, simple and sound. My devoted dialogue was meant to point us in a direction of never folding our tents; while sharing powerful and poisonous ultimatum of words, where finding answers could be neglectful to the strength of our cause. We were desperately weighing in on the matter; although sympathetic, I have to say that my song writing is somewhat insensitive when it comes to popularity, so I sang to myself with an operatic symphony of stillness as I crooned, "So take it easy and relax, because we have plenty more horses for saddle in this barbaric race; and when trembling with fear comes crashing down on you, do a double-take and live life at an uncharted sense of pace; do-dah, do-dah, do-dah hey!" We were steadily inching along with no comment of submission, as we finally and adventurously entered the graveyard boundaries, where something was going on within us that couldn't be held back, while still staying alert and having doubts in our hearts that we didn't have a chance; and at an instance we could be gobbled up by a trusting anchored point of view. Kevin was beyond cracking this case with his fiery and free-for-all attitude as he yearningly stated, "Guys, it'll really be like trying to sneak past tragedy and terror while looking at madness through a broken glass of mirrors; so, Daredevils I don't know what's going to occur but I fear the worst." "Every person should admit their fears and express what's lingering inside your hearts; and although I know my heart is emotionally self-disciplined, it still has a tremendous apprehension of the unexpected, so beware!" After Kevin's words of "remember the fright in the night", I could see the summer darkness smiling with the stars aligned like a sneer, and I instantly knew that everyone was frightened like a swatted at fly; but instead of saying "shoo" the mysterious spirits that inherited this cryptic cemetery were saying "boo", and welcome to something you'll never get used to, and on the contrary; get ready for the scariest shenanigans on this path to hell that you dare to travel through. The other Daredevils and I were appreciating Kevin's valor of honesty, and by truly witnessing animal gratifications face to face, it was like catching up to our greatness in directing the outcome of these unfounded rumors that lay in wait. Our frantic pace at humping it through this unwanted Undertakers appearance of ugliness was sped up considerably to double-timing it; as the not so fast pure and pressing apparitions were beginning to make their mark on reality, but we knew they could sense our desperation to live. When all of a sudden, the whining wind rolled in a loud extended howl that was holding on to the sinking feelings of our uneasiness, that couldn't be recognized at first by its overboard antics of "scare or be scared", but we knew something wicked was out to capture the hearts of the ones willing to play. Charlie alarmingly said, "Only Sacman could part the clouds and summon such a full and frivolous moon; and now I know that Kevin was right, were all doomed!" "This graveyard is alive and it breathes bellows for the scent of revenge, leaving no room for escape or a south paws chance in hell." I instantly replied with my eyes flickering feverishly of anger and dread filled with anticipation as I said, "It's nothing Guys, so keep on moving ahead, and speed is a necessity!" I could feel all things were possible, as the tombstones to the graves started looking like blood-drenched slabs of meat, fresh off the chopping block of mutilation and murder at its peak of being brutally clear through these separated hazes of unholy smoke that were silently choking the miracles that happened to seem unachievable and very far from our willingness of acceptance; but we knew that God was embracing our struggles while showing us that he was the Present and the Past. As I glimpsed behind me to make sure everyone was accounted for, I could see that Lil Tom was very uneasy as he prepared for us to be attacked;

by brandishing his "ready to fire" BB Gun like a Geronimo or Sitting Bull riding through sacred burial grounds with the belief that facing life's challenges with a warriors mentality could somehow save us from courageous consequences. The wind was becoming stronger and healthier as it blew with a whipping-up and battering appeal that most adventure seekers would see as a sign of the elements trying less, but succeeding in its urges to let you know; here's a reason to opening up to change. The tops of the trees were presently flexing inward, causing a claustrophobic sensation to spread throughout our insides as well as stir up an eye full of natures penetrating power with that slash and gash attitude of "going-off"; just to set the record straight. Our overly trusting bodies were moving so fast that we forgot that sometimes it divides to multiply and that opposites rarely attract, but we were physically and mentally trying to touch base with the inner secrets of fear, and when it actually first arose. We were steadily and spontaneously approaching the outer boundaries of this nightmarish existence that was shattering the calm, and greedily preparing itself for slim hopes of a sacrifice as I started to feel like a Legend being freed from the stone with power supreme; or was I just sleepwalking in a featured delusion, where the conclusion was in an obliteration of confusion? When all of a sudden, four stagnant shadows appeared with the looks of "moonlight mayhem", and were exhibiting wide open arms toward evil while displaying a unique timing in their sounds, as they swayed back and forth under a large tree with vines of snakes slithering to the sound of a Violin Soloist playing hypnotically with a Snake Charmers melodic tune. The nostalgic night was becoming a canvas of hearts beating a lifetime of adrenaline, while these visions of "up to no good" hovered in the air with the dirt mounded graves beneath them from which they emerged, vibrating and shaking like a seismic tremor of terror. We were all impulsive and passionate in our desires to flee from this bad choice of journey; where chance was being encountered by horrid situations rotating over and over again through our minds, but our new possibilities of escape would be handled with care and craftiness like skipping stones on a frozen lake. My Daredevils were mightily overwhelmed, but in our cores of certainty we would never bow down or lay puppet to this risky pressure of these Frankenstein like Phantasms floating with awkward choreography through this misty and "devour us" new moon, hovering like a wicked witch on a spell casted willingly broom.

As we made our way around these mountains of no return with spooky spirits of satanic seizure barricading our departure from this jungle dense like vegetation of Hell; we silently called for our thoughts and feelings to Goat at it, heads first. Our risks were blind hunches, which inspired us like the "Book of James"; where believing that destiny brought essential parts of having the right tools to make life simpler, while trying to get ourselves ready to one day hold in our arms the Almighty; who will be wearing the thorn bearing crown. It seemed that everything was coming undone and out of sorts, as I reached into my knapsack to retrieve a special powder of "Mississippi Mo-Jo", which had two very different kinds of results: one worked like salt to keep the demons away, and the other was meant to evaporate their metaphysical presence causing them to ache and yearn for a new task. I reactively threw this fine mixture of "make me free" into the center of the apparitions like a knuckle ball of kick a** that was moving too fast for the naked eye; strike one, through strike three, now you're out of here like a roundabout wallop of the umpteenth degree. The other Daredevils and I were shivering stunned like Simon said freeze; standing by these front row seats near the heat of the action, where there was no exit before a round of applause. We could clearly see these ghastly ghouls "with secrets of the dead" lingering in the air, as they slowly started to look as if the mood of the present moment was playing out our lives the way we wanted it to be, while showing them that evil lies in everyone's hearts, but God judges as well as he gives out new life to open up locked doors. The thrill of the excitement was immense, and we were looking at things with new eyes, witnessing the presence of our parents, while standing firm beside these graves of doubt and reluctance; but our warrior's stance was like a dance of wolves that were hungry for more, sort of like a hunt and trek error, where fallacies could be deadly easily leaving our mistakes in a state of fragile denial. Anywhere is nowhere, but when traveling to somewhere, it somehow forces you to beware with your faith never shaken, although sometimes pausing and striking a balance between engaging rivalries with hair rising antics, you have to reach for that firm grasp that ultimately leaves you falling behind; when instinctively, a passionate and relentless side emerges. Suddenly, the Fourth Little Piggy was out of the gate and the Fifth wasn't close to heading for home, because it was still getting acquainted with the strategic properties of a full scale war, while convincingly thinking outside of the box where optimism beamed throughout the never ending night; which quite frankly was too much for us to handle. We were on a destination for truth as we started running silently out of this forsaken hellhole with long periods of non-communication, where the words that brought positive responses could have been words that you should never use; rebelling like an angry crowd of millions, while the world is being close to no more Native Americans; but don't cry my heritage of Honor and History, for the good Son will return. So, heed and witness those that were forgotten about, while slightly feeling at ease from this fateful turnaround; for we were a handful of seekers finding the time, and eagerly manifesting our desires, for my brothers and sisters our genuineness will live forever, and always be told. We had managed to slip past the spiking tensions and the universal laws of yester years with the strength of our intuition; reminding us that while Walter was at the home front looking after the hens pinpointing and clucking the settling of scores, that we had hit a bump or two along the way where we couldn't erase the drastic night sweats from these nightmares, as we finally reached our destination; which was a passageway to overcome. My fellow brethren and I were zeroing in on guerilla attacks and bush whacks, where our voices of reason and being chosen from heart were still feeling concern, while keeping a slim lead in these sumptuous reproves. Although unusual but very much dynamic toward strategy, we had at last set all our booby-traps, manned our peripheral, and handed out communications; where everyone had walkie-talkies set on low in case the slightest odd behaviors that may occur, or if we come in contact with this "man" or "monster" that we were doggedly pursuing. It seemed that we had talked up a lost treasure of pandemonium; when out of the "palm reader's night", Sacman arose from the gloom of wickedness, stealthily making his way through the foggy, tortured mist. He had distinct characteristics, where he resembled a Lurch or a surly figured Sasquatch that looked wild and crazy as he stomped down the overgrowth of the surrounding brush, blazingly making his way a recognizable path toward the tainted train cars that we had encountered earlier, as he looked like he was aware of his history and its results, while slowly letting go of his rigidity. The "No such Luck" wind was whispering in our ears and being more responsive than ever, like a little bird telling us that "kids have a funny way of touching our spirits"; but this was no place to be stuck in, because in a "huff and a puff" exploitation of weakness, and seeing flashing dots and can not's was conniving, cleverly masking over our souls like an umbrella, steadily rejecting and protecting us from unforeseen complications, which was stealing the lime light and developing a certain courage of "To have and To hold". We were trying to adjust our maneuvers in this unjust world that brings surprises and back road songs of blues, where making things happen and having a trivial turn of luck releases some of the pressure when concerned with offensive off-hand problems; while miraculously being pulled out of the fire, still staying anchored to the senses of difference, and the withdrawn lures that was blinding to the young and eager to prevail. When over the walkie-talkie, you could hear Kevin's rattled and shaken voice nervously sounding like an evening serenade being less certain of the words that he was about to display, still struggling to spit out the right message to us secret partners camouflaged in the "meeting your match" madness of acting out our courageous deeds of how it's done. He said, "Guys, hold your positions; just watch and wait! I repeat, stand down for now." Lil Tom had already placed Sacman in the cross hairs of his bountiful BB-Gun, keeping an eagle's eye view on the overgrown outlaw, while Charlie was edging his way closer, tree to tree trying to get within numb chuck reach; although disliking the brimming intensity, an order was an order. We were all watching intensely; as Sacman dropped his oversized sack that he was carrying like a wrecking ball that quickly fell from its secure position of dangling six feet in the air, causing the broken windows of an aftershock to seem measly, but very much igniting to this no end "game of life"; like immediately awakening to Celtic thunder with an eclectic mix of tunes stating "this is war", with a nervous screamer in the mist. This brutal time was ticking, while we were trying to know our enemy and his tendencies, as we were slowly but strategically crossing that bridge of exploring grief and the idea of desolation; yet always having second thoughts when fighting for survival beyond unforeseen penalties. My Daredevils were swallowing big regrets and feeling hopping mad by being black-hearted by this tall tale of monstrosity, but never-ever looking back; while opening up to adhered adjustments, and all the extraordinary challenges that brings about that dynamic gusto towards careful approach. Meanwhile, Sacman was leisurely and casually rummaging through one of the train cars, as he pulled out a sharp tool that seemed for digging and a long pole with a hook on the end that resembled a Sheep

Herders staff, which would have seemed symbolic, but on this haunted night was being considered as a clue to the "canvassing of the sights" eyes that were watching and anticipating his next moves. As he finished his collection of "curious questionable", it was leaving us with thoughts of many aspects of why and what for; but our main demand was to find out where this Gravedigger of hearts was holing up and placing his victims of vindication. The once Miner and dedicated family man was now staring through his hardened eyes, out toward the wooded surroundings where we were hiding under the blacked out basin of the trees blocked from his view, but days before we were very much alert to his aggressive and pursuant mentality, and when being on the receiving end; it's no telling where your emotions and adrenaline will lead you. We were two-stepping like Doce-Doh, as we began to square off for an epic battle of wits that would take us out-of-this-world and past yonder lands to reconnect with the cold, stark reality, anxiously consuming our true hopes that we so dearly treasured every day. As we turned our attention back toward the confusion developing right before our eyes with heavenly horns blowing silent, motivational notes of "anything can happen"; the fine traces of twilight was exhibiting fierce looks that would spark, and ignite big shocks to rattle our frames, as if our thoughts were drifting off into another place. Stunned and tense as we were, it seemed that we were inhaling our last "gasping for air" breaths, with our hearts racing like a Pole Positioned Racecar Driver worried that this could be the last stand of a band of motivated, mischievous thrill-seekers barreling toward the edge; of sanity. In the distance, we all noticed that Sacman was slowly disappearing into the darkness, heading toward the Willow laden river, while maintaining a desired pace and not knowing that we were in hot pursuit and quickly closing in from behind. We had to act fast, as everyone moved in on Sacman's last position, while immediately sending Lil Tom to retrieve our reinforcements back at the home camp; because we needed help to solve the root of our problems that had us running around in circles and trying to regain a sense of normalcy. Charlie had taken off through the brush in a creeping, crab crawl looking back and shaking a warning finger of "halt", which meant for us not to follow until he gave us the "all is safe" signal of bird calls that repeated in three short vocals like, "coo-coo-coo, coo-coo-coo, ah-ah-ah!" Lil Tom was rapidly on the fast track for home, like he was on an undertaking to reach his destination before the light of day; as I willingly took command by grabbing my walkie-talkie from its hip side clip nestled like a narrative of "need help now", by spitting out precise direction of leadership and skill for bucking up to the moments of manhood. I instructively said, "Tom, you have to cover our movements with fragile, creative craftiness my brother; it's your job to motivate the other Daredevils to toughen up while keeping a centered focus on our major objective; for this war has begun with fearsome fiction and finality that only the mind can capture." There was no dilly in his dally as he quickly came back across the airwave with a simple reply of, "Copy, barricades and bigoted words couldn't stop me; for I am free!" His witty and worldly response was like words of rejuvenation as Kevin and I huddled in a kneeling position in the thick growth of bushes, where Charlie had slithered away like snake; discreet and hidden from the predators and prey of nature that triggered our imaginations to elaborate on many unusual insights. We waited, and waited as thirty to forty-five minutes had passed like a clock with a long, winded tick-tock, with a lit wick climbing a giant ladder of heartbreak; but was this actually the time that counts in learning from our lust of the thrill, or was it just twenty-five acts of worthiness getting us ready for dreams that are deferred. The airwaves were extremely silent, and there were no bird calls to be heard like a countdown of riveted reflections; because Charlie had cut off his walkie-talkie before he had jumped into the trenches of his solo-seeking, frantic game of hide-and-seek. Meanwhile, Kevin was peering intently into the pitch dark surroundings with his eyes seeming to be on a swivel, almost like he was being very insistent and persistent on taking control of our brethren of brave hearts with his "all or nothing" attitude that shamefully flawed his patience. He quickly said, "Jayme we can't wait any longer; we have to follow his tracks to make sure that he wasn't found out!" Then suddenly, through the misty air of despair we heard Charlie's mimicking bird calls, although faint and shallow, it was enough to guide us in his direction for a reunion of free "galley slaves" rowing the boat ashore, rowing the boat ashore on this military tour of commanding justice for the Lord. As we neared the spirit of his calls, we were hearing the rapids of water raging in the night, when Charlie abruptly crawled from under a fallen tree that was neatly tucked and cozy lying by the riverbed with his numb-chucks wrapped around his neck like a pearl setting of protection. He immediately placed his finger on his lips, which was his child's way of letting us know to be silent, zip it up, and mum's the sound; because the monster is still on the lurk and we definitely don't want to be found. With his finger still pressed against his mouth, he eagerly waved his other hand for us to follow him under the log that he was so invisibly nestled, while Sacman's presence was still expressing now you see me, now you don't antics causing our imaginations to lead; while our minds followed somewhat clumsily behind. Charlie's attentions were glued on what looked like a patch of fallen trees encased with large rock debris that was about twenty to twenty-five yards away, while off to its port side floating aggressively on the raging waters was a boat covered with vines and brush; where it was barely noticeable in the fogginess of this "racing to the finish line" moon lit night. Some of our dreams fizzle and die, and some of our dreams have a yearning to fly but the one's protruding with wings will always carry you to the deepest parts of the sky, while never asking why? My young Daredevils and I were living our dreams with wings, through the good times and the bad, as we laid in the darkness hidden from sight and filled with shocked reactions trying to piece together the clues, while being inquisitive by nature we were spending a lot of time and thought on judging and making tough calls; but we were arrogant young fools, just learning how to use our "Heaven sent tools". Our thoughts of some battles were worth fighting, while not knowing forgiveness should have found a place in Sacman's heart, but we were all standing together on an adventure of a lifetime with renewed perspectives and established boundaries. Yet, time after time, after time, we had a very special, secret weapon that only God could have graced and placed so divine; it was a weapon that could never be defeated or depleted; we had "UNITY"!

CHAPTER IV

Family Man, "Hearts are forever!"

There once was a crook, who lived in a nook, and what he stole was vitality from reality, but in actuality he had been driven to sack hearts that he hung like trophies on his troglodyte type of hooks; as we were taking baby steps in wisdom, where the concepts of "beating the wild" and facing ourselves in a true mirror had us awaiting chance and bad consequences. We were praying to the Lord to give us insight and courage to confront the wrongness and needless fear being caused by a killer that seeks young hearts through the neglect of the night; like a fish swimming upstream trying to capture that satisfaction of achieving a life's effort of wearisome experiences and dangerous exploits. As we unwearyingly laid under that fallen log it seemed like a secluded place of refuge, and even though we had primitive weapons, our far-out ideas to this point was immature and ineffective with our faith still being a little unstable and weak; when really all we had to do was "hear and obey"! It seemed that Sacman was just a stone's throw away, while the violent river beside us was echoing like a storm with trickled, fiery displays of us putting out the flames, that steadily flowed like a Roman River calling forth the warrior inside, while trudging through key areas of our lives and showing the seeds of beginners to summon that nerve to stand up to that new bully on the block. Still, we were somewhat fragile at this time, but being just a swing in what was happening was extremely reactive for us to get the lead out and get back on track; while lying beside my comrades, my true brothers that were willing to funnel our frustrations into vindicated victory, and pleasurable pieces of the mind. At this particular moment, I was beginning to feel like "I would forever be a just man", as Charlie finally spoke up with an enthusiastic eagerness to tell what he had learned on his Kamikaze mission of sight. He was talking wildly and rapidly like a politician spitting the "flim-flam-flarth", to get us enticed and rejuvenated about things that no longer work; while desperately being put on the front burners toward the path of future success. He said, "Guys you see that tree stump over there with all the brush surrounding it like a hidden oasis." "Well, Sacman had did a hocus-pocus and disappeared into its opening using a Shepherd like pole to open a rusted metal grate covering the top of the entrance; and then he vanished within a split second." Kevin was attentively listening with his slingshot clinched between his teeth and wielding a lasso that Lil Tom had given him before departing to get help; and he was so proud to get an extra weapon to add to his arsenal that he was carrying it as if pigs could fly, thinking that he could somehow snare them in mid-air like a heat seeking missile with fatal justice for bitter blood. Charlie continued to inform us with information from his recon as he let out a long sigh of relief as if he were finally being grabbed from the clutches of these "going crazy" mental gates from which commitment and concentration were very much overwhelming. He knew this was a burdensome "Hell Night" and that there would always be a last challenge, but he still centered his focus of watching the tree stump, while nervously waiting for what would happen next. We all were exhausted and sleepy, because we had been trying to follow this handed down story of a Boogey Man relentlessly and with little rest, like we were safari bosses leading a group that was searching for pride and glory through the wild, where walking a slim streak of suspicion was unswerving and heart stopping, on this nowhere road toward this diabolical freak of nature. He was surprisingly wood-shedding our methods of capture, where we were left approaching the situation with a greater understanding and a strong confirmation in our own minds, noting that harmony was more important than we had realized. The need to slow down was rolling around the rim like ring-a-round-rosy while opening up closed doors, but getting a greater grasp on things as we continuously fanned through the flames; for they were searing and scolding hot, knowing that tomorrow was all so near, while Hell was still scavenging on the way we were. Charlie was still conveying his thoughts of how to approach and finish our quest, but really not seeing the big picture; while Kevin was less hopeful as he played out the scenario much differently, but still honoring the taken children's sacrifices being slightly shaken awake off the "running in, and helping" warpath. We knew there was a flip side to this rare Buffalo nickel, where on one side there was a warrior, and on the other side a close to extinct prey fighting for survival to exist, like plenty of planets unfounded and without a name. Sneaking up through the mist, there were mournful wails of the wild echoing past our safe place of haven, and although we were listening closely, it dramatically made the pressure still continue to build; while pressing a terrible reality on our nervousness. We were remaining in motion with stress felt-tears watering our eyes, where black-and-white thinking was heavily weighing the problems at hand like always and forever, yet for our hearts content it was slowly finding strength in finally burying the hatchet; while toughing it out. Our ancient, antsy, and anxious "art of warriors" were fast, like fizzle pop fizzle journeying to the core of our integrity, while quietly lying hidden on the battle field like a beached mermaids "never forgetting" body, bringing the imaginary creature to life top leveling the Richter-Scale like attacking a Fort and taking a slight spill; but still climbing the challenging hills steadily moving in silence through the dim murk of going berserk, so please my brothers chill. It was like Little Bo Peep when she lost her sheep, where we wanted to grab some shut eye, but we were too far on the edge of making sense to find time to sleep, count sheep, or continue to let this monster creep like Jeepers; on our way to sentencing the Keeper of the key, to this puzzle of endless intrigue and mystery. So much of our communications had been stifled, as Charlie was drawing his B-52 boomer-rang like a gunslinger pointing it in a certain direction toward the gong sounds of branches being snapped against the water logged forest floor as they fell heavily to the "come and get me" ground. There were so many shadows approaching our position in a leery and eerie manner that Charlie took aim and threw his Rang, as it sang and bellowed mellow tunes across the noisy path where the forest animals were now astonished, and heeding the clap of thunder shifting like turning pages to an encyclopedia; because there, all is known; or just written to ease the tensions of unanswered questions with words for bootleg beggars.

We knew there was always a price for getting revenge, but what must unfold lets life flow more easily when things are turned upside down dealing with the same old grind; but the night was belonging to us, while being strung together and steadily moving past the harder to find problems. Now, should we share more of what is on our minds or should we be more secretive about committing our sorrows to anything but that; standing on the summit like Cochise of winning from within. It was like we were helping with a heist, as the so-called unsuspecting thieves in the night made their selves known to our half-way covered faces, still peering through the strained fingertips of fear and hindrance. When out the corners of the wind, with thickly fogged shadows hovering over our backs like weeping willows with tissues for the many issues that concerned our detrimental of "off the tracks" burning realities of rage that flares and scares our inner sides, for no more loss of innocent and precious lives that deserve more than what's being offered; being handed out like government cheese, **Please!** When frequent flashes of red lights were blinking on and off like a lighthouse, making us quick to realize that the rest of the Daredevils had arrived to help find the answers to what we wanted to know; and what we wanted to know was lying within the confounds of his hidden hideaway and being oppressed objects of desire that just had to be fulfilled; we might have been far from home, but we were still within an ears link of Father, Amen! As the sun seemed to be easily walking nonchalantly without a care through the timid air, it was in fact sneaking and peeking from behind the sullen mountaintops like a snooping neighbor with an outlandish curiosity for gossip. When Walter suddenly appeared from the ebony darkness enhanced by the giant shadows of the trees that only welcomed limited rays of light with Charlie's boomerang held in his hand, while encouragingly holding it in the air above his head with its curved structure facing upwards forming a strong-willed "V"; which was an image that we had embraced as hope, through these digging deep days of getting our point across. All of the girls were following close behind him with Lil Tom pulling up the rear, looking smug and smitten while working with the concepts of finalizing some crucial details to this war of discovering, "What is possible". I excitedly rolled from under the log with the swiftness of the wind, to make room for our warranted reinforcements that were so noble and well trusted; as nature's bandage of security was wearing thin, for now we were sitting ducks in a lake of revealing light and shallow voices of reason. It felt like we were attached to the past, while desperately dealing with a smidgen of "a matter of luck", as we once again were together still welcoming the hate that had really hurt our hearts, but being in constant contact somehow relieved that "going back and forth" sensations that was jolted by this "rock-a-bye baby" predator. In actuality, some of us were favoring this devoted Dawn which was an insight toward justice of righting the wrongs, and being left alone with our tumbled thoughts that had fallen to harder places to find; greeting this day, where truth was to be heard, repeating word for word with no one there to hear our screams in our own minds; and all I could say was, "Woe these are trying times." Kevin was barely holding on to his last wits, but he still had that zest for an open and neutral attitude as he quickly said, "Walter, you old military pimp; I see it's just another evening out with the ladies, huh?" As he smoothly leaned from under his dug in position, Kevin chuckled with secret intentions, while proudly patting himself lightly on the back of his shoulders. Walter immediately replied like a crooked eyed carnivore craving a challenge of cleverness as he said, "Well, Captain Marvel I see you're tucked under that log real neat; with them pink panties riding up the crack of your edgy, sweaty anal canal like they're as scared as you are, huh Kev!" "I think you better take off that thong and get back in this game of seriousness, because it definitely speaks for itself; but be wise youngster, for we actually have a chance at moving this doubt and that's plenty of reason to believe." You could sense that the intensity was racing with the Sun, while running from the Devil; struggling with the transition of admitting to the demand of dares and hardened stares, as Charlie inadvertently drew our attentions back to our objective at hand as if we were losing time, and our tightened tenacity. We all knew that there were no ifs, ands, and buts about it, that there would be a price to pay; and this sentient was opening up questionable possibilities in our minds like a mortal storm had been swept through in this "betting room" of the last word. The scene sounded like mournful poems that contained untold stories of fear and fright, to cause the night to evaporate like liquid; but the wicked was still casting a shadow of the most evil night stalker, moonlight walker that ever haunted a dream at close range; so evil and deranged! Now the day had slowly arisen, but we were still imprisoned by these nightmares with entrancing anguish; and although some blessings were uncommon, we could feel that this loneliness was really a piece of mind that catapulted our awareness to a sacred level of improvisation, which expels the vice that plots and plans its advance; but our silence was being reluctantly agreed amongst, between our passionate personalities. We knew that what we did really mattered, and even though we were seeing issues differently, we were close friends and families playing follow the leader to the sound of the lightly drizzling rain; but we had to thank God Almighty for its cosmic cadence of clarity and its leniency of pain. This exciting morning sky was a dim-viewed dark gray and the trouble was just starting to simmer; as we were actually realizing that we had finally tracked down our long time coming of razor claws, Halloween and Hockey masks, and Children's Dolls overtaken by sin-seeking souls; but we were urgently chasing our visions of establishing our renegade rendition of a more appropriate "marshal law!" It was like boot camp arrivals huddling in a pact; fresh on the scene with snot noses, and no clue of terrible regrets, as Charlie was beckoning up the right words at the right time to raise our spirits, before we stepped in the direct route toward this threatening weather and this two-time unverifiable, unknown mystery of mystique; but Dear Lord, somehow we knew we were bound for "Newsworthy Glory" with more trials and testimony to seek. We had been chosen like eenie, meenie, miney, mo; like one potato, two potato, three potato, four; we were chosen like sweet addictions, and wicked attractions lionized as hungry young lions, yet somehow we were feeling guilty from the painful choices and the unpredictable instability of our heartache battling the caresses of unhappiness. So, some of us were keeping quiet about our concerns, but we were still remaining sensible while finally grasping the full picture of this extremely withdrawn, worn-down man that seemed to enjoy his solitude, like a flameless candle facing off with the wild gushes of the wind. My young Daredevils and I were approaching broad, bold visions with the shedding of some glimpses of faint light, while being mysteriously protected in a preferential way, like receiving a blessing that seemed vague at first, but actually ended up being dear as Love Poems written in "inner carved" inscriptions. Except on this finicky fiasco of daybreak, where we were odd ducks that went cluck, cluck instead of quack, quack never lying on our backs, but crouching like kids do; and pondering the disappearing stars like picking up a penny on heads will truly bring you good luck. We were all witnessing locker room activity as Charlie was giving a pep-talk for us to beat the field of content contenders that anxiously awaited our A-game of abilities. His words were beginning to climb mountaintops that were unreachable by desire and grit; when he suddenly said, "We need a similar key to open up his sardine can of a haven guys; and Jayme it's definitely your time to shine, because we need you to go to the train car that Sacman was scavenging for pay-dirt and find that "chance to face", Mr. Spectacular of Illusions." "There has to be another mechanism for entering his deadly domain, and if anybody's going to find it, it's you with your bloodhound bravado of finding Waldo!" We were dreadfully battling birds of a feather; and although I seemed like an unlikely Angel, we were all living in tomorrow's world while trying to discover the truth with alleviating sighs of relief, and dumbstruck facial expressions that spanned across time and space like a forsaken foreshadowing of frenzy and fierce fidelity. I needlessly not question the moment, because we were on the move again and I knew I was the best one fit for this "bring me back the answers to this Sudoku puzzle of numbers leaving a hint of strategic accuracy." My Daredevil family and I were trying to start over again like erasing a blackboard with our bare hands, while realigning our concepts of craftiness and central modes of creative craziness by beginning from the top, step by step, and carefully working our way to the bottom of its endless edges. This was a definitive payback like Lumber Jacks with an axe chopping away relentlessly and out of control; where death lives like trolls manning and bridging the gap, but we were hearing the mighty rumble of the railroad tracks leading in from our backs with this talked-up torture technician sneak attacking his confident foes with a speed demons cry of unhearing; as suddenly a peel of awakening thunder was leaving a mark on our senses and heading us into chaos with tight holds, while steadily getting us ready for nearly anything. As I started my departure, I was feeling my close connection to the Lord like an anxious Angel, as I bravely spoke as if these were my famous last words that flowed like a river of righteousness ready to crest its banks of containment. I felt like a lion-whisperer as my words were meant to tame and save thy soul like a soldier of fortune with a verbal commitment for the heart with my expressions leading through thick and thin; so please forgive me my Lord for I have sinned. My self-confidence was now fully surging with the spirit as I smugly said, "Only God knows the planets, moons, and stars; and I say you might win some and lose some while feeling conflicted in some ways, but today is a day of feeling far more deeply than accepted acknowledgement, because stars often shine less in the face of adversity." After my hallelujah of henceforth, I gave my crow's nest salute; for I was going at all costs to improve upon our position, as I faded like camouflage into the gray unknowing mist of daybreak looking back to notice an all thumbs-up vote from my dedicated Daredevils still manning our perfect attack location. I was moving like the cartoon character Speedy Gonzalez; which is really fast but definitely controlled, as I made my way back toward the "train cars of beware" still soldiering my surroundings, while knowing that the Devil can be very convincing in times of danger trying to intimidate ones faith. He purposely leaves some elements missing, where you're having wandering thoughts, but in this stormy weather there were strange skies setting in with awkward messages that just didn't make sense at the moment; however as time had passed the clouded was now clearness, leading a straight path to our needed knowledge. It felt like I was actually being eaten alive, and my soul was barely surviving the realities of "hours of devour" in this wreaking havoc of slip and slide, but I was trusting all the things that made me feel safe steadily edging me forward, while churning my insides with all the bottled up memories of loved ones I couldn't save; that had regretfully died. So, I was pulling back a bit and observing more than usual, while being cautious and wary but holding onto my desire to prevail, and at the same time sending Lucifer's fabric of time that was adding a fake luster and shine, back to the depths of his miserable Hell; Jehovah knows that I'm trying! I know some might have thought that I was just a candied "sweet" headed into the rodeo ring of requite, but not in this twilight, tomorrow, or forever; because I'm far more clever than any of their personal endeavors, that I easily ruffled like feathers. So, as I approached my objective discreetly, I could feel a warm sense of insecurity slightly altering my keen awareness, but it was still moving me toward a direct path of chance, as I started creeping quietly alongside the back of the train wreckage that rested like a secluded Ghost Town. I boldly entered its boundaries with a journey of challenges that lay with inside, like it was inviting me for a Bronco busting ride that had the ups and downs to throw off my persistence in Pride. I could suddenly hear barking noises closing in from afar, but they were still out of range for me not to complete my mission; so I continued to belly crawl to the train car entrance, where we had seen Sacman clamoring like a crazed killer from our insensitive intrusion. Still, my timid thoughts wanted me to take a quick look inside, and if anything went wrong I would hurry off toward my reinforcements that were waiting on nerves edge; although staying alert and ready like it was no doubt that they were going to conquer this jungle with their unique ability to come across as tough-guys in this "tease or be teased" terrain. I knew God was love and I had so much to give; so I was no longer fearful as I freely started envisioning weird circles of synchronized subtlety, that were bringing an end to an age of persecution and mean spiritedness with its lighted- lash of unforgiving for some; because as you see, all is seen from the emotional scars that sinks deep into a compassionate mind and heart of Heavenly hereafter. I slowly started to reach up from underneath my cover of "curiosity and concealment" to gently slide open the rain soaked train door, as it screeched and creaked with the eeriness of a violated violin. I just knew I had to search this Death Trap with nimble hopes; but very delicately, not to set off any snares that Sacman might have placed for any uninvited intruders. As I started to rummage for only a short time, I immediately discovered a similar shaped-pole that Sacman had taken with him on his previous search and seizure of sentimental values, where he could easily disappear without a trace or clue. I couldn't believe this fair-shake that had been forwarded into "find and keep" as I grabbed the imitation pole with no delay, and spun around like a coveted Cyclone ready to leap out of the train car, when I suddenly noticed those same yellow glowing eyes from earlier lurking beyond the trees moving about predatorily, as if they were about to drop in for an unpleasant visit; like they were itching to ask, "where do you think you're going with this sacred treasure, without a violent scuffle of payback from our prior encounter?" I was now being hurriedly thrown into the saddle of responsibility, knowing that I had a special delivery to make; and if anything got in my way, I was to speak like a Classical Poet before I started to let go with my fierce flow; which would only add more problems on my plate. However, I would start to speak arrogantly and forthright, for fear should not deter your trust in something that's greater than mere man or beast. So, I believingly said, "Alright you fiends that lay in wait with tempers that are scorching a flare;

why don't you lighten up a little, and buzz off, because I'm not easy to scare"; and although my guilt was lingering in the air, I knew it would always be there like a negative nightmare. Therefore, to all my foes and fake-jakes all up in my face looking for information on a constant basis let me lace this so you can get a taste of bliss while you're sending your secret messages; now that's what you call sweet, and I really don't care if you get pissed, because climbing this mountain to miracles is just too steep for anyone of you Judas's to reap. Deeper understandings will evolve, so I continue to say a little of this and a little of that, as I attentively watch for the **Black Cat** giving me signs; for I am an intuitive soul destined to make a comeback for all of mankind. Indeed, with greed you'll reach deep into your little bag of tricks and treats, while I pray to God to see who the miracle that he decides to embrace and bring home with open arms with a lifetime of peace. I finally started to truly witness, like a Kings command of obey and oblige, when suddenly coming over the small rise of surprise it was those same glowing eyes trying to hide with stealth; but their shadowy reflections were crisp in this dreary morning sun, as I prayed for protection and health. If I were to escape, I knew I had to run like a bullet discharged from a gun, while asking rapid fire questions with no answers; but I could feel this added pressure weighing a ton on my lungs as I sighed and gasped for relief knowing that I was the "chosen one!" So, there was nothing slow about me getting up out of Dodge, while standing in this abyss of "ain't any shame in bringing the pain" when it's a drastic choice of them or me. Without any hesitation, I drew like Quick Draw McGraw, as I reached into my kosher holster of tricks and treats grabbing some Baby TNT's for a bigger impact of instilling fear like the end was near, and I really didn't care if Sacman could hear; I was only trying to express my resourcefulness as these hideous onlookers drew closer, and closer like an emotional moment of sweat and terrified tears. I shouted out with a violent vocal of "Fire in the Hole, you dastardly heathens of Hell", while I quickly started pacing myself with an accelerated trot of retreat; when I suddenly came to a "Hell Naw" halt, and hurled the lit La-La-leery Looses like I was throwing up my deuces of peace; but these boom-booms known for clearing a room were going to disturb the stillness with the willingness and might of Glory. I felt like a repetitive curser of words as I said, "Go to Hell Dog Demons of Death, and kiss where the Sun don't shine because I'm a warranted warrior; and in this particular case your behinds are mine!" All I heard was a thunderous boom, and then I seen dirt flaming like a flare; which looked like mists of hairspray heavily combusted and falling like volcanic emissions from the air. As I looked out to witness my wage of wrath, I could see those yellow piercing gazers, sharp and honed in to my proximity like razors, were now a bright orange filled with a "shedding of new light" to their unblinking eyes; as I scampered toward sunup obsessed and infatuated with my ability to see their "any day now" surprise. I could clearly hear their whimpers and whines as they started to run away from the situation like landslide debris flailing, and wailing like pebbles being snatched from the hand of the master from a student with special focus and concentration that excels at "hand quicker than the eye" mentality. I was once again hopeful as my poetic side was fulfilled, and I was now riding with the wind at my back, because my discipline had been intensity driven scurrying and hurrying me back to my family across the railroad tracks near the raging river with my trophy held tightly from this tug-of-war give and take. It was like a cold hunk of clay being molded from my fearless feelings of an adventure, where faint hearts would automatically fail; but today my accomplishments were grand in scope, and sharply cutting to the hilt of a means to an end, which left me to believe in good times or bad our coming out on top would drastically improve. I was just barely touching base of expressing my thoughts when I finally seen Charlie tucked like a shirt in pants, hugged tightly to the skirts of hems, latched onto the bottom of an old Sycamore tree that resembled a drooping and sagging bedraggled tragedy of what should have been. I red flashed him with my flashlight to give him warning of incoming advances, and not to attack a friendly, non-descript face; because I only wanted to embrace our lions share reunion. We were evenly riding the updrafts, successfully skimming the tops of the battle, while eventually finding a voice for these new rules added to this game of "anything", still having a ton of thoughtfulness for all these new facts that continued to appear like a Genie in a lamp granting wishes on our list of stargazing and mountainside miracles. Charlie easily came out of his situated, side straddled stance with a look of relief and conceit that emotional walls couldn't hold back like a dam with a leak, and sleek relevance of strength. He instantly said in an excited low tone, "Jay the Barbarian of Bad A****! Man, I was ready to come save your Brave Heart behind after you woke up the whole countryside with your Lion's rage of a roar meant for disturbing the peace; but really, a whole powder keg of Ba-Boom!" "My brother, Thank God your safe; but I got to say, crazy is an understatement for you letting everyone know that extreme measure is your soul inside and out bro; dang a little more discretion and a lot less Prehistoric passion, you Bighead nut!" As he proudly approached, we aggressively bumped chests and slapped together our hands, as if the world had finally understood the true meaning of friendship. I said, "I got the prize from the Cracker Jack Box Charlie Boy; so let's gather everybody together to plan our next advance of nabbing this murderous mad-man." We confidently crept through the quaint, quietness of these odd uninhabited woods for everyone that was still dug into their hidden havens, with their eyes peeled on the spot Sacman had disappeared like a Casper, a Gizmo, or a Geronimo with nowhere to go; but we were willing, and ready to broaden our search to find this vanishing vagrant with an abundance of vainglory for his memoirs of his actual story. As I glanced slightly toward the sky for a gesture of reassurance, I noticed Walter was blending in with the shadows on a high perch in the trees overhanging the secret entrance to Sacman's unseen and unnoticeable lair with a foul mood stretched across his face because he wasn't in on the action; but it was guaranteed to soon come like a catastrophic storm passing by with the intent to destroy an everyday dream catchers, hopes and aspirations. Walter stared down at us, as his laser like leer became more focused to finally notice my speedy return; where now he was expressing a spirited smirk, which erased that scowl of a frown of disappointment that had been plastered on his mug like a grimace of pain from neglect, and the feeling of torture from being left out of the mix. Now, I knew for a fact that we were all scared of this Boogey Man, but we loved every minute of it; and our emotional temperatures were gradually rising as we all clustered together under the fallen tree where most of the Daredevils were lying in wait. Walter was still above our position, as he stood up and walked to the edge of the limb, where he was aggressively overseeing; when he suddenly bounced up and down on the secure branch and flipped his body into the air like he was Aqua-man or the Man from Atlantis taking an ocean dive; but this was just Walter showing off again his superiority of fenceless flight. He came down on the soggy wooded terrain, landing gently like a snowflake with his precision dismount, as he began slowly kneeling down while sternly saying, "It's Time!" But, before Walter could begin his hoopla of strategies, Kevin playfully wedged himself in between Charlie and I as we laid under the fallen tree, and wrapped his arms around our necks when his comical side was abruptly awakened by the show boat antics of our "needing a hug" Leader, who was seeking our attentions like a baby displaying its full arsenal of goo-goo ga-ga's; just to get its admirers to ogle in awe. Kevin eagerly began to whisper lightly like a breeze, while grinning from ear to ear as he softly said, "Walter should be an actor my brothers, with a stage name of Ham it up Hank; walking around with his chest poked out like his dookie don't stank!" We were so amused by Kevin's clever, craziness of talking smack that our immediate laughter lunged out of us and shattered the mere silence that had been expected from discipline soldiers that were in the middle of a war. Rene reacted to the outburst like she was juggling a jack hammer; quickly smacking all three of us on the back of our heads like rat-a-tat-tat was at bat for the **Padres**. She looked us up and down as if she was daring us to make another sound, when she rolled her neck back toward Walter and quietly said, "The classroom now has your full attention, so please continue and I promise you there will be no more interruptions!" Her serious demeanor had us shaking like a broken rattle trying to catch back onto the rhythm of the wise words that were about to be spoken, as Walter gave her a respectful salute and an acknowledging wink of the eye. He had been stifled for a moment but his words were still ready to convey, as he continued with his direct plans of attack and allude. He said, "Thank you Lord for our gracious gifts of gallantry and compassion; for we are strangers boldly walking into these dangers that has been presented like an open book with an arrow pointing to the key points on the page which is of our main concerns, as we believe and trust in you; amen." Our Mighty Daredevil of "listen closely and heed" took a deep breath of calmness as he continued with his song that was remaining the same, but his focus and forcefulness of his essence was finally being summoned into the problems that really exist; where it felt like a point of no return! The Devil that you know; he can't survive the "Hammer of God" or, the "Staff of God"; he can only dwell within the realms of pretense and fabrication like this alienated civilization of so much evil; and though, he so desperately wants to be accepted and loved; his sheet of armor that protects his invisibility is nothing but uncomplicated glass through God's eyes. Walter paused for a mini-moment, as he pressed on with his efforts of moving mountains with his instructional words of "we can"; as he slowly and clearly said, "Okay guys, once we get inside the secret opening, we'll follow in a column formation with a two-to-three foot gap between us in case we run into any unwanted booby-traps." "So, take this time of congruence to get all your weapons armed and ready to attack on all sides if necessary; and be aware, be very aware of your surroundings because if you have to hit the "Kill Switch"; it would be okay with me!" We were living life like scavengers on a hunger hunt, and our getting past these problems were feeling strong, as if we were seeking God's forgiveness for recent past broken embraces that ended in differences of opinions, but we were now following with dauntless pursuit of this "shadow" that had only left behind limited clues of his existence. It seemed that we had finally figured out the puzzle to his elaborate hoax, as I held the Shepherd like pole out in front of my heart, as my fellow Daredevils chanted with spiritual hums of harmony as if they were saying, "More! More! Please, Mr. Maestro of Madness, let us dance like wolves while feeling the moods from this barbaric stillness of Death." Therefore, I delayed my forthcoming on purpose as if to rally the troops before gradually making my way into a triumphant pose that resembled a stone statue of greatness, like Moses crossing the Red Sea and leading his people to safety; while cherishing the beauty of the better concepts of life. As I made my way forward, I pushed and shoved my way playfully through the ranks of righteousness, while narrowing the gap between the tree stump and I. I suddenly jumped like an agile Antelope over the large brush that surrounded the metal grate, which happened to be slippery and slimy like damp rocks laying on the edge of a river bed, that resembled gems of superstition; not rare in a sense, but very much a crushing of spirits when it comes to simplicity! Yes, I was always to proud to beg, even if I wasn't making any progress; but sometimes there's no other way to make it to level ground, without that sound of request flowing from your chest; feeling like some juries before a decision could be made, where they were already convinced of the accused guilt in a "hopeless case"; while swearing to be brave. I carefully placed the Shepherd like pole into a vertical position, as I slid it cautiously into a semi-round gap proportionate to the second key; when it suddenly dropped sharply to a certain point, but maybe I didn't push hard enough because nothing occurred within four minutes till dawn to tell its single truth to the day; yet, I instantly began ailing from a warrior's wound of finding out that maybe my hard fought efforts to uplift our hundreds of reasons to battle like never before; could actually be a dud of a bombshell being dropped right smack into the middle of our laps. Kevin suddenly jumped to his feet as the break of day was amongst us, and his sleuth like temperament was forcing him to give his two cents in solving this "dilemma of deduction" that had all of us scratching our baffled heads like constant confusion, while falling to our emerging emotions that were being controlled by the ill humors of this magical illusion. It was as if the final chapter was beckoning its beginning; but the caution in our climax of "no time for delays" was postponing the actuality of surviving this terrorizing tempest. Kevin really wanted his words to be helpful for our despair, as he boldly started to speak like tough guys never die; while urgently unleashing his hard-hitting words that were like "death play", as his voice sounded like verses from a frozen slate of vengeful rise and fall. He critically said, "Guys, we have been training for the way we must go, it seems forever; so please don't give up!" "Cuz, I'm telling you bro, turn that dang pole counter clockwise, because backward time is all that this fiend knows and if time stood still, what could you take from him besides surprising revelations." The entrance to Sacman's hideaway was made with critical design, barely lit by faint flickers of flaws; like being locked in a Shark's jaws, where the thoughts of being consumed was an assumption in this fifty-fifty chance of doom; but I was hearing Kevin's message loud and clear. I aggressively started turning the pole toward sun-up like a wrestler's grip on a head lock; when all of a sudden the grate swung open like a knee-jerk response; impulsive and unexpected to the entranced onlookers, who were awaiting a dramatic rescue from a "sparkle of hope." Everybody started swarming around the open "rabbit-hole" like a semi-detached mob, or an anxious posse that was forging though Hell; who were still exhibiting looks of awe from the exuberance of the darkened, eerie black hole that raged with conjured caskets of curiosity. When out the corner of our eyes, we noticed that Walter was now speaking with heeding hand signals, as our whispers and low tone talk immediately switched to silence and sociopathic suddenness in the eternal words of shut-up! We quickly began to form in lines, like a squad of sovereign soldiers; step by step, and play by play with every movement toward our pre-emptive strike, as we gathered the ropes for our descent into the depths of darkness that was quietly awaiting our offerings of hope and help. Without hesitation but very slowly, we each started dropping into this pit of precious challenges, one-by-one and single file as teachers, preachers and suddenly the main feature on this scale of balances and electrical outages; where past obsessions were under fire like a choir singing memoirs for this desperate hour of "What I did for love!" Defense was working a major transformation on our thoughts, but this Devil of deception was like the fog; blinding and tricky with its thickness of deceit, which was misleading to the eyes; but for the mind it was specific and solid like a slab of concrete. We were so darn alert, that I felt sorry for the Bumpkin carved like a pumpkin of scariness that was testing our limits, but he was actually honoring them by adding more obstacles than usual, for we were living a life of passion fulfilled with purpose to stop this unsuspecting killer; we were truly Heaven sent. As we landed at the bottom of this caged heat of chaos, it reminded us that we had an appointment with this monster that was living like there were no rules; but we continued to press on by Faith, as we cautiously walked into the "gloom of, please go back!" My young Daredevils stutter-stepped, and crept along for about ten to fifteen yards; when we started to smell a concentrated venomous vapor, that was so strong that it smelled just like ammonia. As we continued to peer harder into the darkness, we noticed a circle of water on the left and right sides of the tunnel, with a haze patiently rising from its surface like gaseous fumes that were looking to breathe; while being directly divided with a narrow plank laid across the middle for a nimble balancing act that would require steadiness with God providing a way; as we nervously edged past this off-the-wall obstacle. The Lord painted the sky with stars, while having a Heavenly voice that if you listened; it soulfully encouraged the heart with reassurance that he was there to shield you from harm with reflections of a Paradise that he had so trustingly found. It was as if being surrounded by Angels with quivers of arrows, fending off sinister spirits that never broke a promise; while laying all the cards on the table and cutting the deck with favorable intentions, and always coming to a certain conclusion for different needs. So, we accepted this challenge of following orders; even as we started to notice that the mist-filled waters were swirls of motion that moved strongly like white-water rapids of peril; but somehow we relished this golden opportunity. The raging ripples of water that seemed ceaseless and content could never be calm; because its torment screamed its menacing movements like a force fighting for freedom, while making waves that formed as warriors preparing for war. We instantly started to see the heads of shadowy figures roaming through these infested waters like piranhas that were swimming side by side, and focused on a bone ripping meal; while being direct and slightly belligerent of our unawareness and carelessness, that could certainly be an issue if our game plan wasn't played right. It seemed that there were a thousand ripples of galvanizing predators treading carefully across the top of these two watery moats; as we tramped along on this side-trail of mystery and missteps. The cavern looked like a lost city, with stalactites and stalagmites covering the ceiling and floors that poetically paved a way through these underground taverns, which was fixed and unmoving; and it actually seemed like Sacman had built an Empire like the Incas that had finally been discovered; as we tightly clinched our weapons of choice. Our minds were flying all over the place and unable to stop, and because there were no ceiling lights; Sacman had lined the cave walls with medieval torches, as we started to look at things in a much different sense of light. Everyone's dreams were now fusing with reality, as our attention to the movements in the waters were growing dim; but very noticeable to a Keeper and Collector of snakes like Kevin. He said, "Daredevils, those are Water Moccasins in those pits of death that lay below." "Look at their texture and prowess as they swirl along so aggressive, and agitated." "If you look very closely, you can see that they're waiting for a sucker to bite into; with their venomous vindications of instinct, trying to find the weakest link to sink this Armageddon of Artistry and Adventure." "Now, I've seen many Horror Stories whispering songs of innocence in this school of life; but this one has a new beginning causing an emotional frenzy that could trigger the strings of our hearts to graciously feel the pull of God for present and future fears; while caring deeply for strangers, and loved ones in direr distress." As Kevin's words walked up and down the inner walls of this old-school observatory, chaos was swirling around our Tenacious Ten, as we steadily made our way through this mist of mayhem; but the answers to our own prayers were failing to keep up with the nature of this day, while feeling shocked and surprised by some family members allegiance; like they had turned the color of blood into a puddle of wasted water. Our true understandings were starting to evolve; as we drew closer to the sharp as a musical note, unlawful acts of this problematic predator of youth, set on stopping its growth before the roots had a chance to sink into the soil, and blossom the way the Heavenly Father intended. He was definitely carrying our curiosities through this awkward moment that felt like a weighted down wagon making a long journey through a rainstorm; but our visions were beginning to clear for us to hold our own, and we knew our hearts would go on; strong, while forever searching for this demon of wrongs! We were oh-so determined to keep everyone together; but some split-minute decisions are often flawed, as we quickly lined up in a single-file, while making our way across this unsteady, unreliable plank that was either leading us toward safety, or more tension-driven reactions that would lure us closer to finding the slightest traces of his terror in this unthinkable dark. Walter sternly said, "Be easy my friends, or be a trophy for this beast of a man that's trying to cover his tracks; but also be aware of the things that are happening beyond our sight!" As the plot began to quicken, and thicken Walter was in control, as he bravely took the lead like a Blood Hound without a clue; and his legend of humping a dog and bragging that he had dog babies running around these woods was as sick as him drowning kittens on the mighty river; that was widely known for death and tragic fatalities. This type of madness immediately put him in our Hall of Fame, merely out of respect; with his tortuous techniques that only children with mental instabilities and crazed killer tendencies walked easily without question or confrontation, which raised our fears to anoint him leader and warlord of our Daredevils; because his insanity was seen as strength and security in getting the job done. He was gambling on this game, as if our odds were extremely good; while confidently ushering out verbal commands that would define our success in this new venue of vindication and disturbing secrets. We were all frightened; but whatever happened to never living in fear, while trying to figure out this scenario of long-shots, as we constantly kept score of how much of ourselves were really out there. It was really a shame that our eyes were eager to see life with more openness, as we were entering new phases of our lives where now all we imagined was terror, torture, and twisted take-backs from what appeared to be a long-held sunrise of surprise. It was like entering amongst evil that was trying to hide from the morning Sun, as the chamber we were quietly moving along and creeping under his radar, suddenly branched off into two tunnels that both looked toxic and horrifying from our minds-eye view. We were not sure of which way to go, but we were going to pass right through it by brushing aside all the distractions, where our rewards would be with relentless effort, while staying senseless to our unique and exquisite mixtures of eating away endeavors; that were unleashing those shining postures of positivity. I guess we weren't supposed to get this far, because we all had different approaches to solving this solution; but we were walking heavily into enemy territory like neglected flowers in our garden of hope that propelled us to take another deliverance look, before making vital decisions that went against all our beliefs of trust and faith. It seemed like we were trying to make it up to those who were gone; whose essence was still brilliantly beaming like rainbows bordered with soul-soothing sunshine, while looking down from the skies with ancient harps strumming in the background; so that we could actually hear the grace of God's words telling us, "I know my children that you're carrying a lot of added weight on your shoulders, and there could be more than misgivings lying ahead; but heed my flock and be wise to my Fatherly love that is untouchable to any evil that quietly falls on deaf ears!" "So listen with close relations to my mysterious miracles that "do happen", in the dark or in the light; for I am a Father to a much larger community than you could ever dream, with a harvest of endless love held together with just a cornerstone of might." "So, I beg you my children, Praise thy Lord and I'll make all things to be all-right!" They say that evil exists inside and outside of us, but our stubbornness of hearts and wills are so easily confused by its trickery, that we must be like river horses that are still unbroken; while being tightly wound when the pressure starts to build; so, just let it all go when the walls come down and be eager to win the approval of a demanding Father with worlds of love. We all believingly gathered like manifested ideas toward the center of this eclipsed cavern, with a smidgen of hopeful light shimmering off the caveman like torches that provided us with a slight light; but not a glimpse of insight. Walter with his "going haywire" achievements was now trying to offer sound reasoning to our problem, by dividing us into groups of five; for us to split up and search the separate tunnels while staying in radio communication, and making out the scene for an on the warpath rumpus that seemed just right for this particular division of forces. He said, "Rene, Jayme, Kevin, Nece, and Lia, follow the path we were headed on to the left; and be very cautious to the unknown." "Don't take any unnecessary chances, but please radio or come and get us if our plan has the slightest mishap in executing our in between the lines, traps of "take down." Walter continued on, by speaking clearly with his well advised instructions as he said, "Serena, Tammy, Charlie, and Lil Tom will follow me into this barely open Hell Hole over there toward the right; so, keep your flashlights on low everybody and that's an order; because the low beams of light won't attract or give a clue to our unsuspecting arrival, just like an UFO hiding in the clouds with a downplayed watch and see. Our daring group of "peril players" of this gruesome game had been divided into squads, but was still very much unified; as we gathered in the middle of the cavern making our final preparations, and honing our weapons to be ready to rock and roll. We could feel that sudden swerve in momentum, as we were pushing so hard at trying to solve one of Life's deepest problems, while slightly being changed into stone; and although we were watching our surroundings carefully, our hearts were pounding powerfully like the pistons in a high-tech engine purring for prominence. We were all giving this now landmarked Looser-Ville a once over before we hugged and slapped hands of respect; and yes we offered spiritualism in our individuality, but together we felt close to unstoppable. My courageous renegades of readiness were mending no fences, as we evenly divided into our first ever "Five Pact of Commandos", as we called to mind the underlying causes of the problem at hand, with a hymn of spiritual reliance. As the words began to flow like H2O, it was like we were hearing our ancestors struggling through their trying times; where we imagined ourselves kneeling in a candle lit church singing soulfully in our minds. We could see the words for miles as they sang,

- "Rest in peace young soldiers, for life is a chest match;"
- "We were seeking get-back with faithful attacks, for innocent children getting tossed in sacks."

- "Hearts were being ripped apart;" "by a Maniac telling the story in reverse, from the end to the start."
- "From the Coalmine to chaos, with thunder and lightning pointing to the "All Answers" of the skies;"
- "But, we had an awareness of feelings; that our Savior only knew why."
- "There was no close end to the story with small amounts of time collectively counting massive amounts of dread and worry;"
- "But, we would still rise by knowing our Lord; and that's our Soul-driven Glory, Amen!"
- "Rise, Rise, Rise toward the mountains…"
- "Heavenly Fountains pouring through our blood; while constructing that Mighty Ark of Witness; yes I'm a Witness;"
- "Believing in our hearts that we will survive this flood."
- "We say, Rise, Rise, Rise young children;"
- "Father is there for you, with endless embraces; for his faith-filled millions!"
- "Rise, Rise, Rise….!"

We were now feeling Devine and this extravagant entrance into this vast house that was divided into secrets rooms; where surprises could come from out of left field was casting a hazardous haze over our thoughts; but we were still looking desperately for the easy way out. These treacherous days were tugging sharply on our boldness and bravado, as our two groups sifted our way up the two damp and chilly tunnels, nervously looking behind our advancements to see the perfect pieces being laid toward Death's door. My special group of the "fearless five" was like Peacekeepers being poked and prodded into defiance and self reliance; but we were on point and moving in the slow lane with military stealth and lethalness, that only a "Sergeant of Rock", who was sly as a fox could maneuver so timely and precise; like the hands on a clock. We continued to move gradually and carefully, but it seemed the further we explored the cavern, it opened wider and wider; and with the slyness of secrecy in our steps, the darkness seemed spookier from the speckles of dust that bounced off the cavern walls like a light snow drift that was absorbing a horrible odor that smelled like rotting corpses of dead Possums that laid lifeless on the sides of Deepwater's country roads. The wicked torches that lined the walls were flickering from the caves steady draft like they were calling out for this Killer to "come out and play"; and as we approached a second chamber that was lit up like a Chapel or a sacred place, it seemed like someone was meaning for this eye catching wonderment to be seen; with no little Birds to tell! As, onlookers in awe and amazement the scene seemed damaged; knowing that our lives were endangered, but it immediately felt like it was telling a story where unintended consequences were more elusive than this Madman we were pursuing. We were looking at this Grand Sculpture of a carved out cave that actually seemed stolen from an unforgettable memory; but it was glowing brilliantly, as we suddenly noticed on top of its entrance that was full of enticing curiosities, that there was an unrecognizable figure imprinted like "no acceptable loss." The more we honed in on its odd placement and disturbing deficiency in luster, the more it resembled an upside down carving of a cupid with his arrow pointing downward to an unpreserved organ that looked like a heart shriveling around its confines. There was also a jet-black marble rolling back-in-forth in a crevice below it, which was creatively chiseled; leaving us all in admiration, as we wildly wondered how this magic trick was even possible. Lia was the first to break the seriousness of our silence as she boldly blurted out, "Something smells bad; like Kevin on a dookie drop of his hot number two; that really smells like a stinky, sweaty Old man's shoe." Everyone let out a controlled snicker of amusement by placing our hands over our faces to stifle the laughter, but the hums of our harmonized heckling ran through our minds as if it said, "Mr. Booty-licous, Stank Butt Ma-Gila-Kutty, and better yet; Doo-Doo the Crap smelling Clown!" She was so satisfied with her "putting down" of her older brother, that she became careless as she moved closer to the entrance of this Carved out Coo-coo's Nest; which immediately triggered Kevin and My protective preservations of "don't cross the dotted line." Kevin started whispering his advisements of no advancements, with a stronger tone; so that his instructions were heard and clearly understood, as we rapidly moved out of our safe positions and raced up behind her with a physical tongue lashing of, "No Lia don't do that!" It was already too late though; because as I grabbed her shoulder, her forward momentum still pushed her frail frame further into the unwelcoming room, causing our perils of panic to weep uncontrollably, for we knew this "Sheep Thief" was up to no good. We were earnestly trying to cope with this foreknown knowledge, as Lia looked up with a fluctuating fever of fear like a kid that had entered her first Haunted House; and the house happened to be made of Ginger Bread with a woodshed of pita bread, where no clues of crumbs lead to the Head of the table that was avoiding Justice like the blind truths of the dead. For Jesus; but at a quick drop of a hat, a wooden fence layered with flinted fangs ready to impact like a falling tree with a Lumber Jack's yell of "Timber!" came crashing down blocking the entrance and having just one smile at a time, in a place of miracles and mighty mind misleading. Our eyes were popping out of our heads, as we glanced around this Fox-trap that became ice cold like a polar cap, when our chills and shivers alertly started witnessing this massive room of doom with bloodied hearts bludgeoned and lining the walls with railroad track spikes through their centers, decorating this trophy case like Bear Skin rugs or stuffed Buck Horned Deer that had suffered a fit of rage by its facetious flaming presence; and now we were trapped! We thought the sound of the gate thundering to the grasps of the ground had given away our "surprise for unsuspecting eyes", while having a used gift of yesterday's youth for this Bad Guy, but as anxious antiquated Angels, no retaliation was beckoned from this turned to liquid metamorphosis of sweat and tears; Thank God! The three of us had been surprisingly isolated in this chilling cooler of enclosure, where time was no more than a hindrance for happiness; and it seemed that Tata's and Bye-Bye's were masking the interior design of this "facing off, slapping in the face, horrible time walls" that screamed out loud the words of, "Please help us." The plan had now gone terribly wrong, and we were on the fringe of having our inner-selves collapse; but we knew there were shreds of hope with Rene and Nece still being free, because we trusted that they would find us help, and this surprise of being "put in our place" left us Dutiful Daredevil's in a Hell of a fix. Lia spoke out with an alarming panic of principle as she shouted, "Fiddlesticks!" Kevin angrily responded as he said, "Fiddlesticks! Sis is that all you can say is Freaking, Fiddlesticks!" "Our situation is much more serious than a stick with a Fiddle, being played like a banjo whose musical strings are savagely strummed by a Mythological Maniac, Lia!" "We're at a critical point of being beaten decisively, and every misstep is like a mindless Moon without a thought of its shine or servitude."

His comments had a ton of validity, where no one knew our outcome; as his scared, baby sister coward in a corner of this horrible chamber of chastise, where she was feeling very dense; while being entrenched in pure panic. I could really feel Kevin's warranted anger, but our shock of being trapped was slowly wearing off, and this episode was no more different than the run-ins we had faced while making it through these tormented trenches, and surprisingly surviving thus far. I lurched onto the wooden gate and started shaking it with all the strength I had within my bony, lean body of mere nothing; as my efforts were recognizably deterred by the sturdiness of its trapping structure. I gaspingly said, "Everyone Relax!" and instantly it was like my crazy spirit was now kicking into my soul, where all I needed was a horse, a spear and war paint with the Lord giving me the courage; to never retreat! I was barely able to control this fearless feeling that had consumed my heart with might, and the words of my Mamma saying, "If things get tough and your life is in danger; pick up a stick, brick or lit candle stick and light their a**** up, Momma got your back!" So, I continued to speak with the words of "Wisdom the Truth", where the words were righteous and ready like a pattern of praise. I said, "Guys, this is not a problem because everything that seems broken, barely balanced, and swaying on the extreme edge can sometimes easily be fixed by just taking a deep breath, while keeping an open mind." I had just calmly and rationally spoke, while feeling a hundred percent assuring, that I had not held anything back as I slapped my fist into the palm of my hand and gritted my teeth with a snarl of my favorite collective saying, "Fallen Idols could never exist in our minds, but Heroes blossom from our hearts; and that special combination can't be deterred by the freakish décor of these grayish, haunting "after souls" plastered, and neatly driven into these chilling cave walls." It seemed that the shock of seizure was finally wearing off Kevin, as his rage had now turned to level headed thinking and his "backyard bravery" was at last showing a re-found confidence as he said, "Jayme's right Guys!" His focus and thoughts of freedom were boasting with obedience, as his courage continued to flow his words with perfect instruction of "forever and eternal" with brilliant belief in Calvary. He was relentless in his pursuit of prayers being answered as he seriously said, "Rene and Nece listen up, my Sister Soldiers of Sovereignty; we need you two to go find help quickly, while we try to figure a way out of this mess!"

The Girls didn't even have a chance to respond, when suddenly a gust of wind blew through the tunnels extinguishing several of the torches, making the darkened scene seem like "startled cries" in this dismal Dungeon of Distress. Rene and Nece shakily backed away from the fallen gate, and gradually faded into the shadows like an evasive thought that was meant to be unmentioned, but was still somehow expressed with authority. As our two-way callers of connection disappeared into the orphan black, they were shedding tearful requests of, "Please be safe, and we'll promise to do the same." They pinky swore amongst their selves that "Daredevils live forever", as the two scampered back down the tunnel trying to retrace our tracks through this spacious Spook-Fest. The Girls had miraculously made their way back to where the two tunnels separated; quietly pausing behind some large rocks for cover to catch a quick breath from their frantic pace of escape and rescue that existed in their minds as "Time of Beware!" Rene said, "Nece we need you to go get more help for this rock-shop curiosity of a Caveman, that has almost completely wrecked our pursuit of him; where acting impulsively has put us in the thick of things, and baby girl that isn't even the half of it." "Hurry off and go to Sacman's boat hidden in the brush, and take it down river to find Thomas." A college football player with the strength of five men, who played defensive lineman for West Virginia Tech, which was our local college of choice; and he was also Charlie, Serena, and Tammy's older brother, who really liked putting the hurt on people on the opposite side of any line; straight, narrow, or curved like a "S", he was the best at "Bringing the pain!" Nece had an accelerated edge for Seamanship, because she had been taught how to navigate a boat at an early age by her Uncle Sparky, who used to take the family out on his boat on numerous fishing trips that always ended in "catch and nab" victories. She was now making her mark as the official seek-and-finder of relief; sort of like a go-between middle man with many, many years of knowing what was happening before receiving a lot of grueling details. Our two Heroines were mindfully on their way, as they held hands and crossed the narrow wooden plank to exit "Henry the VIII's house of indelible design", with its sacred poles of strength that was holding most of its infrastructure like Atlas holding up the world that evolves. Even these states of continuous change seemed like it was tipping one's hat to the current situation; where Seeing eye to eye had taken a break or even split, when the sh** had hit the fan. The girls hugged each other like tomorrow was a treasure of forever, as Nece hauled a** to the brush where Sacman's boat was hidden, and immediately threw off all the camouflage on this rusted structure into the rapid currents slightly bouncing the boat like a baby on its Momma's knee, learning that listening carefully, and having a sense of spirituality was an expression of boldness and tremendous effort in heart. Rene was pitching in her motivational advice, while standing by the secret entrance like a coach who had lost some games, but was still having the willingness to win, when their backs were against the wall of failure, as she desperately continued to try and make radio contact with the other Daredevils, with no prevail. Nece had successfully found the boats motor, and vigorously started yanking hard on the ripcord to get the old rusted bucket of "improvised hope" to finally start, and purr like a kitten getting its belly rubbed gently, where the response was kind and thankful; when all of a sudden and like a blessing from above, the engine started to hum spiritually sounding like a time of reflection, while heeding that thin link of chain connected to a wishful rabbit's foot. The Girls knew that God was present, the past, and the future, as Rene shouted out as if the spirit had lifted her devotion to a greater level of liveliness. She said, "Go Girl! Go Baby, and journey like the gist of the wind!" "Bring back the help we need at God's speed; just remember we love you and our hopes of success lies on your ingenuity, and your ability to find the answers to get us past this Killer's restrictions on the boldness of belief; May Heaven be your guide!" Nece saluted like a Private First Class, or an Ensign obeying orders as she spun the boat from its undercover location like she was actually a Captain of the Sea with the skill of a Christopher Columbus or Ferdinand Magellan on a search to discover. As Nece disappeared rapidly down the river, Rene stood and watched her fade across the waves in the water like a Mother Hen sending one of its Newborn's on a survival test for self reliance and confidence that would only increase the whole flock's longevity and their hunger for life. She slowly turned to re-enter this swamp vaporous underground stronghold that seemed only meant for death, and with one last glance towards the "Wading in the Waters" that raged with acceptance of carrying us all back home, safely; Rene finally felt what was meant to be; the true assurances of Hope. She furtively started making her way back toward the other Daredevils with covert quickness, and a need for resolution in the rises and falls of temperament and tenacity. Confidence was starting to build with a new strength of will back in the locked chamber of dried out hearts, where Lia had braced herself against a boulder that resembled a big chunk of ice with the Artic shine of the moon reflecting off its sleek and defined texture that sparkled like a diamond in the rough. I had reached a final point on the thread of fears, as I went Melodramatic like a maddened mercenary being meshed in a minds-eye of massive panic, where "get it together" had struck my fearlessness to fight, as if I had to question my structure of sound outlined substance. I said, "Kevin we have to get out of here now!" "We can't wait for the other Daredevils; we have to exit this heart-filled Hell Hole ASAP cuz." Kevin had a sharp sense of awareness that loved to work backwards for some reason; and although he knew the pressure was building with the odds stacked against us; his resiliency was gaining altitude like a helium balloon reaching for the skies. He spoke with seriousness in his voice as he said, "Guys, let's dig our way out!" He immediately reached into his back-pack to grab his trusty mid-shovel that he had only used to bury his animals he collected; that had sorrowfully past away. Kevin moved like a locomotive as he lunged to his knees, and plunged the shovel into the soggy dirt beneath the wooden "got your a** now" fence. He was digging like a Miner Forty-Niner searching for gold in an unknown, dangerous territory; where nobody knew what they would find, but pay dirt was an acceptable load. Dignity and dedication was pouring sweat from his brow like a mountain blessing had been performed for his unwavering spirit, as he slung the soft Earth into a heap of a pile; but no one knows the power you wield, when opportunities merge causing the senses to reach for Galaxies far above and beyond. The answers were starting to come to us at a steady, but rapid pace; which was extremely quicker than Kevin's shovel could scoop the entrapping soil, even though he was moving faster than the clues in the clouds. He looked like he was carving a canyon, while bringing evasiveness like a fault finder to this defensive wall that was implanted firmly, as if a **son of a gun** wouldn't give it a dog on try. I wanted to ask him could I take a turn at the freedom that was insight, while he grabbed some much needed rest, but I could tell by the "left in the lurches" look on his face that he had the tenacity of a stray dog, and that he wouldn't be denied his "bone" of glory; even if it meant feeling exhausted and pressured despite counting the minutes toward "flee brother flee." He had finally dug enough room under the fence to attempt an escape, as he motioned his shovel at Lia like a summons for her to come out of her shell of an igloo dweller stance. She slowly began to approach our positions, where the newly dug out rabbit-hole was beaming a way to the other side of yesterday; while everything else was nervously on standby. As she hesitated for a split second, Lia began to realize that this was her chance to see the high road that should be taken in this case of lowness; where how much was actually enough, when being hit with a whammy of the unknown. She made-fast by quickly lying on her back, while slipping and sliding her way under the bottom of the spiked pointed tips of the fence, and refusing to let the rest of the world see her moments of vulnerability. Once she cleared the fence, Kevin told her to go hide in the shadows across from the chamber behind some large rocks; and like a bratty kid, Lia held up her middle finger and said, "Don't you tell me what to do anymore, you Ma-gill-a Gorilla faced Ape" as she hid quietly on the edges of the lack of light. The weight of Kevin's words earlier had scarred her ego and shook the handle of her confidence, but it didn't touch her fiery soul or tomboy stature that gave her such a unique personality. I instantly followed her lead, as I dropped to the moist dirt and rolled over gingerly with my face staring upwards at the "poke holes in a prisoner of war" spikes; who's only answer was if you're not very careful, your failure would be taken to the limits of puncture and pierce. Kevin patiently waited until I had cleared the barrier, and then he carefully slid his backpack through the hole like he was dealing cards from the bottom of the deck; looking around our surroundings to make sure his shadiness wasn't discovered by the man whose game was beyond change. He smirked proudly at this lucky break, as he burrowed his way under this weighed down obstruction like a groundhog looking for his shadow on the other side of reflection; while desperately trying to handle the vagueness of our fates, which was putting a vast strain on his Daredevil ego. After he had cleared the fence, Kevin strategically scanned the tunnel up and down noticing that there were narrow strips of daylight or flashes of existence coming from the tunnel ahead, which was causing him to rapidly join Lia and me in the shadows of the stalagmites and rocks layered to the side of this cave of risks. He squatted down beside us in exhaustion, as he reached out with open arms giving his little sister a hug of brotherly love, as if he were asking for forgiveness. I was working to communicate with the other Daredevils through walkie-talkie; but for some reason being underground was causing a major static interference. We all looked at each other with relieving eyes, knowing we were all safe and sound; for the light in the darkness was promising and reassuring, and we knew we were a family reading beyond the obvious. I passed a word or two in a low, discreet voice as I said, "Often we may walk along, but we all sometimes need a helping hand, so we'll wait here in safety until backup arrives; however we need to keep a close eye on both ends of the tunnel, and I promise we will all be okay." They both nodded in hushed agreement, as we huddled in the dark like Hindu fire God's without the fire to keep us warm, or the slightest remembrance of a week ago, when our success was unmatchable; but we learned by heart, that our Father rules from the skies with vigilant eyes. Meanwhile, in the lofty grasps of the other tunnel; where Walter and the rest of the Daredevils were advancing further into the quiet unknown, softly and slowly; while making their way up an uphill incline following one another with more cleverness in their closeness, as they divinely walked through the dark. They were giving this humongous cavern the once over, when all of a sudden there eyes were instantly directed toward more water-filled trenches on both sides of this "not-so-certain" path, but oddly there were leaves floating across their tops. A tree there was none; however leaves they were plenty as if someone was mixing a potion of sarcasm with its special ingredient of phantasm to ward off curious and mischief intruders. The courageous group of Daredevils continued on, but with their minds now twisted in knots, as they had finally made their climb up the testing terrain. Flickers of shapely light were splashing off the darkened cave walls like ambers of lava disintegrating with its mere touch; through all the shadows that lingered with leery and eerie excuse. As they came upon this torch lit chamber that had three massive deadened walls everything started to look more ancient and magical than the repeated falling of black rain, or the staggering search for redemption while sorting through the torn pieces of an ended affair. The young seekers of truth were hesitantly changing their pace and being very cautious, as they were all in awe of the front wall that displayed pictures that were so life-like, one could hear the screams of terror bouncing off its surface like they were reaching out to its onlookers for an elaborate plan to save their cast in stone souls. There were also four large letters and symbols plastered across the top of this gigantic craft of skill that was etched in distinct letters of an **H**, a sideways heart with the bottom tip facing the right that resembled an **E**, followed by two liberated **L's** that longed for its freedom of explanation. Now, all that could see with insight could actually tell that the written message looked like it spelled "HELL", but to the naked eye it seemed far more sophisticated an eclipsing when the hidden, eventually becomes evident. I've heard that the bigger and stronger more often survive; but the Daredevils were feeling empowered by their bottled up bravery that had undoubtedly been uncapped; which made their actions flow like a ravenous river that was strict and unrefined, but was still able to stream with passion and poise. So, as they eventually came to this fork in the road, where they had to try and solve this difficult and unpredictable situation that had the curiosity factor of a Fat-Jack cat, with a four leaf clover dangling from its hat; now imagine that! Everyone was steadily admiring the beauty of the artistry displayed on this unique and crafty canvass of a wall, as they all gathered at its base staring intently at the drawings of a man with a pick-axe chasing child-like figures; where in actuality it seemed like they were eluding vultures of pain and punishment, while slowly awaiting death. Their attentions were being drawn like a magnet to the bright colors on this oversized caption of neglectfulness of life, when Serena slightly stepped to her left and mashed down on a rock that was placed so craftily; that no one noticed its purpose. Then immediately and from out of nowhere, a large log with wooden pointed spikes protruding out of its ends, had finally been released sending it flying from out the darkness above like a killer's swing of death being attached to two ropes and hurling its momentum; to do bodily harm to all in its path of destruction. It swung silently, but very violently from behind our position in attempts to pin us against this wondrous structure of distraction and attraction, with heinous and unexpected developments of hopefully slow reactions. Charlie and Lil Tom responded with the quickness of a rascally rabbit running out of pure habit, to evade its predators with effortlessness and a keen awareness of danger. Lil Tom jumped on Serena and tackled her to the ground, as Charlie pounced on top of Tammy latching onto her like a fumbled football that he was destined to recover; as he immediately swung her to the safe havens of "swing low", with all of their hearts being instilled with the pinnacles of fear. Walter was sure he had more alternatives, as he stood erect and tight like a warrior Indian facing an oncoming Calvary, while honorably protecting his chances to go down in History as a "Legend free from the Stone." He was standing his ground like a taunted Bull, as he was definitely being pushed to the limits; when he confidently sprang from the sandy surface as if he were a seal flying in the air accelerating out of frigid waters to show its graceful talents of circus-like performing of perfection, by accomplishing a feat that only its brethren could admire with envy. "Instant Death" flew under his air-borne body, while whispering a la-la-bye to this courageous chance taker, as he sang serene attack words like he was seeing a War movie; where the First Sergeant was screaming "Charge…" with the passion of a thorn-to-paw Lion. Walter avoided the log with enormous surprise from the rest of the Daredevils, as the momentum of the aftershock from it slamming, and smashing against the mighty wall with its speed and force hitting so aggressively, caused the landing of the great Gymnast to stumble and fall on his "Thank God Almighty" rear end. Pieces of broken wood fragments flew all over the place, as Charlie and Lil Tom scanned the air to make sure there wasn't another follower to under estimate the spirits of "For God's Sake!" When the air was clear, everyone stood up and ran for a more secure position, as Lil Tom shouted, "Hurry guys, run for cover behind the boulders in the shadows of the cavern!" As he made it to safety with quickness, Lil Tom immediately followed up by saying, "Did Ya'll see that kick a** maneuver by the Heroic Sir Walter?" "Wow!" After their quick stint behind the large protectors of patience and primitive perils, everyone started high tailing it back down the corridor to escape; while speedily grabbing Walter up from his bummed out, laid-back posture like he was in shock from the outcome. He had a slight smirk across his face, with his pants sagging and dragging against the dirt while knowing that he wanted to land a perfect ten; but deep down he knew that he had to put in plenty more work for such a score. The Daredevils were glad to be alive as they cautiously started making their downhill descent from the chamber, when Charlie suddenly held up his fist for everyone to stop; because he had alertly noticed a shadowy figure headed up the cave trail toward them making up ground like a "march of madness." As the shadowy figure drew nearer, the scarier it seemed with its "so strong" presence of overwhelm; that it seemed more visible than what they would have liked. So, without hesitation the Daredevils drew their weapons as they crouched low in the dark awaiting to be attacked. They all saw three rapid flashes of red light, as the shadow crept around the cave corner slowly, and walking lightly with its steps; when Rene abruptly appeared from the darkness trying to blend in with the surroundings, while clinging to the floor of the cave like a Tigress waiting to attack its prey with persistence and on the double prowess. Now, this brave group of warriors had just faced a deadly booby-trap that could have killed them all, but now they were approaching things in a new way; where they had come to a peaceful place of understanding. Everyone at this "moment of miracles" was really sensing the vengeful side of the whole scenario, by this Unheralded Undertakers personality; while steadily trying to help restrain his evil with a "Strong Man of Myth" mentality. Rene had shocking news for our Family of fearless Freedom Fighters, as she began to speak with panic and relief in her voice; sprinting toward their defenses with a shotgun formation, fifty-two fly do or die bootleg, that left them clueless in her approach of scoring readily with her words of Truth. She gaspingly said, "Thank God, you guys are okay!" "We have to hurry back to the others, because they are trapped in a bloody chamber of hearts with a fortified wooden gate blocking their exit; and we didn't know if Sacman was coming soon to take what seems to give him his very essence!" "So, I sent Nece with Sacman's boat to bring back T.C. (Thomas Crowder) to help us out; because our plan had busted and his strength could be an asset for us to come out on top, while looking down on things to come." She didn't have time to say another word before Walter cut her short with his built up passions, as he shouted out, "Hurry up Daredevils let's move out and regulate with relentlessness!" His fierce image was coming across like Uncle Bobby that would often have a look of worry and agitation with an uptight tenseness stretched across his face; which made everyone know that he was ready for this war of wits, because Uncle Bobby didn't play; he just won. So, they all charged off into the dark to save our careless hides, all ready to lead with their hearts while feeling Jesus and his mighty Angels inside their souls, with his believing and trusting Disciples still spreading the word for the world to hear. Rene and Charlie were posted on point, while Walter brought up the rear just in case Sacman had more surprises up his sadistic sleeves. No one spoke, or told about their rare escape; they just continued on their "pressure rising, saving mission", but you could see that their hearts were instilled with bloody fear intertwined with anger, while feeling like it was being pulled in two seemingly opposite directions. Everyone was following the downhill path that had numerous routes flagged by instinct and remembrance, because there were no street signs that said, "This Way, or Warning Kid Killer just ahead; Be Cautious!" Now, the young and eager rescuers had finally tracked their way back to where the tunnels separated, when Rene started sprinting away from the others like she was the Road Runner; but as she kicked up dust and took off, all you could hear instead of Beep, Beep was the sound of the dirt beneath her shoes flinging with the speed of the air making a more realistic resonance of the Earth's surface being lifted with every warranted step that she implanted into its secretive soil. She was hectically heading in our direction, with the familiarity of the caves layout, as if she were breaking the speed rules of this nightmarish path leading toward this "Hellish feign." The rest of the Daredevils tried to keep up with her velocity of vigor, but none was quicker than her track speed with genes from Blush, that rushed her legs to reach her destination at a pace of committed quickness; because there was no time for haste trying to save family that was destined for the House of Grace. "We've got to hurry, we've just got to hurry", were the thoughts running through their minds like they were in a movie consisting of a strong posse trying to bring back the bad guy who had fled the territory with tactical navigation; but God is good, God is great, because they were now hot on Sacman's trail. It was if their souls had been awakened with fright by God's might, as they observantly noticed overhead that there were bats hanging upside down stretching across the span of this enormous maze of ambush; where meeting their potential wouldn't be an easy task, but throughout all the horror they had witnessed, they were willing to deal with this Monster in their own way. It was like kids crying at the Circus from the unexpected that had suddenly surprised their one life to live; so in retaliation they had insanely lit the fuse when the room was full of hot air with erroneous, and unreliable mental processes; where they had somehow lost sight of what had brought us to this onetime major breakthrough of clarity and penance. My fast-paced Daredevils were heading toward the next level of melting insufferable barriers, while trying to evade seeping into a bottom line of finality. They were in quiet mode, as they approached the chamber of hearts twenty yards from where we were thought to be trapped, and like a last line of defense for trust; Kevin recognized their approach and gave them a bird call to show them that we were free like a Jay bird singing restitution rhythms that had a certain "can you feel me" spoken ideology. Walter and the group that went with him on their mission of "counting on resourcefulness", looked in bewilderment and fright at the bloodied chamber; as they suddenly stopped in their tracks, glaring and gawking at the worn out hearts staked to the chambers walls with illusions of cries and moans, verbalizing Sacman's vision. Dread was being drawn together like an Army gathering for war, while it reflected a creepy presence off the slight flickers of light coming from the chamber up ahead; like we were reaching for the far-fetches of stars that weren't quite shining in this Evil Doer's domain. We all quietly mustered in the shadows for a quick power-shift, before attempting to leap this final hurdle of blowing the whistle and charging to the finish line. It seemed that the answers were there all along, standing and staring down the middle of the road in which we traveled with its contented sighs that were sounding off; as if to say that our greatest problems lay within our eyes sight, and very close at hand. Lia started whispering covertly with her secretive, sneaky-sly female deceitfulness that ruled like a spunky Princess demanding that all hear and obey. As she looked around shamefully with wrong written across her face, she realized that her Pig Latin of provocative pulling the wool over the eyes had been found out; as she openly said, "The problem is within us! "We have to stick together; and no more splitting up unless our lives depend on it guys, because this Monster-Man is thwarting our challenges and making things extremely cloudy for us to see the big picture." "I'm not a gambler, but even I know that ten against one is better odds for any creature or being to withstand!" She was starting her next words, when I gently placed my hand over her mouth and said, "Shhhh…! Do you guys hear that?" It sounded like muffled wails of misery falling softly on the chilly atmosphere, causing major goose bumps to endure that sunken-in feeling in our guts, while the deranged cries were trying to detach and go their separate ways. We all immediately leaped toward the side, and lined our selves closer against the cave wall to sneakily advance forward toward the bellowing of aggravated assault and tortuous transformations that were taking a whirling spin through our minds asking, "Is this really what we signed up for?" Our group of tough and rugged Sleuths was keeping our enemy in the dark like saying hark who goes there, while not being seen like a warning in a detailed nightmare; where you remember everything, but the vital attentions that were meant to elude. There were strong words that wanted to be said about this enigma living against the law, but everyone kept silent; while feeling these fits of curiousness, where we knew in the end that ingenuity and strength would save the day. We were slowly approaching a volatile situation, and we could feel the wickedness of energy masking the air like a glove that didn't really fit, but was undoubtedly guilty; although little by little something extraordinary was showing us the way of toughing it out, and patiently waiting to see what God had planned. When we had finally reached that point where the light was the brightest; we were still hiding in the silvery dimness that was close to where the cave opened up into an even bigger set of caverns, which made us feel like Alice in Wonderland looking at a new world of mystery, and amazement. As my Daredevils and I furtively continued to edge our way into nestled and secure locations around this massive playground of deeper problems, it was at last presenting us with a newer side to Sacman's horrors with its unique undertaking of utter unusualness. We were all shocked to what our eyes were confirming to be the purest form of ungodliness that had been so naked to the eye; that even these facts of truth were in doubt with our own witness of clarity. It was the elusive Sacman standing before us, lurking in front of two cages that were dangling from the ceiling of the cave with an iron prod in his hand; poking and jabbing at the two children that were in each cage like he was herding cattle or provoking a wild beast in captivity. The panicked children trapped by this deranged madman seemed so terrified that their shadows even resembled ghosts, who were shook by the mere presence of such a barbaric zookeeper; where his captives lived with constant intimidation of his unknown. There was also a large antique table placed in the center of the room behind their present location, with a wind up record player sitting like a center piece in the middle of its sturdy structure. It was blaring out a tune like a well orchestrated symphony that was serving its purpose well; for music was said to be pure as promise, but we didn't know if this beast could be reached with sounds of sun rays that warms the Heavens with spirits that are free. Everyone was canvassing his intricate lair, while listening to the hypnotic melodies bouncing like a trampoline off the favorable acoustics of this hollow haven of classical times and ancient Anathemas (curses). It seemed that this iron-willed killer had a flair for music, as the melodic words spiraled throughout our minds like a cork screw unplugging an unlikely source of intoxication, because soberness was too sedate to handle the repercussions of this reality. Our concentrations zoned out and really started listening to the words of the song, as if the lyrics flew upward and vaulted over the minor hassles of acceptance with its mighty statements of importance. The expressions were like tunes of terror that were strong and memorable, as we closely listened to the singer flow his feelings diligently and determined to heed a sense of beware. As the words rang and sang against a new community, the singer said,

- I'm walking through a world of constant death and pain,
- Letting tragedy and revenge drive me hellishly insane;
- Reality is cruel, where the sky and oceans are blindingly blue,
- But what's a man to do, trying to withstand the test of times; where nothing seems true;
- I found truth to be in the heart of the soul,
- But after sacking so many, I still feel cold while growing old; never easy and slow;
- I'm well aware of this nightmare that I've been so calculatedly placed,
- Like before I transformed, I still wore that expressionless anger on my face; while setting the pace;
- Now, I'm lost and never can be found; and if I should drown in this river of sediment and hurt,
- Then I smother the hearts of little kids hiding under their covers, taking revenge for the memory of the evilness with intentions of traitorous works;
- Never could say goodbye, but can you remember every grain of sand that filtered through the hands of time,
- Still distraught from the failures, but with this pick-axe in my hand my future seems dim, with no satisfaction from the tears of crying;
- I just travel through this misery until its final and complete;

- But for forgiveness in my heart, it seems that it has skipped several beats, with boundless leaps;
- No love, no soul, no feelings of remorse, no pity, no chance for me to surrender of what I've been made,
- And as you enter this cave of invisible war; your confidence will fade, as you continue your accolades of counted days;
- Time is up, but the time is now; so throw your weapons to the ground and submit,
- Because a killer such as I, am ready for your advances; for I've already seen the answers to this test, and this is as far as you get!

The song had finally went into its eerie and sinister chorus; but to us the song was about a soulless man making his way in a world of weariness, while looking for clarity for an evil frame of mind. So, as we planned our next moves, our hearts were feeling touchable, and very much sympathetic to the children locked like pigeons in those hideous cages. It looked like bird bath slime had fallen beneath these iron cells of capture with the prisoners wailing arms looking like wings, as they weaved through the haze that surrounded the oversized cages. Sacman just stared at his prey up and down, as he sat on a Rooster's crest of a boulder fully entranced by the musical sounds of his liking; but he was definitely running the show like a Conductor of power, and prestige. He seemed satisfied with his works of wickedness, as he finally stood again and started walking toward a secluded cave room behind the cages with no worries coming across his shadowy, fictional, ghost like face. When he suddenly leaned to his left, and then to his right blowing out the candles that marked the doorway that were placed like crisscross patterns of light, as if to confuse the cleverness behind its sight. We noticed that most of the walls to this cavern were in a symmetrical slant throughout this oversized dungeon, which aided in giving plenty of hiding places for us to advance for a spectacular showdown. As Sacman was wondering off into the "darkness of seclusion", it seemed like he was leaving out bait in the center of this spooky, extraordinary cave for us new fish to come out and bite; and what he really wanted to do, but didn't realize was that we were looking at the basics on our agenda with smug resolve, charisma, and patience about our overview of "crush and capture". Things were being tipped-off in the favor of the home team, but everyone was pitching in with insightful questions and ideas, because as Daredevils we were surly not going to admit defeat. The scene was extremely questionable, but only in a traditional manner; because the Lord was continuously working his wonders, and with our faith growing with every trial; we knew we had unfinished business to attend to with our super-duper heroes of a crew. Now, at this instance of insanity, getting out alive was our maximum priority; yet we were feeling nervous and antsy, as we all huddled and exchanged tactics of survival while glancing over our shoulders to notice the huge, bloodied chopping block that resembled the smiles of death. It was sitting next to the large table, where the record player sat like a symbol of a madman obsessed with revenge, as it continuously rang out lyrics of dread and dyer needs for help. We had finally realized that this war was our truth of dare, and we had built up the gall to go through with our "take off and landing" excursion with no regrets, no remorse, and no nail biting Nay-Sayers to stop us from showing the world that the Daredevils were for real and fearless, when facing evil injustice; so can I get a witness?

CHAPTER V

Strength in Numbers

We had entered Sacman's "traveler's morgue of mischief", which was steadily increasing with hostility; as we sat in the dark feeling restless, but very anxious to make our next move. Everyone was crowded in like pack rats in a darkened nook, when Tammy pointed toward a large blood stained sack hanging on a spike outside the door where Sacman had relinquished his duties. Our emotions were twisted and being roughly abused like they were meant for running out of control from this nightmare that we weren't quite prepared to face. Jesus opened the doors to a powerful Heaven, as Lucifer had opened the gates to this bellowing Hell; but we were trying to keep death at bay, while trying to catch this impossible enemy of our fears. Walking with the Lord had our resolve brightly shining, while definitely stealing the stage from the monstrosities of this everyday maker of **Tom**foolery and livid lunacy that had us on the edge; but we were graciously being pulled toward infinite Heavenly love, and concern. Several of our schools of thought were being forthright and direct, like a War Council debating strategies that would lead a band of warriors to a successful outcome for a rejuvenation of our spirited youth that had been so tactically aged. We were integrating new ideas, while staring balefully at many options that had lively exchanges, but we were also trying to lead a careful comeback by settling down with a calm endurance; slightly yanking on the reins to our wild dreams that seemed never to be tamed, because Heaven had placed us here as "Adventurous Angels" to conquer the evilness in Death's power with our dedicated belief in the Son of God. We were cooking up new approaches in Hell's kitchen, while trying to eke out a miracle or two; sort of like stacking up building blocks and scratching unnecessary things off our list that weren't so realistic, but having the composition and attraction of a Heavy Weight Boxing promotion. Walter was our rock, as if he were "David" putting in a lot of man ours to defeat this Giant Ghoul, who was no fool to the rules of commitment and sacrifice; and although our minds were jumbled and confused, which made it harder to stay focused as we kept our slight advantage aflame with eager burning inquiries being asked by our testy congregation; the challenge had still been accepted. His quick wit and humor to lighten our moods were his strengths as a Prince in the playing fields of territorial terror; where whoever was most clever would never, ever be light as a feather when the weather is a storm with gushing winds being born. Walter had no second guess in the jest he had chosen as he decidedly said, "Err-hmmm! Guys; thought you weren't going to have any fun at this amusement park, huh?" "Well step right up, come one, come all to challenge this Phantom Traveler with a violent spirit of rage; because we aren't without purpose or rectified reason." "I know we're all having hunches that our plans could go up in smoke, while protecting our self imposed boundaries, but the things that were meant to be groove-like or slick, still calls for the simplest of prayers." "Our survival could be an iffy attempt, while seemingly being misplaced; but I see everyone has recognized that we're playing for our Brethrens seeds, and not metallic marbles being plucked from a circle of misbelieve." I really loved Walter's take-charge attitude of blasting through this day on our own terms, while waiting and watching for the final curtain to fall, but there was no applause for the bows being introduced like an incidental enticement of conceitedness, that was way too cocky to prevail. So, to make a long story short; we were urgently investigating alternatives with our strong-willed ways, like a wild feline tracking its prey from the trees, while living in a jungle of bounce-back; where in actuality it wasn't wild at all, but in plain view seemed like a God send that was doing the ground work from above and laying a path for the way back home. We had all decided for us boys to fan out and explore the surrounding caverns for other exits, but we were to meet back up and try to secure the room where Sacman had vanished to make sure our cover wasn't blown, before we attempted to free the frightened captives hanging like not-yet slaughtered animals; but knowing that their demise was growing near. Walter told Lil Tom and the girls to stay to the shadows, and wait for his signal before tackling this daring and dangerous "snag and grab" task, that would have made Harriet Tubman feel proud from such a riveting rescue attempt. The four of us; Walter, Charlie, Kevin and I broke off into two directions, paired up of course; because we stood a better chance at pulling off the impossible, while being somewhat camouflaged by the pitch-blackness of this Monsters domain. The moist air started to flow with a great amount of intensity and exactness that was surprisingly spurring us on to accomplish the things that we held so dear. Charlie paired up with Walter, as Kevin followed behind me like a lost puppy trying to get its nerve up to bark like a Rottweiler if things went awry; but truth be told he shouldn't be surprised if our last-minute plans fail, and we have to fight for a pass to freedom. As we separated like the swiftness from the swing of a sword; Kevin and I continued to sneak and creep, while ducking and weaving through the dark on a straight ahead course to an unfinished cavern, where a chance to change your life was yearning for redemption from the sins being solicited in its confounds of captivity. It didn't look like much work was being put into widening its exterior entrance, but we quickly noticed that there was a wooden gate hanging above its passage like in the chamber of hearts, which was causing us to examine the situation more closely. We looked back pure in heart, as two distinct shadows that were Walter and Charlie faded into the other cavern like the writings on the wall they had witnessed was actually erasable. Yet, there were no torches lit for the truth but the words was still there and full of life surrounding the insides of the chamber like a "will and a way" that had its own light and presence of foreseeing. As we reached to pull out our flashlights and place them on dim, I had to ask why didn't we believe and just follow the light; but we were lucky not to attract any attention from the brightness of brilliancy that was there, so why kid ourselves with the secrecy of conceal. We nervously peered inside this heart thumping horror of havoc, as we could plainly see a blood drenched chopping-block table made out of stone with shackles in the four corners of its square structure of gloom and agony. I immediately turned and looked at Kevin with serious and solemn eyes, while nodding my head in disappointment; but I was simultaneously pointing to the ground beneath us, to have him to watch out for any mechanisms that would release the gate to fall from its stationary position.

We had entered a chamber of underground bushwhacking, hidden beneath this big tent of brutal bombshells that only a breath-taking Buzzard could respect, and learn from its enemy all the deceit that lay comfortably on his offering dish. We were keenly attentive, and there certainly was no bickering amongst us; because Kevin didn't take my advice lightly, as we eased our way passed this table of torture while making our way toward some stone steps with droplets of finished blood. The trickled path that had been laid as stains of pain was leading a defined trail up this sullen staircase with streaks of dark red smeared across them like something had been dragged away with no struggle; only total submission. It seemed to us that Sacman was destroying the minds and bodies of the innocent before discarding of their corpses with no remorse, while being waged with an undeniable revenge; and if you had happen to come across meeting a treasured Wish Master, who could grant you those "keeping dreams alive" wishes; they would also be hesitant to face such evil in his grand scheme of things, without the trust and belief in our Savior. We had reached an intensity that couldn't be hidden anymore, yet we were nervously sweating fervency and passion; which was seeping through the atmosphere like the Sun, Moon, and the stars itchy triggering us to be centered with aim, and knowing which way we wanted to go. My pragmatic platoon and I were aware of our limitations, but we also knew that Sacman had broken many spirits that we could clearly hear like the sounds of no guarantees; and where hope always springs from the bottom then up, while trying to get past all the confusion; although silted and neglectful when entering into chaos. We gradually edged our way up the stone staircase feeling like we were on the winning path, while slowly cutting through suddenness and those large changes that comes to terms by accepting our deep reflections that were edgy with spontaneous actions; causing strong feelings that our restrictions were somehow self imposed. As we ventured forth, listening and toning our instincts; we were peeking behind the facts of life that was offering "chills and thrills" with a lot of ground to cover in this longtime coming of a brutal confrontation with this man made of ice cold stone; creatively carved to the bad of the bone. The Girls and Lil Tom were still on the lookout; but Kevin and I were confirming our insights of sadder days to come, while advancing up the bloodied staircase with so many twists of truth and twice as tricky of not understanding what was being done and said; which was quite similar of us not feeling as sure of ourselves as we would have liked. Sacman was far from a "laugh at me" Town Clown, and the evidence he left behind proved that he had incorporated a strong manner, as he weathered Life's storms that would eventually tumble into his lap; for no umbrella, can support or protect a man from the realness of the **"Reign"**! Somehow, he still stood like a Tiger slightly crouched in the brush, ready to pounce with a mouth-watering vengeance of a starved Barbarian looking to single-handedly conquer the world, and all those who have stolen his love and humility. Kevin had passed me on the staircase, as if his pace was frantic and five steps ahead; while it seemed to me that he was certainly trying to maintain his fears, because we knew that only a few were chosen. As we neared the top of the staircase covered with bushes and brush, he had a scared-looking intimidation across his face as he nervously swallowed; and then reached up with both hands to give the intertwined rummage a good heave-ho, so we could see if so; that this was our course. When Evil instantly appeared like a trip hammer; as the covering of bushes swung open and upward faster than Buccaneers to bones that showed the realities inside, but we were wide-eyed and mystified by where the secret entrance had lead us to; but not satisfied! Now, scared and shocked our block heads were on a swivel; pivoting and peeking out of the opening like a zoomed-lens telescope doing no harm, with surveillance and transparency of this secluded area. I said, "Kev, he's the Harry Houdini of surprises man!" "Look, it's the same cemetery we came through earlier before we found his secret lair!" Kevin boastfully responded with, "No sweat cuz!" "Now we have another way of escaping from him if we're put in a difficult position, only leaving different possibilities for our retaliation of rapid-fire ideas to aggressively counter his next moves." Our adventuresome nature was emerging with good sense that was lifting our awareness to higher levels as to what could happen, while we carefully moved back down the staircase eager to give the other Daredevils details on our successful recon mission that had been long overdue. Meanwhile, Charlie and Walter were ready to go toe-to-toe, and blow for blow as the exhilarating rounds counted down with this Master of Mystique that had a crook's method of moving about, and then suddenly disappearing without having any magical powers. He unquestionably had a reflective mental process that was absolutely making him look like he was sitting on a High Horse, as he leered down on the incredibly foolish and awkward ones that was too lazy to meet his challenge of solving the encrypted handwritings that he had left on the colorful gyrations of graffiti plastered on the walls in the chamber that my fellow Daredevils had barely escaped. There was no turning away, as the two cautiously watched their steps while easing into a suspicious cavern that was very well lit, but had black coals spread all over the floor surface with a Comet's cloud mist from a wonderful waterfall; that to their eyes looked vibrantly illustrious, but dangerous with its heavy raindrop sounds smashing to the terrain far below. The dull clangs and bangs of rapid pitter-patter seemed to have the strength of a Samson like storm that had the right to get even by smashing violently against the rocks beneath its massive force, sounding like a Marching Band performing a cadence for a well in tuned audience with its percussion section having the musicians step heavily across the layered surface as if to say, "I can hear you, and I can see you!" "So, watch your step, or be a victim in this world of fears and sinister anticipations." They were ready for life, and all its demands as they silently made their way to the edge of the large cliff; which was horizontally spread, and had them both looking in amazement from the darkness that the waterfall projected from its depths all the way to the top, where they stood with one hand across their foreheads, as if this would enhance their curiosity of view. Charlie with a sudden sigh of relief said "Looks like a dead end, my fearless friend!" In All, and actuality his words sounded like a Revival shout of amen, and Thank God that they didn't have an encounter with this Seeker with the deepest, and deadliest secrets; which only left them with definite differences of opinion regarding their potential risks, that had begun like a race through their minds searching for the truth. Walter rapidly responded with the bold manners of his persistence by saying, "This isn't the way God meant for the world to be!" Which alarmingly shook and woke up Charlie's faith, that had seemingly took a short nap; as he now listened up closely to Sir Walter's words that felt like a vicious uppercut that had ultimately rattled his insides to release "the what is more Salvation", that could sense the power thrusting their souls as they yearned for righteousness. He continued with, "Peace give us strength, and comfort while knowing that we desperately want to change, and although these days are growing into a haze of rage and at its best it will be nothing, compared to our chance at triumph in this rude awakening of an Aftermath." "So, keep your cool and walk with wishful steps Charlie, because we have a lot of things to consider and if we make an "all out effort", Sacman's terrible retributions would seem like they were meant to erode, crumble, and tumble downhill at a perilous plunge." Charlie was intently observing what was happening while being preached, but he was feeling overloaded as he was now making steps to get back on track; and at the same time letting go of all his fears. He was alert and on deck with a serious salute of approval, as he gently reached out and patted Walter on his shoulder, while he convincingly said, "Let's tear-off into this Maniac's madness like a black box of boom-shaka-laka; now we got you!" "Where this horrible monster will have to pick up and go with a referral to see a doctor for being a kid stalker; and Walter my bro, I don't mean to sound so uppity and proper!" Walter readily replied, "I got you, Mr. Head Knocker of being smarter than the average bear, I got you even if Father Time after many years leaves you with no hair on your head that's shaped like a pear!" They both smirked and laughed at their little child like rhymes, as they wrapped their arms around each other's shoulder, and faintly faded across the obscure flooring of coal; as they finally made their way back toward the other Daredevils to fulfill their dedicated Destinies. They were alert and alive like an arrow crossing through a heart of love, to feel that irresistible influence from the specialness of affection, as they reached the cavern entrance; where they immediately noticed two shadows moving in concealment against the darkness of the "to be next to" walls, doing an awful job of not to be seen. They traveled as troubled young men, while feeling that they could never be wrong as they cautiously nudged forward trying to get a better view of these critical circumstances. When Charlie came to a "Hawk hazard halt", and let out a whispering Birdcall that was only familiar in pattern to a true Daredevil with "buckle up for the ride awareness", by having the characteristics of a clever clue collector to guide them, while implementing a stronger communication system; because only God knew where they go, as they maintained this course of extreme danger. Kevin was alert like a Rabbit feeding, with both eyes taking over the sureness of sensitive surveillance, when the hooty-hoo call rolled across his obsolete observance like a 911 distress, as his ears puckered up toward the skies letting Heaven know he was listening; I mean really listening! It was one of those calls where the caller squalls all the information to the responder, who really shouldn't have mixed feelings, but even with faith it's anybody's game if you're paying detailed attention, but not having a true commitment to the strength of the **Word**! Kevin reached in his knapsack and grabbed his flashlight, blinking three quick red flashes toward the direction of the discreet call; similar to a can attached to another, with that vibrating string carrying a ring, ring with the words of "I'm calling to see if we really have air beneath our wings, so please answer me, because this dream of a crooked scheme is ready to bring this so-called fanatical King of feigns to his knees; deposed of ruling anything!" Charlie and Walter had received their confirmation that it was us cloaked by the gloom of the cave walls, as they responded like a bird ready to fly, with a "coo-coo" to let us know they would be joining us soon, but we all knew that our mission was more than anyone wanted, and we had a long way to go under the absence of jubilation from the Sun lit skies. The two of them zipped through this maze of meet us at the far end from a delightful place in Frankenstein's lab, while being covert and rough like a snake's slither as they neared our position through Sacman's devilish actions of consequence, and chance that left a smell and reek of flesh and blood. The howl of the wind had wandered into his domain once again blowing through the "spirits within" caverns while portraying menacing sounds; but the moment seemed to take over the heavy burdens with its compressed feelings of pressure, yet we were prepared to root out the real cause of our minority changes of minds, because we were children bred for action and justification willing to figure out how to prevail upon these disagreeable tasks of the impossible. Charlie was juggling through the shadows like a night walker with impressive alternating skills, who was born to blend in with the downcast of this dreary habitation, as he jumped head first into our laps saying, "Anybody want a soda to wash down that bag of terror, because my throat has a knot tied around it like a non-caring noose on a stuck out neck trying to get a quick look at the near future." Walter was five steps behind him, but more suave and smooth with his approach looking like a Cheetah in a white wife-beater that was toned, rippled, and chiseled like a sculpture of Zeus with a thunderbolt of order and fate. Now, throughout all the stories of his myth, it was said that his pose of power resembled a posture of pure luck, but Walter made it seem like he was gracing this living darkness that surrounded our full circle of dreams with a convincing Champion construction of heart and soul. He suddenly came to a complete stop as he drew nearer, and wildly placed his hands in a rare ray of light that was beaming from above, as if it were a sign of "where there's always darkness, there will always be light!" Walter immediately connected his hands and started making different projections of animals that boldly bounced off the unappreciative cave walls and although his crazy classroom shenanigans was brief, it had the brilliance of a classic film room animation session that was poor in taste, yet rich in character and spiritedness that let us know; that all was not lost. When he had finished his framework of a Festival, he hurriedly made his entrance which seemed exhausting and ridiculous for the present moment, but he made his actions seem like he was wrongly convicted of "selfish broken embraces". He had a stockpiled smile, with his eyebrows arched high, as if curious was sitting on the summit of notable times; when he slightly gasped while awaiting our judgment, as he said, "What's wrong with a little humor in the face of danger?" "Loosen up guys, because you never know what's going to happen next, but wisdom and imagination is on our side." "So, don't be overly concerned with the mixed messages I'm sending, because we've accomplished more than any solitary Hunter, with no amusement for the thrill of the game of "who's going to make the first move." Before anyone had time to respond to Walter's arrogant and touchy rant of justification, I attentively noticed that the children in the cages were clinging to the bottom of their "secluded spots" of a jail; where nail biting and pacing would have been useless against the anger, and lust for vengeance that held this mysterious man captive in his own little world, just like his frightened prisoners that he displayed; as if he was drawing a line between freedom and the thought of nowhere else to go. My well polished observance had granted me a chance to think before blurting out words that could be detrimental towards our faith; which was only growing stronger, even though Walter was acting shamelessly bold, it was his gung-ho way of reckless brave heartedness that was truly needed in the crowning points to come. God had given us unity and **strength in numbers,** but we were caught between unforeseeable circumstances while trying to make our way, and being left with only one way to start this war of wit and resiliency. So, I calmly said, "The more the merrier fellas!" "I see out of menace comes retaliation, and we'll need the type of luck that a Leprechaun has clamped between his butt cheeks; lined with a four leaf clover carrying a penny on heads while dragging a Rabbit's foot to climb out of the crack of this mess!" "Even if we confidently lay it all on the table like a trumped playing card incased with an angrily thrown club that's ready to pulverize the man we don't know from Adam; it's going to be hard to overcome." "Are you ready Daredevils, let's go!" Everyone nodded in agreeing alliance, as we all slapped hands in relief and belief in my speech, while single file lining ourselves against the shadows of the wall ready to get this deadly incursion underway. We calculatedly inched our way closer to where this villain had gone astray, through the darkened doorway, while still being able to hear the music play with a tune of mayhem for our listening pleasure. Kevin and Charlie slid and hid to the left of the door, while Walter and I climbed the rock structure above its entrance; leaving Walter crouching overhead to pounce on the Giant if he happened to come out, as I slyly jumped to the right of this dark "come right in" open invitation, of only enter if you dare type of free-will corridor. All of us were drawing out our weapons and getting ready to tee-off, while being well equipped for this advised against mission of warfare; because we knew that Sacman was unpredictable like a territorial Hippopotamus, but somehow we couldn't ignore his lurking in the dark like antics that had our whole community in despair. Charlie was ready like set, go was to slow; as he kept his numb-chucks cocked back like a sledge hammer, as Kevin was winding up his mid-shovel like he were Hank Aaron ready to take a swing at changing the world in a place far beyond change. Walter was still sitting like a Tom Cat on a fence above the entrance with his blow gun loaded and ready to deploy, as he started waving it back and forth to signal Lil Tom, who was across the way with the girls still hidden in the shadows awaiting for their chance to make the world a better place with no more prisons and unnecessary deaths. So, he was automatically keeping a sharp eye on our progression, while patiently waiting for the signal to save "these tales of woe", "the oh-no", and "say it can't be so"; "Traumatized kids that were sitting with these tortures of time, and their loneliest of visions; while Devil stepping their demise on this Mad Man's Death row!" Our strategy seemed to be flourishing, as I reached and grabbed a car flare from my crowded back-pack of tricks, while using my knees to hug tightly to the outside entrance wall with my nightstick in one hand, and the

"Wake up, wake up Rumple-stilt-skin" burst of blaze in the other; where I had a little too much emotional position to be permissive or discreet, because enough was finally enough. Walter looked down at me with a final go ahead nod, to spark the flames of this thought to be last stand war; and even though it was an out dated communication system, it still got our pivotal points across. Now, please beware because some actions were meant to take part in a message of twist, when you're wheeling and dealing in the depths of punishment; where it seemed like pleasure was this Lunatic's wish. My hands were shaking like the hips on a Hula Dancer, as I ghastly glanced inside the darkness of the room, when I finally got the gall to break the flare for illumination; tossing it quickly inside like a rugged roll of the dice that looked much more clearly than a seven, or eleven winner that takes it all. I remember my Father used to say, "You win some, and you lose some"; but today these old and inspiring hand me downs, and sit down occasions with my Aunty slicing me a piece of cake with chocolate icing, really had me seeing victory plain as the uncertain days that lie ahead. Oh yes, Loretta had a warmth about her that instantly let you know that love and family goes forever, but only if thy inner self is true against betrayal and deceit; graciously leaving forgiveness to be your choice of acceptance. My thoughts of Heavenly dreams had left me with a sense of calmness, because I could see the real in Cil's eyes before this storm had come; and as I looked into this lit up room that resembled a ceremonial fire releasing Sunlit spirits from a "binged filled bottle", there was a chaotic cadence of drumming that was blaring an alarm for us to charge! We waited with fear and anticipation for this Monster to run out into the arms of our unbreakable justice; but Sacman seemed to be silhouetting his background from a shady shadow into simmering smoke. It could have been really stupid, or just really smart, but these faint flickers of unexplained discoveries were causing clouds of confusion to swirl around the chilly, damp air; yet, there was no response when we had stepped up to the plate, thinking we had scored a home run; but our immediate instincts were to run! Run Daredevils run! The sinister of this arena had us thinking about death lurking, while on the verge of completing our goals and unselfishly responding to others needs, as they tamely lay like pets in quarantined cages with a mist of afterglow of here, and now. There was no movement within Sacman's sanctuary, and time had lapsed at a "see what happens" snail's pace; but even time seemed like countless reasons for our true feeling of fear to stand up in this hair-raising situation that was leading us to a new beginning, to an end. I had finally caught my breath from all of the excitement, when I suddenly decided to take a gander for this Fish-Lander of a fool; even if it meant losing my coconut of a head while sitting atop of a palm tree on a desolate Island of dread, trying to get a peek at this predator communicating savage threats with his recent efforts of escaping Hell in those weighted down shoes. The violent flames of this noted nightmare had had its chance at the power for the days, while getting older from the truth that hurts; but the light that shined within this miserable room of doom was still very bright, and hard to deny, as I scanned the interior for any activity; but there was none. There was also no sign of this "stumbled upon" heart breaker and taker of humbled happiness that had us buzzing about with silent screams and shouts, while hot-footing it for definitive answers to our questions of, "why"? I quickly gave everyone the signal of clear; vividly letting my fellow Daredevils know that "the Boogey Man" was nowhere to be found, as if he had left his legacy of torture and bitterness behind; as a trail for us to follow. Kevin and Charlie rapidly followed the brilliance of my bold break-in, as Walter still sat like a Praying Mantis, but in a cooler manner while scanning the cavern with caution lights flashing in overdrive through his protective military mindset. Sacman's headquarters was neat and tidy; which was fascinating to our curious eyes, because we were expecting Ungodly sights; but there was only a bed made of wooden crates with a large mattress stretched across its hardened support, with a table made out of a huge piece of coal displaying a picture of a boy with a smile that spanned from ear to ear. In the corner of this "spick and span", Peter Pan disappearance of like a pebble from the hand of a lost room, that had been found as if given away; sat a brilliant made bookcase with hundreds of books lining its knowledge holding shelves as if a message was left behind saying, "I'm more than what you thought, or even dared to dream about; I'm the heartless Sacman!" We were scared to touch anything in the room, but our eyes were our hands; and the constant thought of booby traps patiently halted our sneak attack while following this "Trail of Tears" like a Cherokee, but being too absorbed in our own thoughts; where the possibilities of a set-up never even crossed our confused and tripped up minds. The flare had finally sizzled and fizzled out, causing total darkness once again; but we instantly crouched low to the floor in case we were bum rushed by this Hell raiser of Heathenness. Charlie was keeping his eyes peeled on the doorway, when something suddenly drew his attention back toward the "bridge for tomorrow" bookcase that was uneasily causing a panic to infiltrate his confidence of capturing the man we had been asking to eagerly meet. His eyes grew wide as if he were crossing a dangerous game of "leap and seek"; where the shock of the sudden surge had him really feeling the cold breeze from this Executioner's song that was blaring in the back drafts of this bottomless pit of pain. He had noticed that there was a shiver of light reflecting from a crack under the bottom of the bookcase shining secretively from the other side of its scholarly frame. When without hesitation he shouted, "It's a trap! It's a trap, run guys like a rocket!" For he knew to escape this seemingly "sand box trap"; that we would have to jettison toward the planet between Mars and Saturn, while finally reaching the outskirts of Jupiter the fifth junction from the Sun; so he pleaded with us, "Please my Daredevils run!" We didn't hesitate to ask any questions; we just all took off like a sprinter hearing the Starter's pistol to a race, with fanning smoke whisking past us, like a pie toward the face. As we reached the entrance to the door with our weapons drawn like they were chiming for a confrontation from retreat, we could feel the lightness in our feet, walking on the wind like rising water reacting to the heat. We exited the doorway like Norway was our way, with frozen ice straddled on our backs; but we felt like a feign escaping from un-forgiveness that was fervently seeping from the rise in the cracks. Walter was mightily shaken from his pose of prestige, as if his knees wouldn't buckle or bend; but he was keeping a lock down lookout for any suspicious activities throughout the cavern, so this "I've got to get out of here" outburst had him stunned from the sureness of sin. The children being held in the cages had heard the commotion of our fearful retreat, and started to scream for our help; and like ripe fruit on a tree for the picking, they were ready to be taken home; but with the issues we were working through, their sense of "Home" was like an unforeseeable destination for any of us to offer. Walter's attentions had been striving to win, but the suddenness of this distraction while confronting our temptations had left a major gap in our dealings with disguise; and our immature plans seemed to be going up in smoke like a cloudburst of blameless rain. It was as if hearing a Ghost Story for the first time, that was wandering through our dreams and had actually been transformed into reality; where our imaginations were running wild with déjà vu, while recalling to mind those cold night sweats of the terror that really exists in these "carry-on's" of Hell! When like a flash of lightning coming from out of the skies of "surprising discoveries", there was a thunderous warning of reprisal that echoed through the caverns; instantly circling around our frightened and over achieving bodies that were hesitantly headed off to a fight, while watching our heads and hinds; but ended up capturing the braced Faith in our "time after time" minds. Walter quickly looked toward Lil Tom and his Rescue Team that was awaiting this King of the Damned; and as they lay in defense, he noticed a large shadowy figure standing in the center of the cavern entrance right beside their hidden position; looking like a Mythical Hunter with the presence of a hideous monster with miles of strange and unique demeanor; as he leaned forward out of the darkness, to prey. He instantly wanted to scream out to warn our unsuspecting soldiers that were equipped, but had no clue; but Thank God he was interrupted by the captive's wails bouncing off the surrounding walls, that was burning at his efforts of speech like old flames in the prevailing winds of fate and good fortune; which still left us with a slight advantage of surprise. Now, as this angered Warden with fear of escape came forward emotionally like the "Tears of the Sun", and the "Menace of the Moon"; his emergence was finally noticed by our startled and much too curious Heroes that seemed to be unimpressed by his stature; and from the darkness of their haven they eyed this Giant impolitely as if to say, "Who's afraid of the Big Bad **Wolfe**!" The tensions that we were all feeling were the uneasiness of the unthinking, but extremely immense; and for me being who I was, caused instant panic to over flood my military blood, when the hard way seemed to be the only way, as I started to run. My direction of flight couldn't have been more unsafe, but under his roof there were no strangleholds on "The Greatest Story Ever Told"; as I headed toward the Timeless table with the record player still shoveling out sinister lyrics of things being six feet deep; where I Chicken Little was crossing this madness of mercy through the middle of the street. Sacman had seen my movements as aggressive bursts of attack, periodically checking over his back; as he stood there like a Mighty Oak holding his ground like a Pitcher on a mound trying to judge the distance of a strike-down with his evil antics swirling through the air; around and around! I could see the look in his never surrender eyes, where there was no age; yet they showed the agony that flowed like tragic waves of pain, and untold numbers of disappointing heart ache that seemed like they could never, ever mend. The stand-stills of Time had my six-sense right on target with a whole new light that had been shown like an iridescent stone flashing all the false clues; as if barking up the wrong tree had finally realized that a stronger force stood above us, and now while being visible; we were making headway toward our coveted chaos that we had created by intruding on this mysterious region that Sacman had labeled as perpetual punishment. His Hell bound actions were under control and nonchalant, as he slowly held up his left hand with a bloodied heart still dripping those large incarcerated cries onto the floor, like muddied waters slowly irrigating into the equation of trying to fill in the blanks; but being very difficult to access the solution of promise with his built-in blood lust, while he stood sturdily on the sensitivities of solid ground. The finish line markers had been set, as Sacman violently swung his right hand through the air wielding his pick-axe and lunging forward to his knees, spiking his impressive symbol of mystique forcefully into the "don't get your hands dirty" soil lying beneath his Gorilla stance of an entrance. He was suspenseful and surreal, as he raised his head to look up at us with a broad monstrous grin carved into his face like a Jack O Lantern, while his lips shivered from anger and the strain of bracing a silver whistle between them; as if fury was his flag's color of war. We could actually define his furious demeanor, by his dedicated and direr efforts to produce a sound, but as he clinched tensely and tight nothing could be heard except the impatient winds hurling through the chamber like a superstitious Mocking Bird, with a silence for words. After moments of realizing what was transpiring right before our eyes, I immediately started thinking to myself of where I had seen someone blowing a whistle that chirped no communication of comprehend. The tears of this absent Sun was dripping a flaming resolve of scorching cinematic awareness, as Dawn had been placed upon me; when I fantastically found the answer that was within reach of my remembrance, as I thought of our next door neighbor Mr. Jacobs and the dog whistle he used for training his obedient Doberman Pinschers. I was now navigating a ship with black sails through these breaks of waves that were problematic, where Hen house noises from an encounter with a Fox had knocked off the socks of my crew standing nearby in silence by the dread dug into the docks. Yet, by faith we knew that God was our Lead with wise and willing love, but we knew that time was of the essence; so we couldn't waste a second of contemplating or waiting for this large Game player of this sporting competition to make his next move. Our decisions were getting harder as this stealth-like cat, for who we knew, was seeing red; which happened to be the realness of fake, because from out of the distance we started to hear the oncoming echoes of belligerent barking and yapping charging from the blackened cavern with the bloodied steps. Certainly the not so rosy smell of this torture chamber had brought us a sudden reek of "ambush and too late tendencies of tenaciousness"; but was still bound to not fade away with its terrifying rotating roulettes, where the bets were set at an unfinished level of fanatical fun. As the dedicated patience of our amazing group had been awakened to the true feelings of Death, we all suddenly turned with anticipation toward the chambers narrow opening; when the appearance of hideous, yellow eyes with a "get at us" glare was charging our lonesome location at atomic speed. The aged wrinkles of instance was moving in with a blur so benevolent, that the darkness from which it came seemed to overshadow its courage to set things right. We could now see that it was the wire-haired rovers that we had encountered near the cemetery, who was approaching with a not so silent arrival of attack; while exuding their resilience like confidence were their alliance; of who had who's backs. Even though this running Brook of major knowledge had Walter still sitting on his perch above Sacman's "Room of Illusion, and Confusion", he was relentless with his sharpness in mentality, as he yelled uninterruptedly with free will, "Scram Daredevils, and demolish this Demon of Darkness; and yes, life or death is our only option at victory!" As his orders had been shouted and conveyed for us to react; Kevin, Charlie, and I all started running in different directions while summoning our strengths of strategy to propel us forward with no back-steps from the heavy-weighted blows in this long bout of confirming our resolve; but our fear was like a leaf on a tree limb; trembling its dispensing despair. We were trying to funnel these fugitive feelings through a positive light that was unusually bright; however never losing sight while being forced to hold forth what's true and right. Meanwhile, Tom and the girls were still waiting on Walter to give the command for them to evacuate their position in these so entrusting shadows; which was actually thought to be our last ace in the hole, and final chance at gaining the upper hand. When like a Great dog of "Under Dog status", Streak came from behind Sacman sprinting like an unbreakable force of loyalty and fearlessness, with agreeable dog complaints from the sadistic actions that this monster displayed. He jumped with the might of Zodiac foretelling the stars, as if he were jumping over the Moon; plus with the velocity of his unfriendly determination to protect, he startled Sacman as he knelt in his crouched stance. One could even say, that Harlequin Romance couldn't have written a better silhouette, when these two started to Tango for their dance; which featured Crazed Killer versus Canine with a teetered two-step that enriched their battle on this Dog Day Afternoon. As Streak landed brilliantly on all fours, it seemed that his presence had made the enemy feel the acute power of family, friends, and loyal faithfulness with his formidable advance. Sacman's demeanor was simmering with rage and shock by this rude interruption while his temperament grew madder by the minute; but his vengeful concentrations were as a military tit for a tat, where witnessing his valor of a villain having prominence; was as strategic as being out of his right mind. In all honesty, it seemed like this clever twister of retreating reactions was giving his Blood Hounds the command to attack, bark, and bite; while having a confident celebration, where he knew some men would die from the fright. Their deadly manners that were responsible for the rhetoric of revenge would leave a malicious mark of might in the wounds of these "Times of Beware"; where terror of becoming his prisoners could be fatal like a huge mistake in this rock-hard "**Scare**" of chance and dare! These events were unfolding quickly as the lead dog made his way toward our direction of escape, and like a big bully on the block he looked larger, stronger, and more dedicated to his loved one than the others. Streak responded with the swiftness of a real and ambitious walker of the bridge; like he was connected to both sides, but knew where his loyalties were accepted as if he were extravagant art hanging from a flawless wall with spectacular visions of admiration and awe. Watchfulness was his wager of capability and compassion, as he came running across the chamber to attack this hideous dog out in front of the pack that stalked like an intelligent, but extremely over convinced prince of "putting it down". He had come to our rescue faithfully, and without a hint of hesitation, as he lit into this under nourished but massive Mutt like a Cassius Clay of canine catastrophe; except he was mauling like a Bear and being fearless like a Prayer as we asked ourselves, "What is more than a ***Man's Best Friend***?" The other feeble looking and neglected scavengers were shocked by Streaks relentless ferociousness that they started back pedaling from where they had entered like "Cool Cats who wanted none of that"; and as they witnessed the demolishing of their leader, their boldness quietly transformed into a Magicians code of disappear. Their barks weren't as boisterous as before, but now seemed like whimpers of surrender as Streak had this "pitiful challenger for protection" gripped by the neck with his powerful lock-down, while finally slinging his dauntless dead-beat body across the cavern like a paper weight champ.

It wasn't even a challenge, as this wild lead dog landed and rolled into a humiliating stance as he let out an agonizing wail of defeat while retreating back through the Torture Chamber with his tail tucked between his legs with the rest of his scared and terrified entourage following close behind. Kevin and I were the closest to their shameful and speedy exit, when we started taking steps like we were walking through the Valley of Death to end this irritating intrusion; but I could feel that trouble would eventually find us again, before we could even have a chance to stop and think about a counter-attack of our own. We both ran toward the gate hanging above the death ridden chamber, where the dogs had cowardly dispersed into the "Darkness of Dishonor" with a midnight Teller of lengthy stories patrolling its outskirts, as it attentively wrote down this epic encounter of right and wrong like composing those words that carry a heavy weight on our minds. The thoughts of having our hearts toppled and taken had Kevin instantly starting to climb the cave wall around the entrance like the excitement and adrenaline had caressed his liveliness of being; while systematically and effortlessly pushing him toward the top, where brief upturns was being extended for honor and pride. He pulled out his Boy's Scout knife, as if to slice a piece of the pie as he excitedly started carving and cutting away at the hardened rope that was holding this bush-whacking tactic of hatching a plot for revenge; when suddenly its extended gates of trapped in jeopardy came hammering in full force into a downward freefall, and as clear as a waterfall pounding the Earth below, it loudly whispered; "I had to let go!" I wasn't positive that the invaders had truly gotten the message that we were trying to send, so I grabbed a few Baby TNT's from my supply while keeping a close eye on Sacman's activities; but it was a mystery why he was still squatting down low to the comforts of the cave ground like an Offensive Lineman waiting for the play to develop. I instinctively lit the wicks on the TNT's, and several Jumping Jack Flashes while still feeling confused as I eagerly tossed them through the wooden gate that was separating hard lessons to learn, from the odd notions that we still had a chance to survive. For some reason it seemed that we were suffering from broken relationships that had been shattered by conflict and petty insecurities about judging others and their mental instabilities; but towards the end, was just a Family issue. Yet, the inside of the cavern was now shedding light on the outcome of the question "could we change the future?" with no strings attached, but by and by we all knew we had to do something. We felt grateful that Jesus was walking with us while this end to an adventure was getting underway, where we were having strong imaginations of resolve, but like in most battles mercy doesn't exist. The dogs had been cut off from their "wine and dine state of minds", and our focus was currently jumping over fences but at the same time trying to reach for creative touches that would seal our victory as we moved to this soulful beat of terror and panic. Sacman finally stood up angry and abandoned, as if he was ready to do some damage like a medieval adventurer searching to accept some good luck that had a consuming rage of an inferno that was burning his soul, while him not being aware of it. He immediately headed in our direction, as Streak observantly turned around proudly from his accomplishments and started a charge toward him that a Calvary would state as "heroic and honorable" in any soldier's range of view, while courageously looking out of his protective eyes. As Streak moved in swiftly he was like a streak of light, a streak of luck, and a streak of brilliance trying to intercept Sacman's passage of prejudice that was planted like a poppy seed where high was low, and its anchor was sunken into obscurity that even a storm of steadfast couldn't resist the look in an Angel's eyes. Our dynamic dog leaped dramatically into the air as if he could soar from his aggressive attack mode like brilliant stars that suddenly explode, but with the knowledge and not a fear in the world, while pulling pieces of loss for words from the cold and poetically being showed as a Campion stepping over the barriers that stood so tall before him. Sacman reactively swung with all his might to deflect the onslaught from our canine comrade, who was glad to put his life on the line to knock off this villain of violence and volition. Streak was out on a limb that was ready to collapse, as Sacman's razor sharp pick-axe connected with his front right torso simultaneously, when his virulent bite to this Monster's neck was rudely interrupted by this Man made of Wolf and Warrior with an "even the score" swing that was trying to dig deep into bones and flesh. Streak let out an undeniable cry of pain and fright, as his Butcher of an assault was harshly cut down; and if he had judged more incorrectly, his head would have been lopped off on this "Mad Museum's" ground like a Hunter's trophy stuffed on a mount. Sacman was motivated and now moving in for the kill, as Streak lay on the cold cavern floor helpless; whining and panting softly, but awfully rapid from his thought to be mortal inflicted wound. Instantly, Walter's voice had finally come back to life as he shouted out the words that rang out like a melodrama; when he said, "Martin Luther King!" which was our honored code for "freedom" letting Lil Tom and the Girls know to save the children at all costs that were being put on display and dressed neatly in their long white robes while sitting in this solitary with its isolation slowly killing their will to escape. Sacman stopped dead in his tracks as he was about to deliver the final blow to Streak; when he suddenly looked up at Walter with a cold, dim, and grim stare where he no longer looked wild, but very much self-reliant and possessing a new found intensity which tipped the weighted scales of "pissed off!" Sir Walter seen this hideous Henchman giving him a good look like a Death Stare; as he came swiftly off his high perch, performing a surfboard stunt with a piece of Tidal wave timber that was laid like an Ark in the rubble structure of reckoning above the entrance to Sacman's lair; like a rockslide or stoning had just occurred. He cried out, "Surfs up of a sacrifice baby, Hang ten", as the plank of wood came rumbling down the steep face of the cave giving off a snake like hiss from the pebbles of stone scraping the bottom of this make-shift snowboard; but there was no snow, only a reluctance to go, that made this ship flow like the waves couldn't stop this magnificent show of "Do you really know?" When his motions of an Ocean eventually came to a halt after sliding for what seemed forever and a long-shot; Walter stepped off the reliable stand-up board in a full sprint, calling out for his Daredevils to detach rather than react to the scenario that had briskly thrown our "at the end of the tunnel" counter maneuvers over a steep cliff, simmering and boiling like a pot of "Get Back" that had a specific knack of a conjuring brew with Rat tails and Bat wings. So, it seemed as if the Graces of God had welcomed us into this Zoo of anything, with new beginnings that were opposed to what-cha-ma-call-its and packed away fat laced shoe strings that were never meant to be tied. We were revealing our real hearts that could play any song, as we proficiently triggered them to beat one heart beat at a time; as we were now curiously divided, but focused on expanding like a boundary line getting to the finish line; bit by bit. I say, "Lenient Listener's did you hear those bellows of woes dragging against those rugged walls while exploiting young souls, tortuously held and exposed; but almost shut off from the real facets of life. Charlie screamed out with a powerful and to the point effect that warranted all attention as he said, "Run toward the waterfalls like fugitives on the lam, or stand there and pose like Piñatas excepting a beating of reprieve; for you have seen this Judge." "I only pray my Brothers and Sisters that this moment is unforgotten, because memory is emotional and spiritual but at the same time it is your friend, so follow it to the end!" We all were forging ahead to the fullest of seek, and if a peek was accepted, then thank you God for a glance of our direction if only for a limited time, because Sacman was blocking our true exit legally; for we were trespassing and whether he be "Head Hunting" or being on a "Heart Pursuit", he was bent out of shape and his rage was ravaging with revenge. As my Soldiers of Morning Glory entered this well lit, coal floored cavern like we were flagging down a Taxi on the busiest time of the day with crucial and vital echoes screaming, "Stop!", "Stop!"; but instead they just kept passing by like our chance for a blessing wasn't intended to be answered. Sacman was strong and ever standing while ruling his domain like Sitting Bull's territory, where living in denial was like falling from a sky that seemed like a magnificent obsession of an important truth that could only be heard by those willing to heed with limited options, while trying to reach that Almighty Kingdom; as I speak for home, and only home is my destination. He ruled like a Czar in pursuit of a stolen car while having a child lost forever where there was no testimony for tomorrow, but I could hear a slight round of applause that was only meant for us luckily making it thus far. We were scraping the roughness of regret off the surface of our charred and challenged lips, from that unimpressive Kiss of Death that had us curiously looking toward the stars and light years beyond Mars. My young Daredevil's were all wondering why Charlie wanted us to flee through this particular chamber, but as we all entered this spacious finality of a Spook story that had us wandering, we were steadily reaching out with hands of hope for help; but not knowing what would happen next. It seemed that we were only doing what was natural, as we continued to run like prey while nervously looking down at the black like gemstones that hampered our speed, as if we had landed on a No-Man's island of quicksand always being a step away of getting it all done, but never close to finally being "**Free**". We were all unknowing to the strength of the word, but I think Charlie really understood; because he had implemented a grand and master plan that had him quickly reaching for his book bag and pulling out his "emphasizing the right point" boomer rang that would certainly make a difference that counted in the word of trust. The Spirit Horse had been saddled as it ran freely, and although our enemy was running the show our efforts weren't always sustained, because we still had that "scorch and burn", "dive right in" type of uplifting passion. Charlie looked behind us as if he was waiting in line for the next man to pass by, but the only thing he recognized from this over the shoulder acceptance, was his "familiarity of fear!" He knew Streak had been injured in this Bullring of controversial ideas, but this hocus-pocus that was being displayed as one deception after another was unusual for all works of life. Charlie's walking stick stride had been tamed, but he had surpassed the right momentum for his spectacular and eye catching take-off, as he raised his arm to sling his boomer rang with the kind of "boom" that the Sonic scales couldn't even acknowledge. The "V" as in victory projectile launched from his hand, whizzing through the air as if it couldn't possibly return, but would actually burn the sound of speed into shreds while facing a wrath on its one way path to defeat this Evil, with a comeback "from out of nowhere" surprising blast. Sacman was quickly closing in on Charlie as he cleverly knelt down on the black coal in a sitting duck position, waiting with patience and poise; as if he was summoning for Satan to attack while boldly daring him to cross that invisible line of too close for comfort. Kevin, Walter, and I continued to run further toward the edges of the waterfall while keeping our spread out, can't reach us type of approach; so that this brutal man would have to make a quick-witted decision on how to snag us all without one or two of us making a mad dash of escape. Meanwhile, in the other chamber, Lil Tom and the girls had sprung the locks on the two cages, freeing the four children that were being prepared for sacrifice; because restitution was this Ghouls tool that he used so proficient and precise, like the shivers of ice that dangled from his unemotional demands for clarity. Although the mirror had no image, the hopelessness that everyone felt, even after this daring feat of bravery and honor; my young Daredevils and the freed children still had the smarts to flee at Gods speed while sincerely searching for help. They all speedily disappeared down the dark cavern that Sacman had recently been blocking, as they regretfully left Streak in the dark shadows of the cave walls because he would have been too heavy to carry, and it would only slow down their return with the aid of "won't back down!" This mystery was now igniting and bursting into flames as it unraveled with the patience of an unseen presence prepared to offer that hour-glass time many considered possibilities of profound effects that was only bringing us closer together; as we were learning some unique methods to war in hopes of strengthening our reason, like a not so quiet "coming to grips" trip down memory lane. My thoughts suddenly flashed back to the waterfall chamber like the quality of mercy had vanished right before my eyes, as the moment had Charlie staring Death in its face; where his depraved aggressor seemed oddly stumped to go along with having one of the eeriest looks on his hardened mug, and like silent thunder he was unwilling to show his true self while getting ready to deliver a devastating attack with other worldly acts of punishment and pain. Our hearts were racing as Sacman stood looming over Charlie, as he swiftly but cautiously moved in for the kill. As he came within arm's reach, it was as if a cloud was bursting an unsuspecting storm when from out of nowhere the lightning fast boomer rang screamed like an old song, as it sailed back through the air as if it were a ship being tossed around on the high seas drifting and reminiscing for a prayer. The boomer rang struck Sacman like a two by four knocking him flat to the black coal flooring, and as Charlie looked up at the huge ape like man falling face first into the coldness of this mountains artificial turf that had been put here for symbolic reasons by the man who had just met it in a "one step ahead" way. Charlie's idea was a masterful stroke of genius, as he squatted down watching the broken down giant squirm, and moan until his body went limp with stillness of soul. The cheers of jubilation had immediately begun as Walter and I shouted out "Great job Charlie boy!" which was a friendly nickname we had given him because Serena and Tammy used to tell everyone that he was their little sister. Walter was extremely proud as he continued to shout out words of encouragement when he confidently said, "That's not the way Jack defeated the Giant in "Jack and the Beanstalk", but very impressive my little witty under study!" Everyone was rejoicing and celebrating ecstatically, when Charlie suddenly glanced down and saw Sacman's right arm move to brace his body to get back up again. Our hero of the moment was still kneeling, as he tried to do a backward roll to get out of harm's way but was hard going trying to maneuver at a fast pace on the sharp, movable chunks of coal. Sacman had quickly made it to his knees, and was within grabbing distance of Charlie as he lunged forward toward Charlie's back pedaling frame, and swung a powerful blow that instantly connected with the side of Charlie's lower leg. The wail of his pain echoed freely through the hollow cavern as he continued to try moving backwards away from this Beast; when Sacman angrily yanked and pulled his pick axe out of Charlie's leg raising it once again high in the air to finish the job he had begun. When like the Commander he was, Walter shouted out with a regulating voice that shocked everyone inside the chamber to come to a grinding, immediate halt as he screamed at the top of his voice, "Over here, Mr. Bad A** Boogey Man; I'll kick your prissy behind!" He started laughing hysterically as if to mock this menace into a change of mind, as he raged his heckling into overdrive like he was running out of time. His tactic had worked like a charm because Sacman turned his attentions sharply in his direction, as he was now fixated on our going berserk leader standing near the edge of the waterfall. Walter continued to taunt this enraged Lunatic as he continued to take cracks at his murderous concentrations by blurting out, "That's right Gorilla face; why don't you pick axe on somebody else your own size, you pissy pants, peanut head, poor excuse for a Momma's boy Son of a B****!" We had never heard Walter curse and swear like this before, but we knew he was pulling out drastic psychology to get this monster of a man to channel his animosities at him. Sacman stood up slowly while staring down Walter with the look of rage that was burning the fires within him, like we had just crossed beyond the gates of Hell and our darkest days were a world of novel realities that he was about to show us the answers to, and had been looking for what seemed like an eternity. Sacman marched over the top of Charlie, who was cowering and lying beneath him clinching his leg that was now bright red from the devastating wound he had received, as he gasped and whimpered like the puppies we all were; but we still had to show our braveness in the mists of this danger that wasn't simply just going to go away. The oversized Hell raiser carefully made his way toward Walter as the silence now owned the cavern and everything within it, which seemed to be humorously making a mockery of the definition of "dividing walls." There were no more words being spoken as Sacman hostilely started patting his pick axe against the palm of his hand, as the taunts from Walter drew him in nearer and nearer; when he himself teasingly began swinging his honed weapon savagely like a Safari Hunter setting up his prey and trying to scare them into defeat. The two warriors were getting closer to being face to face, as I darted from my position heading over to Charlie to make sure that he was going to be okay. I crouched beside him, grabbing him under his arm pits as I started dragging him further away from the action that was about to occur. We quickly found a safe place to hole up close to the cavern's entrance, as the "throw down" was about to go down; and we had front row seats for this intriguing action battle developing right before our eyes. The shock had finally wore off Kevin like he had been snapped out of trance, when he covertly started crawling toward Charlie and I, while sticking to the shadows; but I could see that he was eager to help fight for our lives. As the battle progressed, Walter unstrapped his blowgun off his back and started twirling it like he was in a Martial Arts movie; and that he was actually Bruce Lee himself ready to face the wrath of his deadliest enemy. Now, we had seen desperation beyond this battleground and by placing our lives in jeopardy, we were uniquely set to shine bright like a gemstone on the front stages of this situation Room of Doom; as Walter stood like a Virgin on the edge of a volcano getting ready to be thrown in for a horrendous sacrificial death. The killer within Sacman didn't say a word, like he was facing betrayal with the intent of an ending that would be presentable for all eyes to witness the method of his monstrosities, and how he dealt with unwelcome violators of his vengeance; as he suddenly made the first move. He cocked back and swung his pick axe like an executioner in the mood for a kill with so much destructive force that when it connected with Walter's blow gun he was using for defense, it instantly snapped it in half. Our cocky Captain of creative courage knew that things weren't going well as he reflexively jumped into the air and hit Sacman across his helmet with one half of the blow gun, and simultaneously stabbed him in the shoulder with the other end of the broken weapon while performing a side cart welt to escape Sacman's retaliation. Although, he didn't realize that his evasive maneuver would land him so close to the edge of the cliff and cause him to be thrown off balance, he fell forward into a three point stance unprepared to protect himself from Sacman's counter attack. When the Beast seen that Walter was at a disadvantage by losing his footing, he didn't waste any time to promptly begin his charge toward him like a pissed off kid stomping his feet against the coal covered ground looking like an enraged Bull seeing red for the first time. There was no hesitation as he started swinging his pick axe violently, causing Walter to backup while dodging and weaving until his heels were hanging over the edge of the cliff. It seemed that there was nowhere to flee for our brave Leader, as Sacman stopped his Mad Man assault, and slowly raised his pick axe above his head like he was teasing Walter again; by taking his sweet old time! Walter started laughing out loud because he wasn't right in the mind and when it came to facing danger, it seemed that fear was tickling his funny bone and causing him to react in the craziest way, because to him a laugh was like possessing a dagger in the secrets of survival. He started screaming, "Is that all you got, because you aren't scaring me, you ugly bastard!", as he continued to laugh louder, and louder as if now he was the one with the upper hand. Sacman drew back like he had two six shooters on his hips with a cigarette stifled between his lips before he cocked back to deliver his malicious fatal blow, as there was the sound of fast moving footsteps tracking across the cavern floor, and by the time we had drawn our attentions from the epic battle; we noticed that it was Thomas Crowder making a bee line like a sonic cluster of dust, heading straight for the two soldiers standing at the edge of the waterfall. The Duo that were clashing heads with so much fight in their blood, had been terribly engrossed in their own confrontation to notice that T.C. was drawing nearer to their location as if a few were chosen from a place, where whoever wasn't afraid would be unseen by the self-righteousness of pure evil bent on extinguishing an unforgettable memory. So he slid under the radar like a shimmering shadow of hope with its shine being way too bright; because his acceptance was needed in a world where emotional rescue was the only strings to play to hear those quaint tunes of **Peace**. T.C. launched his body through the air like an Apollo Challenger in a Discovery for a new Endeavour, as if Columbia and Atlantis were an Enterprise for something greater than a mystery in our minds. He shouted out, "Walter, duck now!" His words of concern and command startled Sacman immediately, which made his aggression stand at ease as he speedily turned around to face this powerful attack; but his reaction wasn't to the satisfaction of the seriousness of sin. It was as if Time had spoken, as Thomas's shoulder nailed him right in the abdomen forcing the large Gladiator to stumble and fall backwards; while Walter quickly dropped down into a Cheerleader's split to dodge this Wreaking Ball of once and for all. Sacman's backward momentum was certainly unavoidable, as his unbalanced body connected with the side of Walter's head causing him to slide over the edge of the cliff; barely able to hang on for that last cold, but heart-felt confession. The large brute was now barreling over the edge with the look of defeat never to find a way across his expressionless mug, and with his last attempt for revenge; he swung his pickaxe with the desperation of a devious, demon that suddenly had the weight of guilt, plucking the feathers from his fallen wings. His vicious blow of "not letting bygones be bygones" was thrown with acute accuracy, as it connected with the back of T.C.'s shoulder inflicting a gorge of a gash on his well toned frame. The monster that we had been searching out so relentlessly was fiercely free-falling into the darkness, as he gasped out his only words that we had heard him speak since being in his "no rest for the wicked" presence. His final words were as if he were asking God where art thou; but his fury from his mental pains had him screaming his insides out as he roared, "Squirt, Squirt!" Sacman, the man of illusion and imagery beyond our imaginations had defiantly disappeared into the abyss, as Thomas rapidly pulled Walter up from his dangling position on the side of the cliff, and with their emotions running free they gave one another a heralded hug and slapped a high five for congrats. When like a whirlwind of goblins rushing onto the proven path like they were copying the Ghost in this killer; the rest of the Daredevils and the four children that had been kept in the cages came running across the cavern heading straight toward T.C. and Walter. Although the large Lifesaver was bleeding severely from one shoulder, he had lifted and hoisted Walter on the other like a pet chimpanzee, who could talk and walk in the shoes of his wounded mentor with minor flaws to his willingness to be taught. I was out of my mind with joy and witness as I shouted, "Hey Guys wait on us", when Kevin and I hurriedly pulled Charlie from his seated position wrapping his arms around our necks to make this "parade of the children" easier on his wounded leg. Everyone was standing near the edge of the waterfall, embracing and cheering the way things were meant to be; when I noticed a large Owl with hideous, yellow eyes sitting up high on the cavern wall staring directly at us like it was angered by our victorious celebration. It clearly looked as if this peculiar animal was having a meltdown from these images of truth that were reflecting off its glowing, glass like eyes that were wild with disappointment and plausible protection. I could deeply feel its words that were being silently spoken preaching to us as if it were saying, "Here ye, here all that has found wickedness as their main course to curve an atrocious appetite, please beware; for I am starving with love for my Father and there is an answer for all, but is all ready for the questions of your faith?" "Throughout Time there has been many heroic hearts of hereafter, nevertheless how many hearts now have the courage to believe while quietly kneeling on your hands and knees; asking Father for forgiveness in an abundance of prayer for he shall never leave; so believe in what your spirit can foretell for judgment is obsolete, but very much eternal in its commands for saving thy soul." I was amazed by the wisdom that was flowing from this curious creature's vibes of vagrancy, as it sat so statuesque and surreal like the truth had finally been spoken for us to stop sleep walking through life and pay attention to the things that really mattered. I spoke up with acknowledgement as the key to open that door like crossed swords were coming out as my words when I astonishingly said, "Guys look at that big creepy Owl watching us from above"; and as everyone turned to look in its direction, it suddenly spread its wings and took flight across the cavern diving downward into the blackness where Sacman had met his demise. It looked back like a warrior glancing over the bodies of the fallen dead, as if it had more words to express like the whispers of way-back had carried forth more Intel sternly stating, "It's not over till it's over young Daredevils" as it silently and mysteriously fell out of our view. Walter finally spoke like a champion of now belief as he said, "Wow my Brothers in Arms did you see how normal that really seemed?" "It was like that Owl dove over the edge going to save Sacman because it cared, it truly cared; and I could tell by the message in its flight that it's heart was of passion and poetic poise." As we all stared into the darkness trying to summon a glimpse of this impressive focus from such a remarkable symbol of loneliness for love; our tendered quest of whom it took after was somehow broken down into regretful tears. Rene responded with a calm passage, where remorse was centered in her journey back home like the connection between lost and found that had the past hanging overhead, with our many attempts for ever increasing faith that warranted no limits like a harvest. She said, "Remember there will be a Revelation, and the power of knowing is within thy self, so as we walk down these curious avenues invading at a pace of presumptions; Survival is ringing loud and crystal clear, where sheer terror has the decision of can you hear; but do you understand?" We were headed for home and her voice of forever sounded like sweet music to our ears, as we triumphantly made our way back across the cavern toward the entrance to retrieve our precious protector that lay wounded from his visions of agreement, that loyalty and love was worth putting your life on the line. Once we reached our fearless friend, he had the look as if there were a page missing from our triumphant touching moment; yet soft, but very rigid in its hidden secrets of giving all of our hearts. The boys and I immediately started gathering fragments of anything that was made of wood, so we could start building a carrying sled to take Streak out of this horrifying abode that flowed with critical maneuvers from the purest forms of silence. The girls on the other hand were playing nurse and doctor; as our unleashed, undaunted "Wonder Dog" whined from pain with his whimpers becoming stronger from every rapid breath that he inhaled. We speedily crafted this Ark of "save and preserve" that would route our beloved friend across these flooded waters of distress; and although the situation was treading lightly we had found this Devil in the dark, so the thought of unexpected scares were always on the forefront of our minds as we hastily departed for home. After we had exited these caverns of chaos, and finally reached the warmth and welcoming of the loveliness of light; it seemed that God was standing on the edge of the river with open arms asking us to remember and hold dear our trials, for they were meant to be. I was a witness to our exploits of bravery and dedication to our standards of right and wrong, but I was also feeling isolation from the rest of my brethren; because I had a spiritual and lyrical attachment to the word, that truly opened my eyes to the evil that exists. Once a friend now gone, twice a family that judged wrong, thrice the trust becomes cold as ice; but the heart never forgets the tortured testimonies of life. So, as we continued to journey toward the riverbed with our heads held high and proud, our understanding was to board this misguided maniac's craft to carry us to the sanctity of safety. Yet, as I readily remembered our encounter with this legend of late night after words that were only spoken on the hush, it was kind of ironic that his myth was defeated by Thomas; or was it plainly meant to define that Sacman destroyed himself by fighting with a rage that he couldn't control in his last fight for revenge. I guess we'll never know what was on the mind of this peculiar stranger who brought us closer together as a group and a loving family, while searching for the answers we truly needed to comprehend. Although, tired and weary from our long trek of "where's he at"; we continued to load our able bodies into this pirates ship of "take and break" like jeopardy was just a question of our committed faith. As Nece checked behind her to make sure that her cargo was secure and sound, she hit the throttle to this ship in a bottle and left no messages of despair. These waves of departure were like "rock a bye baby", as I felt so exhausted from our mission of peril and playing fields, that it left scars of "is it real" lingering on our souls, but the slight rocking motion of the boat rolling over the waves were too much for my consciousness. I started to feel like a young crying baby, back when my mother used to lay me on a pillow across her knees and move her legs gently up and down to put me fast to sleep; so I trustingly closed my eyes. When I started blinking rapidly from the fear that was like a ghost at its most, it seemed as if everything had been a dream, and when I became fully alert we were all gathered under the Radford's carport listening to Kevin with his world of brags and boasts; who in our eyes was the greatest of hosts. He was telling the tendered tales of our Sacman exploits, as if we couldn't remember the difference between the cold days of December or the hot heralds of heat that had been scorching our laid on the line behinds like a cinder from glancing out the window. I can honestly say that Jesus stayed with us through our trying walk from beginning to end; he was there as promised if belief was given in him, even if thy path was dimly lit; just ask forgiveness for your sins. Kevin's voice continued to echo like a tropic storm knocking on the door of hear me, but as we all listened with intent and aim to beckon our guiding light of "everything's going to be alright"; past ventures had made us weary. Never had we journeyed so long and so strong, yet we came out analyzing and finalizing the game that had been rolled with loaded dice, where snake eyes was venom bitten into the hand that hesitates and contemplates the chance of snakes lying in the grass like green pastures didn't exist. Adam and Eve were naïve of recognizing that evil is Kin to all who can't see the disguise of darkness, when the light had already foretold his commandments of obedience and acceptance. I thought to myself that maybe this conniving charade was actually a way for someone that was alienated to gain one's trust, which made them feel like they were needed; then like a shark with those soulless eyes in blood infested waters blatantly defies the one who exiled his existence for the pure pleasure of spite; letting them know that he was still here. So, as I was seeing with my heart and deep rending feelings, I suddenly felt the light tap of someone trying to get my attention; and as I turned around from my off into the wildness thoughts, there stood Mrs. Radford with her Bible clutched in her hand like a staff of wise words that was about to express its truths. She lovingly said, "Jayme come on sweetie, were about to start our Sunday school lesson, so gather with the rest of the flock and let's gain some strength that will prove to be mightier than none other." I nodded my head with a smile of belief that could never be taken away, as I held her hand and walked under the shelter with the graciousness that Glory was present, and ready to fill my depleted soul. Her teachings were something special, because she got all of the children involved by asking questions, which some knew and some didn't; but even if you didn't have a clue, she would lead you to toward the light of the right answers. I learned a lot on this particular day and it would never be forgotten, because I was experiencing something that felt Heavenly by just opening up my heart; with her helping hand of course. After Mrs. Radford ended her sermon with a powerful amen; she asked that we all join hands and have a prayer of praise, as she pointed to me to lead us in our quest for hope. I was so nervous, because I was new to the education on the word and not as polished as the others; but I was ambitious of course, which made my prayer to be a moment of recognition as my timid enthusiasm became an obsession. I gently closed my eyes and truly began to believe that I could lead us with the words that were about to unfold from the depths of my trembling soul that were so ready to be heard. I bowed my head graciously, and now without fear I said, "God, I know that you are there and I only ask that you please forgive me for my innocence, because I am ashamed of my lack of knowledge; but I promise to do better with my understanding of right and wrong." "I only ask in the name of Jesus Christ that you protect and guide my friends, family, and I while keeping us healthy and strong; so that we can continue to filter the evil out of this magnificent world that you have created." "I am in awe of your wisdom, and your words are so rejuvenating to my spirit that my love flows through you and my happiness of life is over the limits of ecstatic." "You are our father, and we are your naïve children trying to walk through this Valley of Death, patiently waiting to return home to you someday for your love is unconditional; amen!" As we all raised our heads from a congregational amen, Mrs. Radford looked at me and winked her eye with the glow of an Angel, to let me know that my words were acceptable and appreciated. I knew that our journey was long and hard fought in this never before told saga of death, while dodging past haunts that required a certain amount of luck; but we were righteously serving justice with faith and culture combined, to overcome an elusive fellow such as the legendary **Sacman**! I wish us, "Godspeed toward our guide of light."

Printed in the United States
By Bookmasters